ZEBULON ANGELL AND THE SHADOW ARMY

CHRIS RIKER

Fulton Books, Inc.
Meadville, PA

Published by Fulton Books 2021

ISBN 978-1-63710-705-8 (paperback)
ISBN 978-1-63710-706-5 (digital)

Printed in the United States of America

DRAMATIS PERSONAE

Me: Ill-named and world-weary, or maybe tired of being me, one Zebulon Angell. *Call me Zee, please.* Not quite married, not quite divorced. Songwriter, tutor, Uber driver, and general gig mage. Dream feaster.

Dr. Jing Angell: My long-suffering wife. Amazing lady. Tired of waiting for success, she reached out and grabbed it. Very moral, as long as she's the one writing the rules.

Marqus "Nitro" Baine: Loyal and true. Fellow veteran of AA. Nitro is what remains of a sharp mind and proud spirit when wine and women take their portion. Has certain skills picked up when he was in the Navy or perhaps while in jail.

Gillian Li: Dragon lady who'll leave you begging for another dose of venom. Easy on the eyes but not what she appears.

Kevin Li: Dynastic teen heir (Americanized); selfish and cynical.

Hui Rong: Scholar, gentleman, possible assassin, knight errant, and quester for the greater good, or not. Rong has a winning sense of humor, an unfortunate love of jangly music, a keen mind, and a keener sense of which way the wind blows.

Zack Angell: Better than me, I dearly hope. Handsome. Coming into his own. Chinese American, occasionally self-loathing.

Jessa Angell: Learning the dangers of resentments, I hope, though I am not providing the best role model. Not one to hold hate too close to her heart.

3

Ma: Ruth Anne Angell, keeper of family secrets. Teller of family secrets. Enthusiast of spirited beverages. Friend to all except those who marry her son.

RHM (Chairwoman Takahashi's "right-hand man"): Japanese-issue businessman. Possibly tied to the yakuza. He uses henchpersons, including *Tatsuo*, my, um, athletic girlfriend? It's complicated.

Franz "Frank" Fuchs: Jing's boss, head of ValKnut Pharma and Holistics, GmbH, a company with deep pockets and powerful ambitions. Charming. Agenda-driven.

Henchmen: Four local hires working for Frank. One is surprisingly knowledgeable and polite.

Assorted people met along the way and one crusty old shen.

All my demons came out to dance, and so here is my confession, wrapped in adventure, wrapped in a travelogue, wrapped in a sex farce, served with ghosts.

CHAPTER 1

I WANTED TO CONQUER the world that morning, but my beer tasted skunky, and my head was full of cats.

I thought about getting to a meeting.

As I reached for the door, it swung inward, nearly clipping my face. Jing's five feet four inches of lean purpose brushed past me with a basket full of clean laundry. That meant the maid brigade had blown through the giant house. The star of my heavens was many things, but a laundress was not one of them.

Jing was breathtaking when we first met and lovely still. Back when we were dating, she liked sex as much as I did, approaching it with an enthusiasm I found both wonderful and terrifying. More importantly, we were friends. I enjoyed listening to her talk about her work back then, though I understood only a fraction of it. She listened to my dreams without making fun of me. We never judged each other's failings. *Back then.* I confess I could live in those days forever in my mind, but Jing lived in the real world, focusing on her career in Big Pharma.

Murder blazed up from the unfathomable depths of her sloe eyes as she spotted the Bud tallboy in my hand.

I said, "Just coming to see you. I have the rent!" I smiled. She didn't. "Well, most of the rent. I'll have the rest—"

Jing cut me off. "Keep it." She set down the basket and pulled out an envelope that was tucked among my shirts. Plopping it down on the kitchenette counter, she said, "Here's money." Yanking the beer from my hand and pouring it down the sink, she added, "You won't be finishing this. I need you to watch Zack. In four hours, I'll be on a plane for Tokyo."

"What's in Tokyo?"

"Five-hundred-dollar wagyu steaks and a boss who'll stuff me full of 'em if we finish this project." I was pretty certain that wasn't all her boss, Frank, wanted to stuff into her, not that it was any of my business at the moment. Funny how playing with pharmaceuticals made some men as rich as pharaohs and left others paying rent for a guest cottage in their own backyard. My sometime wife went on, "I need you to stay in the house 'til at least Friday. Maybe all weekend too. Jessa is supposed to swing by. Give her the check on the kitchen counter. It's for Emory, so don't forget. It's fine if Zack hangs out with his buddies, but they can't drink. You either. Seriously, Zee. And yes, beer counts as drinking. You want to rebuild our trust? Don't blow it. Get Zack to bed by midnight. He has summer school, and if he flunks, he'll end up repeating eleventh grade. If he goes out, tell him to keep his phone on…and remind him to actually answer the thing."

"Check. And good luck." She was calling me Zee again, not that name my mom picked out. That was a good sign.

Expressionless, she hurried around the cottage, loading my clean undies into the drawers and picking my dirties from the floor. I heard her hiss, "Chòu si le!" (I knew that one! It meant "Stinks to heaven!") Living in a studio cottage tended to concentrate my slovenly ways. From a chair, she lifted the Martin Dreadnought she'd given me for my fortieth birthday—a day I'd spent alone with the shiny new guitar and a bottle—and placed it gently in its case. I wouldn't have blamed her if she had shaken it to see whether I'd stashed anything inside, but she didn't.

Jing finished and looked me straight in the eye. "Be his father for a change," she said. That hurt. "Remember, under no circumstances are you to Uber with the Lexus. Use your Corolla and stay out of our neighborhood. Don't burn the house down, do a good job with the kids, and maybe we can fool around when I get back." Somehow, the prospect of getting pity poon from the mother of my children hurt even worse.

This was the first time since our big blowup that she was headed off. She'd been to China solo on more business trips than I could count, plus stops all over the map. We used to go together. I drove Jing to the airport in her brand-spankin'-new 2018 candy apple red Lexus hybrid. I-85 traffic was easier to take in luxury. Maynard Jackson International Terminal, named for one of Atlanta's larger-than-life mayors, had speedy curbside drop-off, as opposed to the congested nightmare at the domestic terminals. Porters with strong backs took her luggage.

"What about this bad boy?" I asked, pointing to a big aluminum trunk I'd never seen before. With the other bags cleared from the back, I noticed it was plugged into an outlet in the Lexus's floorboard. Lord, they stuffed enough gadgets into a ninety-thousand-dollar SUV.

"That stays, Zee. Someone's stopping by to get it. They'll contact you. Remember to plug the car in the garage charger when you get home." She kissed me on the cheek. I almost drew her in close for a real goodbye kiss and maybe a fanny grab, but I didn't. It'd been a while since we had been that couple. Maybe this week would go well and…

Giving orders the whole way while simultaneously talking on her phone, my gal led two porters through the glass doors and over to the check-in counter. I got back in the Lexus (which cost more than the house I was born in) and pulled away from the curb.

One good thing about Uber was you could switch vehicles in the app. The Lexus commanded a higher fee than my Toyota. It seemed a shame not to take advantage of being at the airport.

Sure enough, I got a call to the Ride Share lot. A woman named Patricia got in. I peeked in the rearview: nice hair, smart suit, permanent scowl. Business type. I'd had my fill of those during my seventeen years in marketing. I was a free man now. I answered to no one, except whomever I answered to at the moment. No big bosses, anyway. My business card read: "Zebulon Angell—Gig Mage."

"Have a nice flight?" I asked.

She grunted a reply, basically saying, "Shut up and drive."

I fiddled with the dash controls and put on music. My music.

> *The years fly by*
> *We're halfway done*
> *On our way to the sky*
> *I hoped we'd go on and on*
> *But the ache never leaves*
> *And in the end*
> *I never thought that I*
> *could hate the word "friend"*

The Martin needed tuning. Maybe a new D string. Maybe all new strings, whatever. *I'm a writer, not a singer.* This was a demo. All I needed was for someone to hear my lyrics. If I had to drive richy-rich skirt back there, she was going to get an audition. Next came the tear-jerking refrain:

> *We're just one heart shy of romance*
> *One trick short of a magic store*
> *One fool's wishing his life away*
> *Dreamin' up a dream...of so much more*

I pulled the SUV among the northbound interstate turtles, grinning and ready to spring my surprise on Ms. Patricia.

"I bet you've never heard this artist before. Funny thing—"

"Don't let wishes steal your life," cautioned a small voice.

I glanced back in the mirror. Patricia was wearing a pair of those space alien antennae in her ears. A moment later, sabers flew from her lips as she opened a conference call with her team.

"I don't need to know why the numbers are low," she said in coiled cobra tones. "I need to know the numbers are where they're supposed to be. Jack, you need to get your sales reps in line. They're new. Work with them. Better yet, bounce the losers, Kieran and Benjie. There are plenty of good dogs. No need to keep the bad ones. The quarterlies are due in eleven days. Eleven days, people. Am I clear on this?" She was clear on that. I didn't even work for her, and I was terrified.

I switched off my music and put on the radio. Chris Stapleton, the lucky hack, would take it from here.

I let Patricia out at the Hilton on Courtland. She was on another call, reaming some poor wage slave. She offered me no goodbye, and no tip. I thought unkind thoughts. Another good thing about Uber driving is it let me be judgmental. It was like being in church.

As I pulled out of the hotel's circular drive, a motorcyclist with his darkened visor down nearly clipped my front end. He gunned his Harley's engine to assert his dubious masculinity and raced off recklessly through traffic. *I hate bikers. They're such puffed-up jackoffs.*

I headed home. No more Uber calls for now. I parked in our huge garage and plugged in the Lexus. Zack would be back around five. That gave me enough time for a quick beer and a nap. No point in getting to a meeting now. I'd only be getting another white, beginner's chip anyway, and I had a drawer full of those. Tomorrow would be better—or next Monday to start the week off right.

My phone rang. It was Nitro, my former sponsee—the guy who thought I had the keys to sobriety.

"Dude, I want to help, I really do, but you need someone who's got a few thirty days put together. I've gone out." A few months of steady sobriety sounded impossible at that point. Days sure, but nights, no way.

Jessa's orange tabby, Damn Kitty, looked up at me from its cookie bowl and ran away like her tail was on fire. I used to love that cat.

On the phone, Nitro was getting frantic. "I gotta meet with you. You gotta help me."

This was against the rules since I'd gone out and should not sponsor anyone just then, but he wouldn't listen.

As we spoke, I sorted through the mail on the counter. Jessa's envelope was still there. Good, I hadn't missed her. Georgia Power's monthly love letter was (still) addressed to me. I opened it…and nearly died. What the hell was using that much juice? I immediately thought of the Lexus and its new cargo box. It had to be a freezer. Maybe Jing's boss had sent her some samples of his fine beef. What good were free steaks if they cost a fortune to store?

Nitro was yammering on. He had worked himself up into a frenzy.

"Nitro. Nitro. Are you drinking now? Are you drunk right now?"

"No! I'm straight." He wasn't slurring—at least no more than he usually did. "I'm so damn straight. That's just it."

"Just what?"

"I've changed, Zebulon." Nitro took a breath. "I am transformed! I got turned into a god, and it's killing me."

CHAPTER 2

NITRO WAS A DECENT enough older guy, older than me anyway. With yellowing teeth, facial scruff, and a Greek sailor's cap perched atop a frizzy head of hair somewhere between Frederick Douglass and Fred G. Sanford, he came off a bit pathetic. Divorce will do that to a man. Nitro had been run through the mill three times.

Getting to him took time. I knew I had to make this quick if I was going to get home for Zack. I turned the Lexus into a rundown restaurant on Buford Highway and found him waiting at a table—no food, just water. The waitress loved that, I'm sure. I could tell he was upset, though. He could barely hold the glass steady in his hands.

He jumped up when he saw me. "Zebulon! Thank sweet chocolate Jesus you're here!" I held up both hands, palms out, before he hugged me. I sat down and ordered us chips and salsa.

We were supposed to be going through the Twelve Steps, not that I was an expert. I used to have some time put together, eighteen months. A few beers and a wet-brained decision to sell stuff from Jing's professional supplies changed that. Sometimes we read a few pages from the Big Book, but Nitro mostly used me to run his errands. He had been trying for more than a year to get a driver's license, having lost it to a DUI. We studied together for two weeks. Finally, we got up early one morning and drove all the way to Whitehall Street, in a crappy part of Southwest Atlanta. I waited outside the DMV for two solid hours. Nitro had been drinking the night before and flunked the test.

"Nitro, I've got like ten minutes before I have to head back. I've got—"

"That's fine! This won't take only a minute." So this claim of godhood was no big deal? Glad I drove down. He explained, "My Bessie brought me something. Some chewy candy." Bessie was future ex-wife number four. "It tasted kinda fruity, kinda nasty. She said I needed it if I wanted to please her. I said fine. I chased it with Colt 45, and it went down fine. And damn if I didn't please her. Pleased her, pleased me. That's how it went all night and the next day besides.

"Next thing I know, she's so pleased, she's runnin' her mouth all over town." Sometimes Nitro's *ings* had a *g,* but when he got worked up, he clipped them short. "You know Bessie is tight with my ex. So I'm minding my own business, and suddenly here comes Doris."

"I thought Dina was your ex."

"No, not Dina. Not Dina any damn day of the week. She's another ex, the *mean* one." I sipped my Coke and followed along as best I could. "This was Doris standing there, and *she* wants to be pleased. Well, I wasn't gonna say no. Doris is real fine. But don't you know that Doris told Hattie."

"And Hattie wanted…"

He looked me in the eye and nodded. "Hattie wanted. Hattie got!"

"I'm…happy…for you?" I said.

"Well, don't be!" He thumped the table, and the waitress scowled. "That's Bessie and two of the exes!"

"They…all…wanted your attention?"

"Like cats. Just like cats." Nitro huffed.

The phone conversation made sense now—well, as much sense as anything involving Nitro. He was the god of low-rent love affairs. "Sounds like every man's fantasy," I lied.

"No, sir. A man my age has limits, special candy or no!"

I looked at my watch. "Well, I'd love to help, but I'm married…and I'm in enough trouble with the wife, so you'll have to find someone else to help you to…uh…please the cats."

"Jesus wept! I didn't call you down here to jazz my girlfriends. I need a place to hide out and catch my breath. My back's ready to quit me and," he whispered this, "my balls are killing me! It's like someone stuck a knife in my taint." That painted a picture. "Zebulon, I need a quiet place to sleep for 'bout a week," he said the halfway house where he lived was no good. Despite the rules, there were women in and out at all hours. "You gotta put me up." Without waiting for an answer, he got up and walked out of the restaurant, leaving me to pay. By the time I got to the SUV, Nitro was sitting in the passenger seat, smiling and humming to himself. How had he gotten in? I would swear I locked it.

Slipping behind the wheel, I said, "Look, I'd like to help, but Jing would be pissed if I—"

"It's only for a few days, Zebulon. You got that nice little bungalow out back you told me 'bout. I'll be quiet as a bug. I won't cause your missus no headaches." Among his talents, Nitro also knew how to carry on a one-sided conversation. I might have tossed him out of the car, but I kind of liked having him around. He depended on me like I mattered. That made him a rare commodity these days. I also felt a tinge of guilt. He started drinking again after his sponsor (me) started up.

We survived the trip north on the interstates with the gravelly-voiced help of Tom Waits, getting back a few minutes before five. Once again, I plugged in the Lexus.

"A car fridge. Don't that take the prize. You rich folks gotta have your luxuries." Nitro was standing behind the SUV's opened hatch, reaching for the freezer lid. "What's in it?" He tugged, but the lid was secured with an electronic lock.

"Steaks, I think, wagyu." Why the hell had I told him that? "Doesn't matter. It's locked."

"Wahoo? All I heard was 'steak.' No problem. I can get that open, and then we'll have us one or two. You said she was away right?" Had I told him that too? Crap! "She won't miss one or two little bitty steaks. Hand me that screwdriver hanging on the wall."

I stepped over and grabbed the tool from a rack over the workbench that was piled high with pieces of wood from some unfinished project. When I turned back, Nitro had the freezer door open—it swung upward, brushing the SUV's overhead—and stood staring, his mouth hanging open.

"That's not steaks, Zebulon."

"No. It sure isn't."

In the freezer, inside a clear plastic bag, was something not fit to eat.

"That is one dead monkey," Nitro said flatly. "Poor thing. Ain't that a shame?"

"It sure is."

"The little fella sure died happy, though." Through the tented fabric of the bag, I could see what Nitro meant. "Yes, sir, I do believe that is the happiest dead monkey I ever seen."

CHAPTER 3

I DIALED JING TO ask about the dead macaque with the out-sized woody, but she was thirty-five thousand feet in the air and didn't answer. I decided to try later. My phone had two messages. One was from Mom; I knew what that was. The other was some guy prebooking a late ride. Ah, the hectic life of a gig mage.

I made sure the SUV was plugged in. I didn't want the thing in the freezer to thaw out; it would take more than Febreze to get the stink of rotting monkey out of a Lexus.

That's when a Ford Explorer drove up with Zack and a group of his friends. I recognized most of them. They blasted by me and into the kitchen without saying hello and started unpacking the fridge. Someone hauled out a tray of those pork ravioli things Jing makes all the time; they taste good, but they make me windy.

"I could put those in the microwave for you, Zack."

He said without even looking over, "It's okay, Dad. We'll *fry* them ourselves." His tone told me that (a) I was in the way, and (b) I was useless with Chinese cooking.

The others were laughing at…something. I couldn't follow any of their dueling conversations buzzing around the kitchen. They proceeded to fry the pot stickers, filling the air with the smell of chives, ginger, and pork. A few of the boys had plates; others grabbed leftover pizza, balls of sticky rice, or whatever… and wolfed it down.

One of the boys I did not recognize came over to me and asked, "What's your number?" ("Hello, my name is _____. Thanks for having us over. By the way, can I get your number?" is how he meant to ask, I'm sure.)

"Uh, you are?"

"Kevin." I waited a beat, but there was no follow-up. Social skills were extinct.

"Why would you like my phone number?" I tried to stretch out the question to clue him in that he was a dolt.

"My mom wants to hire you to tutor me in English." Kevin looked to be fully Chinese and spoke without an accent or the phantom infinitives used by those struggling to master the beast that is English. I figured his parents had brought him to America as a child. Many in Atlanta's Chinese community were good at making money and determined that their kids would get into the best schools and do even better.

I gave him my number. He texted his mom.

"I'm available on—"

"I have math tutoring Mondays after school and golf on Tuesdays. Thursday nights are good, after swim team. So tomorrow."

"Fine. Tomorrow."

"Zack says you charge sixty. Let's say one-twenty, you keep eighty. See you tomorrow night at seven." I felt/heard a buzz from my phone. It was a text from Gillian Li, presumably Kevin's mom. (Chinese transplants loved to pick a new name for their new life in America, like buying new clothes. Jing was "Barb" to her Chinese friends. I preferred to call her Jing. I knew a bunch of Barbs, but there was only one Jing!) It dawned on me that I had no say in Kevin's plan to overcharge his mother. I was going to make money, which means I didn't have to Uber so much, and that was fine.

Nitro came up to me with a plate loaded with pot stickers. "These are fine! Jus' fine."

"I'll get you settled in a minute," I told him.

My attention shifted back to Kevin, who was now talking to Zack about something. "A sample? A taste."

"No. I told you—"

"Fifty," Kevin said, pulling out a gold money clip. What teen had a money clip? I could never get used to the way kids were able to pull wads of cash out of nowhere. When I was a teenager, a twenty had to last all weekend. Whatever Kevin wanted, it wasn't something I wanted to be sold in my—in *Jing's* house. I wanted them gone. I wanted to use this day for some bonding.

"Excuse us," I said loudly. "Zack and I have a father-son thing to do." No one looked over. Seeing manners were wasted, I gave a piercing whistle through my teeth. "Everyone, out!" I yelled and hustled them out the door. That took some doing and Zack protested.

Once the others had piled back into the Explorer, I grabbed Zack by the arm. Nitro followed us out, stuffing one last pot sticker into his mouth en route. I pointed Nitro to the cottage and told him not to call any of his lady friends for now. He made a face like a scolded child but agreed to behave.

Starting the car—my Corolla this time so Zack wouldn't narc me out to Jing—I glided past the Lexus. "Let's spend some time together. Maybe go get something to eat."

"I *was* eating…with my friends," Zack said.

By this point, we were in traffic. "We could go to the game store and pick out a new—"

"Dad, we haven't played games together in years." I didn't realize until he said it that it had been that long, and the fact hit hard.

"Well, you name it." The words fumbled out.

"I don't know."

"The park?"

"Fine." It was the quietest "fine" I'd ever heard, but I took it.

In the glove compartment, I found some packets of crackers from Wendy's that I would never eat but couldn't bring myself to throw out. Zack and I spent all of twenty minutes in the park, walking around the lake and feeding the ducks. The evening was nice, despite the ninety-degree heat that sweat-glued our clothes to our bodies.

We stepped onto the familiar quarter-mile trail, our feet raising red clay dust. I remembered taking him and his sister there many times. The park was a freebie and a chance to throw them both into an ankle-deep creek and watch them shriek with laughter. Zack and I rounded a bend in the woods and came upon the little face in the bole of a tree. Some local artisan had carved a wood spirit into the living oak long ago.

"Do you remember how you and Jessa used to think this was carved by forest elves? I used to tell you the elves would get us if we didn't get home for dinner. You remember?"

"Yeah," Zack said.

"That's it? 'Yeah?'"

"I don't know what you want me to say."

"I was remembering all the fun we used to have when you two were little."

"Yeah. That was good." He shrugged and walked on.

We watched a couple push their toddler on the baby swing, and it occurred to me I may have missed a few steps between that version of Zack and the nearly grown one standing next to me. I awkwardly said something to that effect.

"It doesn't matter, Dad," he said.

It mattered.

We headed back to the house.

I got busy cleaning the kitchen while Zack disappeared. The envelope Jing had left out for Jessa was gone. Damn. I'd missed her. We'd only been gone an hour. Dammit.

I heard a curse and a sharp thud from downstairs. I ran down to find Zack quickly shutting the sliding partition that subdivided the huge finished basement. I couldn't remember the last time I'd been down here. "What's the problem?" As I said it, I spotted a fresh dent in the drywall, about where a teen-ager's foot would go if it were angry enough.

"Nothing."

"It's something. You yelled." There was an electronic lock on the partition. I didn't remember that being there. "What's that? What are you keeping in there, Zack?" It was obvious what had happened. "Did Kevin come and take his taste?"

"Dad—"

"Open the doors, Zack."

"No. No one's supposed to—"

"Your buddy Kevin went in there."

"Our home security is a joke. I didn't think he could get in the lab, though."

"The lab?" We stood there, staring at each other, more strangers than father and son. "Zack, open it."

"He took my key fob," Zack said with an exasperated sigh.

He was obstructing me. "Open it," I repeated. "You've already seen what's in there. My turn now."

Zack manually tapped in the combination, and the pad chirped. He slid open the unlocked partition, revealing what used to be our rumpus room.

There were cages with two more monkeys staring out. They wore diapers but still managed to stink. *Who was taking care of them?* An examination table stood where the pool table had been. A laptop and something that looked like a microscope from a starship filled a bench, competing for space with racks of test sample vials, a centrifuge, and other lab equipment. The familiar Remington print I'd picked up at a yard sale looked out of place hanging above the pricey gear. Along the opposite wall were greenhouse grow lamps and hydroponic tables filled with greenery. It wasn't marijuana, but something else, more like tiny saplings, plus a pile of rotting fruit.

Zack looked at an opened cabinet that held several white containers. There was a gap where one was missing from the collection. Kevin had known exactly what he was looking for.

"Zack, what the hell is all this? Are you running a drug ring down here? Your mother is going to kill you!" I sensed my mistake the second I spoke.

"Dad…this is Mom's lab."

Of course, it was. Jing had installed all this. My focus wasn't the best sometimes. Slowly, I recalled her saying something months and months ago, about being able to spend more time at home, in her own space, but I didn't know she had all this. Banished to the cottage, I was out of touch with happenings inside my own home. She must have ferried the stuff in using the SUV. She would have needed help to install some of it. *How out of it had I been lately?*

"We'll go over and get the stuff back from Kevin."

"No. It's fine. Mom knows about Kevin. It's just that he's such a dick sometimes."

"Your mom lets him use her homemade drugs? You're saying she's getting the whole neighborhood high?"

"She's not a street pusher. This is a lab-quality product. And it's not the whole neighborhood."

A thought hit hard. "What about you?"

"No! I have…," he trailed off, and my suspicions shot up a trillion percent. It was bad enough that Jing had a DIY cartel. If she had dragged Zack into something…

"You have what?" I demanded, losing control of my own questions.

"I have a girlfriend," Zack said it like it was the last thing in the world he wanted to tell me. It took me a moment to see beyond his not wanting me to know he was dating and realize what he was also telling me.

"This stuff—"

"It's called lǎo hǔ yīn jīng, 'Tiger Penis,'" he said. The Chinese loved tiger penis, bear penis, deer penis, donkey penis. They were gaga for penis. "It's named after the old folk medicine. She gets the fruits shipped in. She's trying to grow her own trees, but that hasn't worked out too well. Anyway, the fruit is the main ingredient." Zack added, "Tiger Penis is super tricky. Mom's been working forever to get it right. Traveling, working out parts of the solution in labs all over the place."

"Tiger Penis. It does what exactly?" As I asked the question, a dead monkey's schlong flashed in my mind.

Zack flushed and said, "It gets you high. But mainly, it makes you crazy horny. And..."

"There's an 'and?'" I asked.

"When a guy takes it, the girl...is into it too."

The pieces were coming together. Jing was building gods in our basement.

I wanted a beer.

CHAPTER 4

I TRIED MY BEST to get more information out of Zack, but he kept telling me to ask his mom. I certainly had questions for Jing. I wanted to know how she could let teenagers use whatever this stuff was. It would be tomorrow before she was accessible by phone, though.

My mind was racing. I went out to the cottage to talk to Nitro. He was poking through my stuff. He'd found all my hidden bottles. I asked him point-blank about the sex candy.

"I don't know where Bessie got it," he said. "I didn't ask." It came out "ax." "My attention was otherwise occupied." He smiled at the thought.

"Has it worn off?" I asked.

"I think so. I could sleep twelve hours, for sure."

I decided to let Nitro get a nap. I told him not to exhaust my beer supply (that I wasn't supposed to touch) and left him to himself. Only then did it occur to me that I'd never given him the key to the cottage; it was still in my pocket. *Whatever.*

Zack was fine for the night. He was good about getting his homework done. At least that's how I remembered him being a few years ago. More importantly, I took him at his word that he wasn't using this stuff, which was another question: What the hell did Zack or Kevin need with bootleg Viagra? When I was their age, I could get hard fantasizing about *Sally Jessy Raphael.*

I decided to take the Corolla for a spin, earn a few bucks,

and let my thoughts sort themselves out. I'd be back to make sure Zack got to bed at a decent hour.

As an Uber driver, I quickly figured out what my passengers were doing wrong. I wrote out a list and posted it on a card in the back seat. It read:

Dear Rider,

> In order that you may have the best possible rideshare experience, please follow these simple rules. Call me from where you are; be where you call me from.

That seemed easy enough, but somehow, folks never quite mastered it. There were other issues as well, so I added them to my list.

> If you're going to have three toddlers in tow, also tow along three child seats. No, you may not eat your catfish sandwich in my car. Yes, when I drive you ninety minutes through pouring rain and traffic to your multimillion-dollar McMansion and you don't tip me, I will give you one star.

Finally,

> If you're going to tell your girlfriend about her boyfriend's bent pecker, don't be surprised when she screams at you. Also, if you don't want me listening to your phone calls, hang your head out the window.

No one read the note as far as I could tell, but I felt better knowing it was back there.

Two thirtysomething women got in the back, sharing giggles, holding red plastic Solo cups of whiskey and mixers, which I could smell up front. They were on their way to a club near Perimeter Mall. I played my music, cruised I-285, and let the time melt away.

I was angry with Jing—furious. I thought about leaving a voice mail, hoping to catch her between connecting flights, but then I thought I'd better calm down first. She should be in Tokyo around eight in the morning, my time. I should let her get settled, maybe get some rest.

She'd probably get a room at one of the city's wildly expensive hotels. Jing and I spent a weekend in Tokyo years ago, back when we used to visit Asia frequently. The city has a lot going for it. It's clean; the people are polite to a fault; and they feed you to bursting on magnificent meals arranged on the plate like works of avant-garde art. The cityscape contains a few surprises hidden among its submissively drab streets: a towering glass needle here, a museum there.

Jing's boss would see to it she didn't get bored. They'd go to some restaurant high atop the city, ten thousand lights shining up from below to backlight an award-winning chef as he prepared ultra-pricey steaks and all the little pickled and diced treats to go with it. Jing would wear something black, tight— too tight. Her figure had laughed off childbirth twice and she could pass for a woman years younger. Her perfumed hair would scent the air as she swept through the room, like a priest swinging a censer in church, though rather than warding off sinful thoughts, her fragrance would incite them.

Afterward, they might go dancing in one of Tokyo's crowded clubs with its electronica music and hypnotic lights. Then he'd take her back to his hotel room on some pretext of going over paperwork. He'd offer her a drink, something romantic—Courvoisier perhaps or sake. He'd be careful so as not to raise her defenses. Then the moment would come, and he'd move in on her, his lips pressing against hers…

"Excuse me, that's Ashford Dunwoody Road. That's our exit," a boozy voice slurred from the back seat. "You missed it!"

CHAPTER 5

I SHOULD HAVE A number of awards. I have been a marketing guru, songwriter, tutor, and father. Successful men have trophies and titles and certificates hanging on the walls. I have done important things in this life, but the Powers That Be decided to keep all the rewards and recognition for themselves. It wasn't fair, but it's where I was.

It's the kind of thing that ran through my mind while rage-texting with Uber, which I did a lot. I'd gotten a call to get a lady way up GA 400 on Mansell Road. It was a twenty-minute drive to get there—which means I was down twenty minutes plus gas before I even got started. So I arrived and waited. No answer. The app had me cooling my heels for five minutes before I realized it was a prescheduled deal. That meant I still had to wait another eight minutes until the agreed-upon pickup time. The reason I didn't see that earlier was because I was answering calls while driving, and if I read everything on the screen, I'd kill someone. Anyway, I waited the extra time.

> I got a text: "Im here. Where you?"
> I texted back: "I'm where you sent me."
> She texted: "Im RIGHT here, apt212."
> I texted back: "That's not where you sent me."
> She texted: "Other drvrs don't have no problem. Pick me up. running late."

It took me a moment to translate *drvrs* to drivers. *Why do people do that?*

I checked the app, and she was a good twenty *more* minutes away. I tried to explain this via text. Turns out, the lady entered the wrong address, got the pickup and drop-off locations switched. That happens a lot.

She texted: "Why you such a idiot? Forget it.
Im tell your boss."

So she canceled. *Dick. Can women be dicks? I support equal rights, so I say yes, they can be and frequently are.* Anyway, I claimed a cancelation fee, but Uber said I wasn't entitled because…reasons. So I spent the next forty minutes in a text war…which I lost. I'm pretty sure no human was on the other end of that discussion, only an algorithm with an attitude and a prewritten script.

It was five dollars for the cancelation fee but really should have counted as eleven dollars, considering the time I'd had to wait. I decided to appeal. I don't like being blown off like that.

As long as the day was going the way it was going, I decided to check on the woman who gave me the gift of life "after thirty-three hours of labor, hard labor!" She'd used her maternal woodburning kit to inscribe that fact on my brain. She had texted me, saying there was something she needed to talk about.

Ma's dark orange car was parked in front of her condo, its wheels and doors coated in mud. I was sure there was a story there, but I didn't want to know. I'm not really sure how to describe my mother, mostly because she'd always been there, kind of like old wallpaper; you're not really sure when you got it or if it was there when you moved in. Anyway, Ma was a youthful sixtysomething and liked to keep active. Sometimes too active.

I walked up and knocked on the door.

"Zebulon! Come on in!" she beamed, her puffy pinkish face and blue eyes framed in a do of frosted blond hair.

That name. Zebulon. It was so damned redneck. I'd spent years working to eliminate the Dixie from my speaking voice (I do turn it to eleven when singing ballads), but the sound of my own name pegged me as a Southern boy. I might as well wear a Confederate flag patch on the ass of my jeans and spit tobacco juice. I decided who I was. I still wore Dingo boots but lost the mullet after high school.

Ma hugged me, patting my back with the hand that wasn't holding the Canadian Club. Half-melted ice clunked in her souvenir Falcons cup. It was not quite eleven in the morning. I will point out that I have never seen my mother soused. I envied her generation's seeming (to my eyes anyway) ability to handle their booze. She knew her limit, a trick I'd failed to master.

We exchanged small talk for a few minutes.

"Do you have everything you need?"

"The checks show up every month, social security and your dad's pension. I'm living la vida loca!" she beamed. I let the dated reference fly by.

We took our usual places around the kitchen table. I knew without looking that there was a case of one-seven-fives under the sink. I didn't want to know how many were empty. Ma kept her drink close at hand, sipping sparingly.

The conversation was tricky. Any reminiscing about the past would lead to memories of Dad propped up in a bed in the dining room, slack-faced, pathetically hanging on, needing to be bathed. I didn't want to talk about any of the recent events, which I barely understood anyway. I danced around my living arrangements and tried to focus the conversation on the kids. Even that was hard. I knew what Zack was up to…and didn't want to talk about that. I hadn't had a decent conversation with Jessa in…a while.

Using her spooky Ma powers, she zeroed in on Jessa. "She's loving her sociology class," Ma said, taking a sip. The last part came from inside the plastic cup. "I think she has a thing for her professor. Ha! She's got my genes."

To the list of things I didn't want to discuss with my mother, I added my daughter's love life. "That's great." It sounded horrible as soon as I said it.

My phone vibrated in my pocket. I reached in and turned it off. It was tempting to pretend it was important.

"She says she's thinking of moving out of the dorms. She's asking if she can stay here." Ma's condo was okay, nothing special, yellow vinyl siding butted against the neighbor's blue vinyl siding, which butted on green, tan, and so on, stretching along the shore of a neglected pond. The home was roomy for one although over cluttered with a lifetime's accumulation of furniture. I remembered the record player and LP rack in the blond wood cabinet from when I was little, and somewhere around here was the toy chest my grandmother painted with horses. The condo had a spare room, currently home to exercise equipment. Not bad, but nothing compared to Jing's—our—house, or the cottage for that matter.

"First I've heard of it."

"So I gather," Ma said at half volume.

"You don't have to say yes. Jessa can move back into the house."

"I don't think that's her plan either." She brightened. "Are you sure I can't fix you a drink?"

"Oh, no thanks. I'm trying again." A half-truth since I was thinking about getting to a meeting. Talking sex and family with Ma was hard enough. Sharing a drink with her frankly terrified me.

"Good for you, Zebulon." And there it was again. My name delivered in that tone that only one woman on earth could generate. It was like sticking pins into all 23,978,534,685 of my nerve endings at once.

"Ma, I prefer to be called Zee." I'd prefer to be called Bill Gates, but life ain't that generous.

"We should take a trip home. You don't remember, Zebulon. We left when you were eighteen months old." And I've carried that name ever since. Georgia has its share of interesting place names. If Mom had been born a few zip codes over, I'd be saddled with the name Hopeulikit, Montezuma, or Santa Claus. "We should go, you, me, and my grandbabies. All of us." A moment later, she added, "You can take Jinny."

"Jing." *Great, Ma said I could take my wife.*

"I've always like her. So good with money, so focused on it. And she's so pretty with her nice clothes and all her makeup and such, bless her soul." A true Southern lady like my mother could say the most horrific things about someone, as long as she followed it up with "bless her soul." The comment matched Ma's tone and she-wolf smile. "Anyway, we'll get a room at a bed-and-breakfast. They have Putt-Putt and…" And that is where my mind dived out the nearest window.

It's not that far, but I haven't been to Zebulon, Georgia, since I was in diapers. I know that Mom met Dad there and that Dad was a firefighter there before he signed on in Sandy Springs, which paid better but still not well. I know Vic Chesnut came from Zebulon; I played his songs sometimes. Zebulon Montgomery Pike was a soldier who gave his name to Pike County, Georgia, to Pike's Peak in Colorado, and to me. I still have family in Zebulon—they used to come north for the holidays every year before Dad's stroke made it impossible to have visitors. They were fun-loving beer drinkers who talked about NASCAR. I haven't kept in touch. I'm not sure why.

"You're forty-two, Zebulon." The sound of that name she'd pinned on me yanked me back to the present.

"Yes. And?"

"Forty-two, good health. You still have a wife somehow and two great kids."

"I know. I know."

Mom lifted her giant cup of C&C in a toast. "Your life is full."

I grumbled, "I don't feel full."

Mom spoke into the cup again, "That's a problem. It'll make you an old man."

I was out the door before she could serve me a Ma lunch of tomato sandwiches and banana rice pudding. I was ready to tell her I had a meeting with my music agent. That was kind of true, it was next month, but my phone saved me the trouble.

One of the texts that buzzed in told me to "meet Hui" back at the house. I figured this was the pickup Jing had mentioned, but the text wasn't from Jing. It was from Mrs. Li, Kevin's mother.

CHAPTER 6

THE EASIEST WAY TO unload a fridge packed with dead spunk monkey is to get two other guys to do it for you. That was my plan, anyway. Nitro started to help but clutched his back in a dramatic fashion and promoted himself to supervisor.

"Keep your end up, Zebulon. Don't drop it, for heaven's sake," he said, making broad motions with his hands.

I carried one end while Mr. Hui, who had shown up with a pickup as promised, easily managed the other. He was nothing but polite. I instantly took a liking to his smile and gentleness. At six-four, he fell into the "gentle giant" category. He sported a spikey hairstyle, Georgia Tech letterman jacket, and designer eyeglasses.

"It's Hui Rong, but you can call me Rong," he said as we lugged the heavy unit out of the SUV and over to his Ford F-450.

"Don't scratch that pretty paint job!" Nitro scolded then turned and spit on the ground for emphasis.

Rong continued, "I have someone coming to Mrs. Li's to help, so you don't have to concern yourself with unloading after we get there." It felt odd adding this errand onto our scheduled sit-down to discuss her son's tutoring. To Nitro, he said, "You will come too. Mrs. Li would like to meet you."

"Is she pretty? Naw, I don't care about that. Is she rich?" I'd heard Nitro attempt that joke before. Why was Mrs. Li interested in Nitro? How did she even know about Nitro? I wanted

34

to ask, but I was busy keeping my fingers from getting mashed between the fridge and the truck bed.

We finished getting it loaded, and Nitro helpfully swung the tailgate shut. "So in American, your name is Rong Hui?" Nitro butchered the pronunciation to make it sound like "wrong way" and then laughed at his own gag. I tried not to make fun of Chinese names, considering the moniker I carried, but sometimes it was irresistible. I blushed with embarrassment and took a breath to apologize.

"Yes, that's funny," Rong Hui (the name was stuck in my head ass-backward now) said quickly. He was grinning. "My classmates at Tech kid me all the time." I put his age somewhere in his midtwenties, except maybe a little older. Yes, I liked him. I envied him his ability to laugh at himself.

"You're a student?" Nitro asked.

"This fall, I'm signed up for international finance, prelaw, organic chemistry, botany, and jazz. Right now, I have online ESL classes," Rong said. It was quite a list. In fact, prelaw wasn't really a thing. It was what you told your parents so they'd keep sending money. As for ESL, he meant he was in a course of English as a second language like most of my students.

"You sound like you've got it down. Too bad because I tutor English," I offered.

"Yes, Mr. Angell. You'll be tutoring Kevin tonight." Odd that Rong knew that. "Get in."

Zack was off somewhere, and my calendar was empty for the rest of the day and evening. I could have driven, but I was taking a break from Ubering thanks to a rich kid with a weak stomach. He had tossed his cookies while sitting up front with me. The smell of secondhand Jose Cuervo Gold was potent. The kid—who was *maybe* twenty-one; I did not ask—was profusely apologetic. I told him he'd done the right thing by calling for a ride in his condition. (How I wished I had never made that mistake.) I also said that Uber would charge him a two-hundred-dollar cleaning fee. He begged me not to report him. He promised to pay me to clean my car. It was late, and there were no detail shops open, so I took him to an ATM. The next thing I knew, he was making it rain. He peeled off several hundred dollars—and kept counting. I handed him back some of the money, kept more than two hundred, and told him I'd take care of it. I got him where he needed to go, drove straight home, hosed out the Corolla for an hour, and pocketed the money. My best night ever.

My right shoulder slammed into the door as we lurched around and past a semi. Rong was a terrifying driver who played K-pop at top volume, chatted even louder, and laughed his way through stop signs. I asked him whether he got many tickets. He said, "Never. I know people who know people."

We drove to one of North Fulton's many gated communities, where Rong offered the guard his license. The guard offered back a rented smile and waved us through but not before taking a close look at the fridge in the back. He didn't ask any questions in deference to Rong but shot the stink eye at Nitro and me as if trying to recall us from a wanted poster. After the gate, we drove for a while. We passed a golf course, a horse stable and riding ring, plus well-spaced homes set on expansive lawns. Some were southern classics with Doric columns out front, calling to mind Scarlett O'Hara lusting for Twelve Oaks. Wealth had incongruously altered those rolling hills, plopping down French Colonials, Tudors, or literal castles of brick and stone complete with crenelated turrets, or so the casual visitor would think. We happened to pass one home still under construction. Men at one end nailed plywood sheets over pine studs while a second crew sprayed on the stones and brick, sculpting and coloring the thin layer to pass for heavy masonry. Let twenty storm-filled Georgia summers lay siege to these castles and they'd be reduced to ruins. Of course, by then, smart investors would unload them at breathtaking profits.

We pulled into a driveway that circled a silvery tree, its trunk made up of gleaming chrome and burnished metals. Oddly shaped fruits made of green-patinated copper hung in clusters from the half-scale tree. I figured it was a Chinese thing, and it struck me as shiny but sterile. The house itself was a three-story monstrosity of concrete and glass, the handiwork of a godchild architect playing with oversized blocks. The upper windows reflected the surrounding area in shades of blue silver, affording privacy. The ground floor windows were clear and revealed generous interior spaces large enough for indoor golf. I swallowed hard. This place made Jing's—ours—look like a shack.

"Nice," I said, grabbing the haversack I used because it looked like something from a Hemingway novel.

"Mmm. Mr. Li must do all right for himself!" said Nitro, nodding for emphasis.

"Mr. Li is no longer with us," Rong answered, and that basically killed the conversation.

He took us to the front door and rang the bell. I looked back to see two men get in the truck and drive it off, presumably to the garage, wherever that was. This house was too big for me to take in all at once.

I half expected a butler in a tuxedo to answer the door, but in fact, what appeared was an image of loveliness: Mrs. Li. She was trim and toned, a few years younger than me, not a line on her angular face. Her hair was perfectly arranged as if a hair specialist had just finished teasing it with a brush. She wore a blouse of subdued aqua over white slacks, adorning herself with elegant gold jewelry. I caught myself before my face gave away what was running through my brain. *Okay, not exactly my brain.*

As I stammered out some nonsense, Mrs. Li took charge of the moment. "I am Gillian." Hard G. "Kevin, his mom." Her syntax was less polished than her son's or Rong's, but the effect was utterly charming. There was a power to her words, a cool confidence.

Nitro's filter was even worse than mine. "Well, dayum!" He laughed and cracked the widest smile I'd ever seen on his face. "A beautiful house and a beautiful mama to go with it! I envy your boy." He leaned in close to Mrs. Li. "You wouldn't want to adopt an older child now, wouldja?"

Mrs. Li was magnificent. "I got hands full to raise teenager now. I think you too much trouble," she said, smiling. I was watching a master surgeon cut out Nitro's heart and hand it to him. Nitro stamped his feet in delight.

I wasn't as amused by his manners. I backhanded Nitro's arm then turned and said to Mrs. Li, "Hi. I'm Z… Zebulon Angell." I used my full name for the same reason I didn't want to allow myself to think of her as "Gillian." It was dangerous to get casual with a woman like this. My marriage was rocky enough. Besides, at some point, I needed to talk to her about her son's behavior in my house. He'd stolen our stuff.

She led us inside. Expensive art hung from the sunlit walls of the foyer. As we crossed the large space, Rong took my arm firmly. He leaned in and whispered, "Mr. Angell, so you know, Mrs. Li is someone you want to please." His hand crushed my bicep almost to the point of pain.

Gillian—I couldn't think of her as anyone's mom—pointed out some of the works on her wall. "This Liu Wei. Favorite for me," she said, pointing to what looked like a child's attempt to fill a canvas with circles, blocks, and lines using all the colors available. "Look," she said with some excitement. Under the painting, there was a tiny card inscribed: *a sentiment of excess, corruption, and aggression reflective of cultural anxiety—on loan from the High Museum.*

"I'm impressed," I said honestly. "I didn't know museums loaned things to people."

"They to borrow from Guggenheim. I from Atlanta High Museum. We are to have understanding." Gillian's smile ripened into many meanings.

"I thought everyone these days was nuts about Banksy," I said. I knew nothing about Banksy. I had seen stories on the news, and in my opinion, his stuff looked like things Ma still kept in a box from my kindergarten days.

"Pretend."

"I beg pardon?"

Kevin stepped into the room and traded furtive comments with Gillian. Then he turned to me and said, "My mother says that your artist," (my artist?) "Banksy is pretentious. He puts on a show to make his work seem more important than it is." There was more Mandarin tossed back and forth between them while I waited. Kevin continued, "She says it's wrong to sell something of no value, and only a fool sells anything without knowing its true worth. She says it is best to wait a decade or two before buying such art, and even though she might one day acquire a Banksy piece, she would not display it in her home."

Suddenly, I wasn't sure this conversation was entirely about art. My mind raced with other concerns. First off, how in the world was I going to broach the subject of Kevin's theft with his mother? The soles of my feet sweat inside my boots. Second, Kevin spoke English better than most Atlantans. I doubted very much that he needed an English tutor, which brought me to my biggest question, What the hell was I doing here?

Gillian spoke, "You act to be tutor for Kevin." It came out oddly, even for her.

I was adrift, so I reached for the AA adage "Fake it 'til you make it." "Yes. I'd be happy to," I said. I patted my haversack, which held some of my favorite books for tutoring. I had a fair number of Chinese American students. So along with *To Kill a Mockingbird* and *Into the Wild*, I liked to assign *The Three-Body Problem*. Cixin Liu's sci-fi saga was wildly popular and offered solid Chinese history as a jumping-off point for its space opera. It was also a Chihuahua killer. I'd save that one for later. Kevin could read one of the shorter books in two to three weeks. I should be tougher than that, but these kids had a million activities eating up their time, so I cut them some slack.

I typically spent the first session talking with a student and maybe had him read a short story such as *The Cask of Amontillado* to see how well he could put together an essay on Poe's dark, dank ditty. I had a whole speech prepared about how Montressor was the real victim. Sure, Fortunato gets bricked up and everything, but Montressor's petty motivations drive him to an unspeakable crime against his drinking buddy, and he carries that guilt until the end of his life when he unloads on the reader (*You, who so well know the nature of my soul.*) Montressor makes *himself* the victim. Most of my students got the nasty murder but missed that aspect of the story.

I explained this to Kevin, hoping to impress his mother who was looking on. I was about to ask if we could find a table and begin work when Kevin spoke up.

"Poe and *Mockingbird*. Okay," he said and left the room.

Gillian and I smiled at one another. She invited me to take a seat in the great room. It was filled with white furniture and bits of cherry wood oriental cabinetry, plus more of the fine art that marked this woman's style.

"You like booze?" she asked, holding up a white-and-blue porcelain bottle with a red wax seal.

I was sorely tempted to accept. The Chinese used alcohol as a social tool and didn't mind when a guest overindulged, which certainly is what I would have done. White alcohol, or baijiu as it's called, can be 120 proof. It knocked my ass into next week every time. "Water is fine," I said.

She stepped over to the open kitchen area and grabbed a bottle of Evian from the fridge then brought it over with a glass and set them down in front of me. As I was pouring, Kevin returned.

"An essay on Poe," Kevin said, grinning and proffering a sheet of paper. "And this is some kind of report on *Mockingbird*," and with his other hand, he laid a three-page report on top of the first sheet. "It's worth an A."

Obviously, he had made a minimal effort to find some things online and print them out. His name was on them. To his credit, they looked formatted correctly, no stray copyrights, although there was an odd mark of three interlocked triangles in one corner. It was pointless asking whether Kevin had read anything. It bothered me a little that I was being paid to rubber-stamp something. It worried me even more that he'd create records of our fake lessons, complete with grades, to get into a good college.

I looked to Gillian and then to Kevin and then back to Gillian. Kevin smiled and left the room.

"Done. Good," said Gillian. "Now we talk business."

"I'm not sure what's happening, Gillian. Kevin has to do the work. Otherwise—"

"Kevin bright. So bright," she said. "He getting what he need."

"I feel like I'm cheating you both. I feel cheated." I meant that I didn't want to miss making my big tutor speech, but she heard something different.

"He pay you one hundred?"

This threw me. "Eighty, actually."

"So. Kevin cheat you. Okay," she said, giggling a little as if she were amused both at her son's cheating and his greed. She moved quickly to her designer purse, which sat on a counter, pulled out a checkbook, and brought it back to where we were sitting.

Looking at her jot-down numbers that meant money to me, I mumbled, "No, I don't mean that."

She handed me the check. It was for sixty thousand dollars. I stared at the neat handwriting. She'd even managed to spell my name right: two Ls. My mouth hung slack. "Gillian—"

"We do business." She pushed the check into my hands and folded them over the paper, pressing her own hands onto mine. This felt either very good or very not good.

"What kind of business are we talking about here?" I stammered. She was in on this little paper-buying scheme of Kevin's. She was fine with it. ("You *act* to be tutor…") I swigged my Evian.

Rong and Nitro walked into the room. Nitro had his right sleeve rolled up, and there was a Band-Aid on his arm.

"We have taken some blood samples from Mr. Baine," Rong said, surprising me with Nitro's actual name, Marqus Baine. "I will run the labs and let you know. However, he looks to be in perfect health, give or take a decade of hard living."

"You got that right!" Nitro chimed in. I had no idea he was going to be tested, but then I had no idea what was going on anyway. Nitro gushed, "Zebulon, you got to see this place. They got a movie room fixed up like the Fox Theatre, an indoor pool, and a real hospital room too! Man! You and I are in the wrong business."

"Yes, business. Good business," Gillian beamed. "Welcome, Mr. Marqus. Welcome, Mr. Zebulon."

"What business?" I repeated.

Her almond eyes grabbed hold of me as her voice took on the gravity of a thousand earths. "Mr. Zebulon, you to be president for Tiger Penis World Distribution."

CHAPTER 7

SEATED NEXT TO NITRO in the back of an Uber, it took me most of the ride home to sort out what had happened. I had gone from being a gig mage to being president of an international company. My qualifications? I looked in the rearview mirror. *Yep, there they were*: eyes of blue and skin of white. Gillian needed a white face to impress her prospective customers. The Chinese say, "Face is more important than life itself." If a White American works for a Chinese company, other Chinese think that company must be doing well. The opposite was not true. No Fortune 500 company would use a Chinese front man to signal success. Maybe that part wasn't fair, but the Chinese I knew didn't dwell on racial slights. They were too busy getting rich!

There were other issues. I had not actually, you know, *earned* a C-suite, but if this was a sinecure, so be it. Part of me worried about what I was getting into. My conscience almost stirred, but the ethical Zee-part was pinned down and gagged by the Zee-part that was getting paid sixty thousand dollars.

In fact, Gillian was vague about my responsibilities. She had said, "Smile. Keep shoes shined, suitcase ready. Good smile. Handsome man." What forty-two-year-old male could argue with that? When I pressed her, she told me I would run unspecified errands between here and China. Right now, my other gigs were flexible (as in nonexistent) so that was no problem.

It was obvious what the product was: lǎo hǔ yīn jīng, Tiger Penis. I was to be thrust onto the scene as the manroot messiah. Gillian intimated that sixty grand was only the beginning. There was a killing to be made in male virility. In marketing terms, we weren't gonna sell these guys the sizzle; we'd sell them their own tube steaks! This was all about that greatest of moneymakers, the male ego. Kingdoms had gone to war in the name of machismo, and no king could rule with a bent sword.

I googled some of the big names in the boner biz. I made special note of the current prices, which were astronomical. Even if our stuff only worked as well as the little blue pill and captured a tiny share of the existing market, it would be worth a mint. It might do better, though. Zack and Nitro both said Tiger Penis put the man in the mood *and* made the woman more receptive. *How would that work? Ancient Chinese secret?* Maybe the man secreted something when it was in his blood, and that aroused the woman. I was no biochemist. All I knew was that people said the stuff was the real deal.

Kevin was a procurement officer. The more I got to know Kevin, the more I disliked his work ethic. He was skating through school on his way to claiming a corner office. I'd had bosses like him—entitled, smug, and ultimately toxic.

Rong's title was more nebulous. He was an executive vice president at large. There's not much Rong could not do. I got the sense that his enrollment at Tech was an opportunity to add to an already-impressive number of skill sets. More importantly, he was focused and resolute in a way that permitted no questions. He said something to me before he put us in the Uber: "I think you're smart enough to know a good thing when you see it." If anyone else had said those words, I could have taken them as boilerplate. Rong had an unexpected way of edging certain comments with menace. No, I did not want to disappoint Gillian, or Rong.

And Nitro? I guessed he was a chief lab rat. Rong was skimpy on the details of the real purpose behind the tests he administered to Nitro, who only said the session involved a Stairmaster, an eye chart, and a blood sample. Nitro had taken the candies and…erm…field-tested the stuff with several of his lady friends. Personally, I was amazed he could still walk. Rong recorded a number of metrics.

When we pulled into my driveway, I stiffed the driver on the tip. I accidentally hit the decline button on the app. There was the check in my wallet but no cash. I did give the driver a five-star rating. Uber brotherhood.

As he walked back to the cottage, Nitro's walrus laugh scared the squirrels in the trees, and he said, "I knew if I hung 'round you long enough, Zebulon, some of your dumb luck would rub off on me."

"Happy to share." I'd have been happy to hand him the risks too, but I didn't say that.

"I's 'preciate ya."

There was a light on in the cottage. "Whoa! Is someone in there? Do you have one of your hoochie mamas stashed in my cottage?"

"Alls a sudden, it's *yours*. So much for sharing." He gave me a sly look. "Zebulon, it gets lonely out here." He was already hurrying inside.

I decided against confronting one of Nitro's former…or future wives, but I couldn't resist teasing him. "I thought your back was killing you."

He held up a packet. In the dim light between the house and the cottage, I could barely make out brownish-purple candies in the plastic bag. Rong must have resupplied him. "A man's gotta be willing to play hurt." Giggling to himself, Nitro ducked inside.

I walked toward the garage. I fished the car fob out of my pocket and used it to get to the opener hanging from the Corolla's sun visor. The big door rumbled open, throwing light into my eyes. Zack was still out. That was fine since it wasn't quite nine thirty. I wondered what Jessa was up to. I wanted someone to talk to. I'd have settled for the cat, but she was nowhere to be seen.

There was still one small detail to attend to. The time difference made it Friday morning there. I took a deep breath and dialed her number.

CHAPTER 8

I CLOSED THE GARAGE door behind me and dully punched in the long-ass sequence of numbers that would connect me to Jing. Walking in the door to the kitchen, an orange comet flew by me. Damn Kitty. Fortunately, the overhead door was already down. I spotted her under the tool bench just as Jing answered the phone.

"Hē?" Her first word was a stifled yawn of surprise in Chinese, then she snapped into English, "Zee! It's the middle of the goddamn night!"

"No, it's not. It's ten thirty in the morning. I checked."

"In Tokyo. I'm in Berlin! Here, it's dark as hell." She croaked out her words in a hoarse rasp. When had she left Tokyo?

As I was trying to figure that out, I moved to grab Damn Kitty, but she darted out from her hidey-hole, screeching and knocking over some gardening crap in the process.

"Zee, what's going on?"

"I'm getting Damn Kitty back inside."

"Zee, don't let him out!" She sounded frantic. I got in close and made my move…and got a hand full of claws. I cursed straight into the phone. Having drawn first blood, Damn Kitty zipped back inside.

"She's in. I'm down a pint, but she's in."

"Thank you, Lord." Jing sounded genuinely relieved.

"What? She's a stupid cat. She used to like me, but she's turned into a bloodthirsty jerk."

"*He* hasn't liked you since day one. Animals can sense things in humans, guilt, anxiety. He knows you ran over one of his kind."

Somebody turned the gravity way up high, and I sat down hard on the garage floor, my back thudding against the door of the Lexus.

"I—"

"I know you didn't mean to, Zee. It was an accident. Even so, Jessa would never forgive you if Damn Kitty Two got loose and something happened. Not again."

Someone stuck my finger in a light socket. I remembered now. I remembered the sickening bump under my wheels and the sudden cold realization of what it meant. I was four beers in, feeling good and wanting to go out to a bar for music and more drinks. I remembered getting out and looking behind the Corolla and seeing the cat struggling to move. Its midsection looked…wrong, not crushed but oddly squeezed like a tooth-paste tube. I remembered the tail twitching wildly and the head trying to rise off the concrete, and then all at once, both surrendering the effort. I remembered Jessa's face as she looked down at the stain in the driveway the next morning. I remembered—

How in the world had I forgotten *that*? In that moment, I would have given anything to forget it all again.

"Zee? Are you still there?" Jing seemed to be trying to keep it to a low whisper, so as not to disturb—

I let myself ask the obvious question. While I dealt with this flood of resurfacing memories, one stupid emotion slipped by my filters. The words came out, "Babe, are you alone?"

"Tā mā de." (Jing said this to me often, and it was a beaut.) There was a pause. On the other end of the phone, I heard her sigh. "I'm hanging up now."

"Wait! I'm sorry! Look, we have to talk about something important. It's about the…stuff."

"Not over the phone, Zee! Besides, I'm really tired. Keep off the booze, and I'll be home in a few days." She made a smoochie sound and hung up.

There was so much I needed to ask her about. I needed to ask Jing specifically. It felt like I was trying to walk with one leg. I stood in the kitchen, staring at the crappy plastic cat that waved its crappy plastic paw at me from its place on the shelf. At least that one couldn't scratch me and run away.

Jing had cut me off, but I got a sense that she already knew what I had to say about the stuff. Had Gillian contacted her? I had never actually seen the two of them together, but everything pointed to them knowing each other. Jing knew everyone in Atlanta's Chinese community. I called it the Chinese mafia. If anyone needed service or a small loan, Jing made a phone call or sent the word out on WeChat. Mostly, these affairs were straightforward: house repairs, translating, minor legal help. I was about to find out whether the Chinese mafia was into stiffy drugs.

Or maybe Zack had spoken to his mother. That made sense. Jing hadn't even asked about him. Were they all in this together? Was everyone in on this whoopie candy ring but me? I was tired of this. I was tired of being left out of the loop. I was tired of seeing contempt or pity or disappointment in the eyes of those I loved. Yes, I had made a few mistakes, but that was in the past. *Hell, I hadn't had a drink in four days, and I wasn't even trying!* Things were changing. I was going to change the world and be someone. People were going to look me in the eye and talk straight.

Wait 'til Jing got home. Wait 'til I could get her and Zack and Jessa and maybe even Ma into one room and sit them down with my news. Zebulon Angell was in charge now, and no one had better mess with the president of Peckerland!

CHAPTER 9

BESSIE SIPPED HER DRINK by the red blush of a scarf-draped lamp as I serenaded her and Nitro on guitar. She was the one who'd brought all the plants that currently livened up this cottage. Nitro was staring at his latest flame to the point where I could practically see cartoon hearts popping out around them. I was grateful he had not brought all the other women in his life here for a fruit candy-induced male sex fantasy. Was this the stuff's work? Was Nitro in love with Bessie and vice versa? I'd wanted to believe that, but the wicked candy raised questions.

I wondered, too, how I was going to explain any of this to Jing. I didn't relish the thought of her stepping into the cottage, laundry basket in hand, and discovering Nitro's love shack.

Instead, I focused on the Martin and chose one of my older songs…

Constant companion…

Hot one!
Let's ride
A thousand million miles
Hot one!
I see
No one but you for me
Hot one!

I was a
scruffy boy beggin' to the gods of Saturday night
You were there
glowin' in the neon beer sign light
Make the other gals turn in their jeans so tight
You thrill this boy in the dark or in the broad
daylight
Hot one!

And when you
Scoot across the dance-makin', floor-shakin' to
tunes in flight
Not a chance
Reaching 'round those dangerous curves—I just
might
Who's this gal, such a gal, got my heart all
a-fright
No searching aching, once you get the one who
gets it right
Hot one!

I added in a gratuitous solo that went nowhere. Captive audience.

I needed time for my mind to catch up. I needed to know who the hell I was and who I'd be if I went along with the deal being offered. What did it really mean to be the white face of Tiger Penis World Distribution? What was Gillian Li going to do with this stuff? Make the world horny? *Hornier* than it already was? In my experience, that created problems. Boys in lust chased girls. After that came a short list of options: marriage, anger…or loneliness.

Hot one!
Let's ride
A thousand million miles
Hot one!
I see
No one but you with me
Hot one!

Constant companion…

It was supposed to be upbeat, but by the end, it sounded like a breakup lament. It's so strange to be married and lonely for someone at the same time, but that's where I was. The Martin fell silent.

"You're too sad for a man who's got so much, Zebulon," Nitro said.

"Who's the girl?" Bessie asked. I smiled at her noncommittally. "You should keep those feelings for your wife."

I knew she was right, but my heart wanted…something. I kept thinking about beginnings—a snowball fight, an artsy film, trips to the flea market at Roosevelt Field. What happened? I couldn't remember any particular fight. It simply ended. Her choice, not mine.

"Well, this party sure is in the dumps!" Nitro observed.

It was Saturday night. Zack was off, as usual, hanging out with Kevin. I wish he'd find someone better, but that was a dangerous thought too. I still hadn't met his girlfriend—didn't even know her name. I hoped she was with them and that she was a good influence on Zack. He needed a green beacon in his life.

My phone rang. "Mr. Zebulon? Gillian. Are you with Mr. Marqus?"

"Actually, I am." I allowed the universe this one coincidence and handed my phone to Nitro. He and Gillian chatted briefly.

I heard Nitro say, "Yes, ma'am. She sure is... She sure did... Well, I'm flattered, a pretty woman like you saying so." Bessie did not look pleased with the sound of that comment. "We sure can. I always aim to please you, Ms. Gillian... Will do. You take care now." He thumbed the red button on the screen and handed it back to me.

Bessie and I stared at him, blank-faced.

"Whut?"

"You two sound friendly," Bessie observed.

"Naw, sweetie. You got that wrong. Mrs. Li and me, we in business together. With Zebulon here. Tell her, Zebulon!"

"I don't know what to say," I said, not knowing what to say.

"Mrs. Li wants us to make a delivery." From under a pillow, he pulled the packet, slightly less full of our wonder candy than when I'd seen it last.

And there it was. I already assumed there would come some measure of responsibility to go along with the title of president. Now it turned out I was going to be a drug dealer, plain and simple. Actually, the idea did not bother me as much as I might have expected. Other people made money doing worse things. How many of my former bosses at the marketing firm were nothing more than jumped-up drug pushers? How many ads had they created for unneeded purple pills and pink pills and even stiffy pills? Hell, Jing's boss, *Frank*, and I were in exactly the same line of work now, selling drugs most customers didn't need. He was a CEO; I interfaced with the consumer. *That was good, right?* I was finally rising to my rightful place in the hierarchy. Still...

My stomach was in knots. "I don't know about this," I said.

"It's fine. It's fine. We're gonna take it to some folks I know. Mrs. Li wants you and me to be more active in the day-to-day business. She wants us to…what did she call it? She wants to give Betty a taste."

In my mind, I translated from Gillian's grasp of the language to Nitro's understanding of words and then guessed at the actual English. "Beta testing," I corrected. "Where? On whom?"

"*Whommm*," Nitro mocked. "At my old halfway house. We'll also stop over at the village afterward, see an old friend." I wondered where he meant by "the village."

"We can't keep giving this stuff to people. Human beings, I mean."

"It's nothing but a little bitty fruit."

"With some pretty big side effects, like stiff monkey syndrome. Remember?"

"Rong says the monkey's death had nothing to do with our dandy candy."

"And you believe him?"

"I have to. He's says he's making me…you and me…the sole distributor. Besides, I've been popping those things like… like candy. Relax, Zebulon. We'll run over and spread the joy, that's all! Mrs. Li says we should offer it to as many people as possible. You call an Uber, okay?"

"I can drive us," I said, surprising myself with my own offer.

Nitro shook his head. His answer, delivered in a singsong way, made my butt cheeks clench, "We're hav-in' a party!"

CHAPTER 10

UBERING DOWN I-85, SITTING next to a nonverbal driver named Bartek, last name unpronounceable, while Nitro and Bessie played feelies in the back, gave me plenty of time to think..

I could not grasp the nature of this Tiger Penis we were about to shower on Atlanta's underprivileged community. Sure, it was a cousin of Viagra, but to hear Nitro talk, it was much, much more. Once again, I searched in vain for clues. Nitro said his lady friend, Bessie, brought samples of the stuff to him, which meant Gillian or Jing got the stuff to her. I'd already used my quota of coincidences. Someone had been keeping tabs on me and Nitro. Creepy, but not really. Jing knew my circle of friends and must have figured that Nitro would make as good a guinea pig as anyone. They must have followed him and met Bessie. That left other questions. What, realistically, was in it for Bessie? Did she need help *being attracted to* Nitro? Did that make sense? Had someone really and truly discovered Love Potion Number Nine? I knew I should accept my good fortune without question. This thing—it needed a better name than Tiger Penis—had put serious money in my bank account. Even so, something deep down began to itch.

We dropped Bessie off at a nicely maintained Tudor off Clairmont. She said she had to get some things done but promised to phone and make sure people were waiting for us. After she stepped out of the car, Nitro made a snide comment about turning it into a love nest. "No more bungalow, no more halfway house," which was our next destination.

I shared my concerns with him about what this stuff did.

"Everybody's happy, Zebulon. Don't fret about the details."

"We're messing with people's lives," I said. "At the least, we should understand what makes this thing work."

"Boys chasing girls, girls chasing boys. It's old as moonbeams."

"We're talking about a supplement that gets women hooked before they even take it. How the hell does that happen?"

"Oh, that! Ha! That's Mrs. Li's ancient magic. You'll see." And indeed, we were pulling up to the halfway house.

Mirror Lake Courts was a former off-campus college dorm complex converted into low-rent housing. A few double-wides now occupied the weedy spaces between the dun-colored buildings, and the area bore the burden of banged-up cars, broken bottles of Colt 45, syringes, the occasional bullet casing, plus other signs of hard living. Children screeched in the buckled parking lots, playing ball, jumping rope, and shooting plastic water pistols at each other. Half the utility lights were out. The out-of-state owners had designated one building as a male dorm for recovering alcoholics. Women were strictly forbidden access.

Nitro opened the front door with his key. We stepped into the large, sparsely furnished front room and said hello to the women.

"Rong briefed me, told me all there is to it," Nitro said with an air of self-importance.

"I was wondering what you two talked about for so long."

"We talked about getting rich. This stuff is better than any little blue pill. It gets the guy's motor running and then some. He starts sweating out something called 'for her moans.'"

"I didn't think *pheromones* actually worked…unless you're a bug."

"Well, they send a signal. The real attraction is something else." He rubbed his thumb and two fingers together. "Women like money, same as men."

"Dammit, I am the president of this company. Why wasn't I briefed?"

"Calm down! You'll get you a part to play. Right now, chill. Bessie's been working these ladies for days. That's the beauty of it all, Zebulon. You get the customers to do all the selling. Now watch the master seal the deal." He proceeded to charm, flatter, and flirt with each of the women, who ranged in age from twentyish to fiftysomething. They were receptive, joking with him and offering easy smiles. The body language loosened toward bawdiness. The women seemed to welcome both Nitro and the chance for something fine in their lives.

Despite my unease, I started handing out the small bags we had counted and packed earlier. On the plus side, I didn't have to collect any money. Nitro's spiel was so thick and fast I could hardly make sense of it, but I got the impression the women were told they were going to become recruiters in the new company, getting in on the ground floor of this Amway of amour. *Magic, my ass*! The women didn't have valentines in their eyes; they had dollar signs. If our feisty little fruit worked, it would be easier to sell than any of the crap the multilevel marketing schemes had stacked in their warehouses. It couldn't be that simple, but…

There were men there, of course; they were the ones who actually lived there. They were husbands and boyfriends, many made prematurely old and worn down by their own misadventures. They wandered in grumpily, none of them smiling. (At least not yet.) I remembered all too well periods of my drinking career when the prospect of intimacy terrified me. What was it Shakespeare had said about alcohol? "It provokes the desire, but it takes away the performance." I understood why these men were not happy. The women probably told them what was coming, but they feared failure and humiliation.

"Not with this special candy, my friends. You will be the tiger you used to be, with *Tiger Pep*." Nitro had found his own (better) brand name.

The women discreetly slipped off to the kitchen a few at a time and returned with drinks, which they gave the men. It was fruity punch or cider, nonalcoholic, anyway. I was pretty sure this experiment violated the spirit of AA's rules, but no one would actually be drinking booze, so there was that.

After a few minutes of mingling and talking up the product, I pulled Nitro aside. "Didn't Gillian say we were supposed to observe the effects? What exactly do you think we're supposed to observe?"

"You have a sick mind, Zebulon. I like that about you." And he bellowed a laugh somewhere between a foghorn and a hippo love song.

I was embarrassed by his display, but no one turned to look at us. The women were circulating. The men were busy sipping their drinks and…changing.

Subtly, they began to loosen up. A drunk in his first weeks or even months of sobriety is a squirrely creature, eyes darting everywhere, dark minute movies filling his head, never at ease. Now these men were moving around the room with a fluidity they had not shown earlier. They began to smile, even laugh. And they began to touch. The back of a weathered hand brushed the exposed skin of a female back or arm or… Then the men took hold of the women, pulling them close for a dance that was out of tempo with the music in the room. One guy had two women firmly in his grasp. The women were willing accomplices, one burying her hands in her partner's back pockets.

As if someone had shot off a starting gun, couples began to kiss—really kiss. Suddenly, I was at an after-prom party. They were really going at it.

"Um—"

"Yep. That's our cue to vamoose, Zebulon."

"So when Gillian asks, we say, 'Mission accomplished.'"

"Smiling people, happy people," Nitro said with a chuckle. As we stepped out into the sodden night air, he added, "Now for the real test."

CHAPTER 11

"SHOULDN'T WE CALL FOR a ride? Why change tactics now?" I asked, trudging after Nitro into the dark, trying to ignore the crunching under my heels.

"No road where we're going," Nitro said.

"The village?"

"Village. Hellhole of last resort. Whatever you wanna call it."

We walked for twenty minutes: out the main entrance of Mirror Lake Courts, left along the fence line, and into some pee-scented woods. I kissed a spiderweb and spat. My phone's flashlight app barely kept us from stumbling over tree roots and tiny creek beds hidden by the scrappy undergrowth. Atlanta had once been known as the City of Trees. Developers had left only a few ugly pockets of mimosa, pine, and kudzu. Not far off, big rigs whizzed along I-85.

Nitro had gotten out of earshot. I looked behind me and saw him several paces back, standing bent forward with his hands on his thighs.

"You okay, old-timer? You're my guide!"

He launched a bird in my direction. "I guess I overdid with my Bessie," he said, grinning but also wincing. We paused for a minute or two then set off again, more slowly, with him in the lead.

Finally, we came to a clearing, roughly torn out of the greenery. A few donated LED lanterns provided all the light there was for this village of rain-melted cardboard refrigerator cartons. Clumps of people wrapped in blankets and sleeping bags filled the spaces in between. Two or three shopping carts had somehow made their way to this place as well. If *REI* got hit by a shitstorm then held a sale, this was what you'd have. Few of the perhaps two dozen people living here spoke, but one woman (that was a guess on my part) wouldn't stop. She jawed on and on about someone named Evaline (it came out Evil-ine), cursing her name to the damp night air. I made it a point to avoid eye contact while at the same time trying not to step on bottles and drug paraphernalia. I might burn my boots later, but for now, I was glad for their protection.

No one looked at us. I turned to Nitro. "I don't think this is a great idea."

"They won't hurt you, Zebulon. If you scared, stay close, little girl. I'll save you." He laughed at his own joke.

"My hero."

"Uncle Sugar taught this boy to fight. Don't you worry."

"Your glory days."

"Fun Time Navy. That's what we called it when the officers were around," he said. FTN, I got it.

I believed that anyone here would kill for a drink, but it was late, and they looked mostly finished for the night. They weren't going to try to take my wallet or whatever Nitro had on him.

Nitro motioned for me to follow him. We stepped between filthy bodies, huddled around the dregs of what they were drinking. I put my hand to my mouth and nose because of the smell, a putrid mix of everything a human being let fly into the world plus moldering leaves and something else. Something gamey. I guessed some of them caught things to eat when they couldn't find a dumpster to dive in.

"Damn drunks," I muttered.

"Yes, I am, Zebulon," Nitro said calmly.

"I don't mean you, Nitro."

"You better mean me. I lived here for a minute. Well, it moves whenever the cops show up, but in this village, I mean. I got out of the Navy with a powerful thirst. For a few years, I managed. I kept things balanced, or I thought I did. Had a family. Had some jobs. Had a dog even. That thirst, though. It's off growing while you're busy paying attention to other things. Next thing I knew, I was here." I'd heard Nitro's drunkalogue in the meeting rooms, but maybe I'd never really listened. This felt like a fresh confession. Nitro gestured around us. "I know one or two of these folks."

"But…"

"But what?"

"You got sober." *At least most of the time.*

"I got dry. Don't pin no flappy white angel wings on me. You know the math," he said. Group leaders brought it up often. Only ten percent of alcoholics made it to their first AA meeting. Of those, 90 percent went back out. Ninety-nine percent died or wound up in prison or crazy…or all the above. "Those are lotto odds. A man he go broke betting like that."

There was something else I remembered vaguely from AA. People talked about hitting rock bottom. Some came up. Some crawled around down there until they died. A man had to get 'tired of throwing up and start growing up.'"

"You and I beat the odds," I said.

"Not yet. Working on it. That's why we here, Zebulon."

Nitro stepped over to an earthen ridge that rose a foot above our heads. At first, I didn't see what he was doing, rummaging in the fallen sticks and garbage. He uncovered a gap, a cat hole dug into the side of the low cliff. It was a rough hovel, the crumbling overhead braced up by scraps of wood. It looked ready to collapse at any moment, and my chest tightened with claustrophobia just looking at the entrance. What must it be like to call such a burrow *home?* All at once, an emaciated face popped out. I honestly couldn't tell whether it was a man or woman, Black or White.

Nitro leaned in closer than I ever could have and whispered something to the cat hole's tenant. I guess what crossed its face was a smile, though there were no teeth to prove my theory. Nitro pulled a sandwich and a pint bottle from his pocket then found a sample bag of our special candies and gave the whole lot to the dirt dweller.

They called me over. I didn't want to go, but I couldn't ignore them. Reluctantly, I stepped over piles of trash and people and joined them. At this distance, I could make out the man's features. He was a Black man with uneven wispy patches of hair, sunken watery eyes, and lips that curled inward. We didn't exchange a word. The man looked at me. He reached into the pocket of his frayed coat and took out an embossed brass coin, which he placed in my hand. There was writing on both sides, which I recognized by phone light. This included a date spread over the three corners of a triangle and a large roman numeral X. At one point in his life, this had been a human being with ten years of sobriety. He was thanking us for the candy by giving us his most prized possession. I couldn't help but wonder if this ten-year chip might also be his last reminder to get back to an AA meeting. My most recent white chip was sitting in a drawer somewhere.

It was only then that a few words found their way out of this man's mouth. In a breathy, wandering voice, he said, "Evil is close to you, my son," and wrapped my fingers over the coin as if it were a holy relic.

I took the coin, awkwardly thanked him, and we left. It seemed a brief visit, though I had no wish to make it longer.

Trudging back to the main road, where we could call our next Uber, Nitro explained what we had just done. "A man in that state loses his power. All of it. If these Tiger num-nums work on *Q* like they do on me, then he'll get some of hisself back again."

"How will we know? I'm not staying around long enough to—"

"I keep tabs, Zebulon. Gillian will get her info."

We kept walking. "Who?" I asked.

"What do you mean *who*? Who was Reverend Q before he lived in the woods?" (*Had that man been a preacher? What in the world led him to this awful place?*) "A good man. A voice. Someone like you and me."

"Actually, I can't help but wonder who he's going to…you know?"

"You can say 'fuck,' Zebulon. We're both over twenty-one." Nitro laughed loud enough to scare the owls overhead. "There were lots of women back there."

"I'll take your word for that."

"They like a man who acts powerful. Then they start acting powerful too."

We stopped below a streetlight. The complex with the halfway house was just up the road. I punched in a call for our ride. The display read six minutes.

"Are we sure this stuff is safe?"

"Safe as candy. Dandy candy." Nitro held a small "candy" delicately in his fingers, waving it in front of me slowly as if I were a dog salivating for a bite of his master's dinner.

I started to reach for it then pulled back. "No. I'm married."

"It's okay, Zebulon. Life goes on. Birds do it, bees do it…"

"That's fine for you. I'm—"

"You're what? Different? Special?" He frowned at me. "*Better?*"

Was I? I thought back on all the times I wanted to get things done but sat back and watched others act. High school was a blur of missed opportunities, girls, clubs, sports, girls. My marketing career had been all about me asking permission to do something instead of doing it and apologizing later. Still, this felt like…*what was I really doing here?* I wanted to take the candy and fling it into the nearest creek. I tried one last time with a weak, "It's wrong."

"You overthink things, Zebulon. That's your problem. You got analysis paralysis. Sometimes, you just gotta let it all go. Live in the moment."

"Now you're a guru."

"My philosophy says a man does his best thinkin' when he ain't thinkin' at all, just lets life happen, like dancing in the shower, like making love with a beautiful woman. In the moment."

"Fine. I'm living in the moment." I stood there, living in the moment.

"I can hear those wheels turning in your head. *Whirr-whirr click.* Ha!"

Overthink, did I? I had a thought. I grabbed the Tiger Pep and jammed it in my mouth, chewing it hard and fast. The candied fruit tasted musty, like a gummy bear I'd kept in my sock while jogging. It tasted like Chinese dates, jujubes, not the Americanized boxed candy but the dried fruit Jing and I got at the Chinese markets around Duluth. That was it. It tasted like Chinese candy.

Our ride crested a hill, past a man standing in the shadows, and came to a stop in front of us. As we got in, I got scared. "Don't you dare take me back to that camp. I don't want to hump any of those—"

Nitro grabbed my phone and punched in a new destination. "Calm down, Zebulon. I got it all worked out."

It was painfully obvious we weren't going home any time soon. I remember grabbing my phone back and desperately texting…someone…about something important.

As I did this, the driver made a U-turn, wearing the tires like pencil erasers, and headed back up the hill, past the man I'd seen. Our eyes met for a split second as the shadowy man looked into our car. He wasn't from around that part of Atlanta. That community didn't get along well with Asians.

CHAPTER 12

"THIS IS WRONG, NITRO."

My words sounded clear but odd, like someone else was speaking them. I was watching myself perform a role on stage, starring as "me" in the story of my life. I wouldn't call it an unpleasant sensation, though. Quite the contrary, I floated on foamy euphoria. I didn't have extensive experience with hard drugs (or I would be dead—period!), but I knew what painkillers felt like, thanks to my habit of dipping into Jing's supplies. What I felt at that moment was similar to the effect from Percodan.

Oddly enough, I would say I was sober at that point. That's not to say I was guilt-free. Far from it. Still, it wasn't a drunk I was on. My worst nightmares happened during sobriety when I dreamed of taking a drink and instantly withered in the shame of betraying myself. Those dreams were always precursors to actual drinking. This feeling was something else…and it felt… wonderful.

There was a change in my time sense. That is, I lost it. Not quite blackouts, I seemed to cycle down in the middle of one action and back up into another. One second, I was stepping into the Uber, the next the wheels were crunching over stones as we rounded the sexiest, silveriest tree I'd ever seen. It was laden with heavy metallic fruit, and I could see many itty-bitty curvy versions of my own face reflected and staring back at me. *Hello!*

Security lights came up in blinding fashion and more beamed out from the glassed-in spaces of the giant house. We got out of the car and watched it drive off. By the time we reached the door, Rong was there to welcome us inside. Kevin was nowhere to be seen, but Gillian was standing there in silky red pajamas that flowed over her womanly form like cherry syrup on nicely scooped ice cream. *Did all Chinese women look that good? She reminded me of my Jing. It was Gillian. Hard G. Hard Zee!*

I said…things. I stared. I willed myself to stop staring at Gillian. I stared some more. Her jammies were colored red like zesty jujubes ready for my tongue. *Food was sex, and sex was food. That was important. I willed myself to remember that for a future song. What had I been thinking?*

Rong and Nitro said…things.

Rong and Nitro were gone. They left. Or they walked off. Or they turned into big metal fruits. Anyway, they were gone.

Did I mention things were a little confusing? But laser-focused and profoundly intriguing. But…confusing.

Gillian took my hand, warmly stroking the back of it with her thumb, on which she wore a silver spinner ring depicting scenes of gods and romance from the Beijing Opera. She led me up some stairs, speaking a little or a lot. I don't really know. At that moment, I remember how much sense it made. She said something about "Not to be overthinking like old man. Be the now, Mr. Zebulon." She was profound. "Live in the now." I said some amazing things as well. I wish I could write them down, but within seconds, those thoughts were on the other side of a plate of rose-colored glass, lovely but untouchable.

More halls, more art. *Hey, I think I finally understood what the artist was saying. If I could remember it, I'd…whatever.*

I lay down. *Wait.* First, I got to a room, a bedroom, and then I lay down. I wasn't tired, though. I mean, I really wasn't tired. It had to be well after midnight, but I was so not tired. I felt as though I had all the energy in the world…and wanted to use it right then and there. I had all the energy in the world because I was…a god. I was a spirit in the night.

Things happened, and I really, really enjoyed them.

I don't mean to be cute about it. I want to recall the details. Well, sometimes yes and sometimes no, but it's as if my mind recorded things in a different language, a different wavelength.

I can't accurately describe the physical act that took place over the next several hours. I don't mean the mechanics. Those were basic, if more acrobatic and of longer duration. What's harder to put into words is the view from the driver's seat. It was swimming pool water, clear, but it stung my mind's eye. I hovered in midair after someone used sandpaper on every nerve ending in my body. I was…stimulated. I could tell that I was not myself, but it was like this Zee was more Zee than ever before.

Having sex when drunk had always been a bestial performance for me. I would feel like a happy warthog rutting around, huffing and grunting. Nothing got between the act and the pleasure. What happened that night with the Tiger Pep running through my blood was more brain-centered. I was hyper-alert to details. Her tail. It's not that Gillian had a better ass than anyone I had ever been with. It was more than that, like something out of Plato's plane of perfect forms. Gillian possessed perfect assness. This quality overpowered my thinking, focused it utterly on her body. Every pore, each curve, the warmth, the scent of exotic fruit ripening within my consciousness. I not only desired her, but I also had to have her, this woman who called me "tiger" and mated in like fashion. This was positively metaphysical: boinking and nothingness. There was a desperation driving me in a way I hadn't felt since college, and it lit the dark hollow where *the* girl had been. *This* girl had me lost in the present and in the unfathomable depths of her sloe eyes. There was also an element of giving that was absent during a casual, nasty dance. There and then in my spirit form, I would have done anything to please this woman, precisely to get the satisfaction of bestowing that pleasure upon her. If I failed, I ceased to exist. *Metaphysical? Maybe pathological.*

I don't know if I'm saying any of that right, but that's what I remembered afterward. Also, unlike being drunk on beer, I didn't have to stop in the middle to go pee.

After what seemed like many giddy hours of strenuous exertion, I lay back and closed my eyes.

I slept but did not dream.

I awoke to bright sunlight coming in through my bedroom window.

My room, my bed, my house.

I was home.

Actually, *we* were home.

I turned on my side to face Gillian. I wanted to ask how we'd managed this move from her glass and steel palace to my house. She was beginning to stir, her silky raven hair pouring in a playful mess over her eyes and nose. I timidly gave her warm smooth shoulder a gentle shake with my hand. This sent her hair cascading back to reveal the lovely face of… Jing smiling up at me and saying, "Good morning."

THE PORTRAITS THAT HANG IN MY GALLERY

THERE WAS NOTHING WRONG with my memory, usually.

I remember the first time I kissed a girl. Holly Freeman, my buddy's sister, in Mr. and Mrs. Freeman's basement. She was two years older and thought it would be funny to break me in as a great lover. I ended up begging her for sex, which she thought was hilarious. I remember exactly how her giggling sounded to my barely fifteen-year-old ears.

I remember every argument I had with Misty Thurgood, my boss at *Daniels, Foye, and Kaiser Marketing*, and her condescending way of letting me know I was never going to win an argument...or get promoted...ever. I remember keying her car—just a little on the rear—on my way out of that job. Days later, I got a security camera photo in the mail, along with a bill.

When it came to Jing, details dug precious grooves in my memory.

We met about a year after college. Educated beyond my native intelligence, I had landed a crap job. She was a graduate student at some big school, majoring in biology, I think—or chemistry. Anyway, she was super cute in her thick glasses. I missed those after she got the LASIK surgery.

We met at Sope Creek Park in Marietta. I was biking around the pond. I passed a group of nerdettes checking out the plants. The prettiest one, Jing, was telling the others what each flower was and which ones were deadly. Ha! I rode another lap and came back to find the girls huddled together. Some were squealing in a panic. On the narrow rocky edge of the pond, three dark oily snakes were inching toward the group. I got off my bike and, in my Superman voice, told the girls to stand back. I grabbed a handful of pointy rocks and whipped them at the snakes. My missiles clacked harmlessly within an inch of the nearest snake's head. The damn thing kept coming. I threw more stones, but not one of the serpents backed off.

"Keep back! They may be poisonous!" I told the girls, maintaining a cool air of control while also stepping backward.

"We're not going to eat them," Jing said.

"What?"

"I don't care if they are poisonous. We're not going to eat those snakes. If you mean we should stand back because they're *venomous*, I agree. We should go."

It was our first fight. She won.

We wound up retreating from the slithering hell-beasts and made our way through the late September woods to the stone ruins of the old paper mill on the banks of Sope Creek itself. To my great fortune, none of the other girls seemed interested in me. They contented themselves with kicking off their sandals and splashing in the cooling waters that ran under the bridge. Jing and I climbed out to a private boulder in the middle of the creek and continued our argument.

"What else are you an expert at?" I asked, daring her to show off. She did.

"I am learning everything I can. Georgia is great for botany and pharmacology, among other things." Looking around expectantly, she said, "Foxglove grows wild here, somewhere."

"Is it pretty?" I was just pretending to be ignorant.

"It is if you have heart problems. It's where you get digitalis."

"I was about to point that out."

"You're a liar," she said with a straight face.

"You're very perceptive," I said. She smiled at this. "And smart."

"Go on."

"And really cute except for that big wart on your nose. Anything growing around here to cure that?" She hit me. Hard. I loved it.

For our first actual date, I picked a movie with great reviews. I sat through *American Beauty* alternating between boredom and mortification. When Kevin Spacey's high-strung neighbor hauled off and man-kissed him, I nervously glanced over at Jing. She seemed to be enjoying the movie. When Spacey was about to nail the skinny teen, she said, "Ew. He's so *old*!" but didn't even flinch at the ending. For my part, I came away cursing the producers for making a film with no necking potential whatsoever.

On the plus side, the night ended well. We popped down I-75 for chili dogs at the *Greasy-V* and talked with onion breath about how great it was to fly in our dreams. Afterward, we bought a cheap bottle of wine and went back to my apartment. It wasn't much, but it was away from Ma and it was all mine. Jing looked at my dinged-up possessions and commented on the general sloppiness of the decor. She was right. I should have retired the Allman Brothers poster.

"Is that your sister?" she asked, pointing to a driftwood-framed black-and-white photo on the far wall.

"No, that's Li—Long Island. It's just a picture."

She moved on to the dining table, which had a pile of old books on the end I didn't use for eating. "Bad feng shui. And you could clean this place better."

"I'll get a maid as soon as the lottery people pick the right numbers."

"Yes. That's a good idea." Then, while I was still trying to plot her trajectory, she said, "I won't do anything on a futon, Zebulon." The futon was in good shape, only a few beer stains on its lime green canvas, but it was a futon, so, as the French would say, 'non humpez vous.'"

I said, "There's a big bed. The sheets are clean. And call me Zee, please." I was hoping—really hard. She kept me waiting a solid minute, standing there, considering her options. Then...

"Zee," she said my name that way for the first time and put her arms around my neck. "Take me to the big bed with the clean sheets."

Yes, I remember how her pencil skirt slid off her hips by the glow of the lava lamp and the way her voice rose in primal song as she taught me to please her and the smoothness of her skin and the way my lungs drank in the scent of her hair. I remember giggling together afterward and not being able to stop or wanting to. And when at last Jing fell asleep in my arms, I remember lying awake and feeling...real.

We officially started dating the next morning, over a breakfast of frosted strawberry Pop-Tarts with sprinkles. We set rules, and I followed them. I agreed to try harder to land a job I actually wanted. I thought it was odd that she focused on that, but in all honesty, she was right. It hurt to wear a college ring on a hand that stocked toilet paper on the graveyard shift at Kroger. She agreed that we were "exclusive"— her word. We agreed to support each other financially. Early on, she explained, she'd need time to focus only on school. Later, when she was established, she'd provide all the money either of us would need. She said I was her "dreaming man." I think she meant "dream man," but I liked the way she said it. Besides, we were compatible because we were both dragons on the Chinese zodiac.

As it turned out, we moved in together six weeks later. We got a nicer apartment with the money I made at my new job.

I was amazed at how well her belongings went with mine. The walls were filled with color and design. I gave the green futon to a friend from Kroger. I worried about where to hang the old driftwood-framed photo, but it was a moot point. It got lost in the move. Nothing else did. I think about that photo often.

I also remember the birth of our children, the day we moved into the big house, and some things I wish I could forget.

So anyway, my memory is usually solid.

It was distressing, therefore, that I had a big black hole in my recollection of the previous few hours.

CHAPTER 13

"BABY, WELCOME HOME," I said. I opened the floodgates of my mind, inviting memory to rage in like a mighty river but got nary a drop. When—I mean *exactly* when—had my partners switched places?

"Morning, tiger." It was a purr, which instantly turned sharp. "I got in last night and found Ruth Anne waiting up for Zack." Jing didn't like having Ma in the house although she didn't seem angry. My act of sending a text last night appeared in my spotty memory like an old photograph fading to red in the drawer.

"Did you…did we?"

"Yes, of course," she said. I hated that I had no clear recollection of that. "You were on autopilot most of the night. In fact, you were out cold when I first picked you up at Gillian's."

I looked at my wife.

My wife looked at me.

"Think of it as a hall pass."

"I never asked for—" Hold on. Had Jing taken a "hall pass" on her world tour with the boss? *Frank*!

"One more thing before we file this away forever, don't trust her, Zee. She's touched by *shen*." She saw the question in my eyes and answered. "Spirits. Bad ones, selfish ones, *guishen*." Demons? Seriously? My head was spinning like a freshman doing keg stands at a pledge party. Before I could get my bearings, Jing blithely added, "It's almost nine. We should get breakfast. Unless you'd like to go back to sleep?"

I wanted to sleep for a month, but I also felt a pleasant reserve of energy burbling up from the depths of this well. Wonderful stuff, that Tiger Pep.

Jing headed off to her bathroom, the larger of the two. I flung the satin sheets off my naked body, swung my legs out of bed, and…nearly doubled over. There was a stabbing pain between my legs, like doing a split onto a LEGO. "Th'FUUUUU—?" I asked the dresser then duckwalked to my shower. Gallons of steaming water and a few limbering exercises later, the pain had all but gone.

Shaved and dressed, I came down to breakfast—and saw my life.

Our kitchen has a bay window facing the garden that lets in plenty of sun. It's decorated with various Chinese kitsch, including the lucky (tacky) waving cat thing and assorted ornaments meant to maximize feng shui. We'd spent a fortune on the brass ox that stood on a plinth in the southwest corner of the room, the wooden carved tiger to the north, and a miniature water fountain tucked under the cupboards. For the very first time, I felt that the money had been well-spent.

Jessa was home, holding a contented Damn Kitty Two and sitting next to Zack in our breakfast nook. Ma was manning the stove like a short-order cook, dishing out plates of the same Southern comfort food I had known growing up.

"Look, Dad, MawMaw made grits…and eggs you can drink!" said Zack, wearing a brave smile while spooning up the yolk from the soft-boiled egg perched in its serving cup.

As for me, I could have lived in that breakfast forever. It was like an extra Christmas morning or a quick visit to the days when the kids were little. I felt like a real father to them, something I had rarely felt lately.

"Everything is wonderful, MawMaw," Jessa added. Her smile was genuine, though I noticed she hadn't touched her pickled okra.

Ma pushed a loaded plate into my hands. "Sit down. Eat. You've lost weight, all from your face, not your belly. You look tired. There are circles under your eyes. Looks like you got rode hard and put up wet."

Jessa nearly spit out her juice. I put on my best poker face. *Smile. Teeth. Show teeth.*

"Fine. Fine, Ma," I said and sat at the table. As I did, Damn Kitty Two yowled and scooted off to parts unknown. That was fine. My daughter was here.

"Jessa, so…" And the batteries in my head died. I looked at my little girl—well, she was a woman now. *When? How?* I could still see the toddler who, the moment I got up for a beer, decided to pick up her toy xylophone and chew on it, then dropped it, yanking out her front baby tooth in the process. And yet right here and now was a full-grown college student. Soon she'd be a doctor or lawyer or—

"What?" she asked.

"What what?"

Jessa tilted her head to one side. "You started to ask me something, Dadda, but you took a little vacation."

Ma said, "I think your father had a full night, Jessa."

"No. No, I only wanted to know how you were enjoying Emory."

"You ask her that every time you see her, Zee," said Jing, coming into the kitchen. She walked over to the stove, brushing by Ma, who was carrying a full plate of ham steaks and a glass of sweet tea. When Jing got to the stove, she found the skillet empty.

Ma said, "There are grits in the pot for you, darling."

Baring her fine porcelain blades at Ma, Jing opened the refrigerator, saying, "I'm sure there's something good in here," and fixed herself a plate of jianbing plus two century eggs and some fresh cherries and orange slices.

I desperately tried to pick up the previous conversation thread. "I'm trying to keep up with my busy college student." I had a million questions, but my daughter was a minefield, so I carefully chose the safe ones. "Have you decided whether you're going to be a doctor, lawyer…?"

"Stripper," Jessa said flatly, her eyes twinkling at my discomfort.

"Good money in stripping," Ma added. Clearly, the two of them were enjoying making a fool of the newly reinstated king in this castle.

"Can we change the subject, please," Zach pleaded. "I'm having a hard enough time swallowing grits without thinking of my sister pole dancing."

"Nice breakfast conversation," I said.

"You got your check, right?" asked Jing, sitting down with her plate from which she took one of the century eggs and put it on Zack's. He pushed away from the sloppy soft-boiled egg and dug into the replacement, though seemed less than enthused by its deep green gelatinousness.

"Yes, thanks," Jessa answered her mother.

"Got a boyfriend picked out? An upperclassman maybe?" Ma asked between mouthfuls.

"Oh, I'm dating my professor," Jessa giggled in full-on devil mode. Had Ma been serious? Or were they coordinating their jokes? "Well, not really dating. It's just sex."

"*Please* stop!" Zack cried. He pulled out his phone and began searching for an online distraction. Anything to avoid the table conversation.

Ma reached over and rubbed his shoulder like she was comforting a lost child. "Maybe Jessa and I had better save the gal pal chatter until after she's moved in."

Jing looked up at this. "I didn't know—"

That was my cue. I was the head of the house, and I was about to bring in a bunch of money. My heart swelled with pride, for my family and for my ability to lead it. Cutting Jing off, I stood up and tapped my juice glass with a fork. "Folks, I have a little announcement to make," I said, shoulders back, chest out.

Jing turned to me and her expression froze. "Baby?"

"I have a new job. I am the president of Tiger—of Tiger Pep World Distribution." There, I'd taken my first official job action by changing the name of the company.

"Baby, can we discuss this?" Jing spoke very quietly, though her voice carried in the breakfast nook.

"We are planning big things with a fantastic new product." At that moment, I looked at Ma and Jessa. "It will help people. More on that later. What I want to announce is that I am taking charge of our operations. In fact, I have a plan—"

"You always do, Zebulon," Ma said. I guess it was a fair shot. She was a veteran witness to my schemes. I looked forward to showing her how things would go this time. This time, there was real money involved, a title, and a chance to get things done. I wondered whether I should go fetch Nitro from the cottage but decided to let him sleep.

I pressed on. "I will be heading to China as soon as I can make the arrangements."

Jing stood up and put her hands on my arms. "That sounds great, baby. Let's make sure...our partner...is in the loop on this." The next second, she was furiously texting—Gillian, I presumed.

"That's fantastic, Dadda!" Jessa said. I loved the word "Dadda" more than any other word. *Capital D for Dadda.*

"Cool," said Zack without looking up from his phone. "Do you have like your own jet?"

"Not yet, but I'm working on that."

Zack laughed out loud! "Whoa!" He wasn't reacting to my announcement but rather to something on his phone.

Jessa, who was to his left, yanked his wrist in a rude sisterly way to get a look at the screen. "Whoa!" she said.

"I'm trying to make a—" My protest did no good. "What? What are you two looking at?"

Zack turned his phone so I could see. And it was an eyeful. He had called up one of the live streaming services that specialized in breaking news with little or no commentary. The site had managed to put up a font that gave the location. It was in DeKalb County, not far from the woodsy village Nitro and I had visited last night. Police were escorting a very dirty man out of a liquor store. We could see all his dirt.

"Ain't nothing tween that man and the Lord Jesus but a smile," Ma observed.

The man was protesting and resisting, clutching a large bottle of alcohol in one hand. As I said, this feed specialized in chasing police scanner news, using subscribers with phones as its eyes. It put events up on the feeds live as they happened with a little perspective and zero filter. This one could have used a filter, or at least pixilation, because the dirty naked man was also as happy as a certain macaque.

CHAPTER 14

"DELTA MUST BE DOING great business flying folks in from China. I read where those international routes are making a mint." Some people think they're clever, but just in case, they cover their bets by laughing at their own jokes. Rong and I didn't join the jail desk sergeant, so he pursed his lips and went back to his paperwork.

A thought occurred to both of us. "Has someone else been here about our friend?" Rong asked the desk sergeant.

"Two other men. Chinese. At least, I think that's what they were speaking. I couldn't make out a—" He caught himself staring at Rong. "Anyway, I can't release drunk and disorderlies to foreign nationals."

"So these two Chinese gentlemen left? Do you know where they went?"

"Braves game, shopping in Buckhead, drinks at the Sun Dial maybe. I didn't ask them their plans, not that they could have told me." The desk sergeant punched in some information on his computer. "Your friend has been our guest since this morning. We cleaned him up and put some clothes on him, but it's hard to tell whether he's still drunk or permanently fried. You've signed a writ of responsibility. That means if he gets in trouble again, you will kiss your bail money goodbye and answer to a judge for a possible fine on top of that."

"We understand, Sergeant. Thank you. I give you my word you'll have no more trouble with him," I said. I didn't know what made me think I could make good on such a promise.

"Okay. Your friend should be up in a few minutes. Have a seat."

We walked over to some benches. Nitro joined us, munching on a Zagnut. "Q on his way?" he asked.

Rong nodded.

"Please thank Gillian for me, for putting up the bail money."

Jing's warning came back to me. This trip to the cop shop did not feel like an act of idle charity. Gillian clearly didn't want Reverend Q telling the police about the stuff.

Half an hour later, jailers escorted into the lobby a confused man whose wispy hair might have been coiffed by rats. He wore shapeless Salvation Army hand-me-downs and flip-flops.

"Aight! You had yourself a good time, huh?" Nitro greeted him warmly, slapping both his arms.

"Yes, thanks!" Q said in a soft voice, barely moving his lips. "But my johnsons hurtin' something sinful." His words were comically sibilant, owing to his missing teeth.

"That sounds familiar," I muttered. Then I dared to ask, "What did you mean last night?"

"Last night?" He looked puzzled.

Great. His memory was as good as mine. "You said something about evil being close."

"I don't recall, but it is true enough. Evil is close. Good and evil circle us at all times, awaiting our invitation." Spoken like a preacher, after all.

"Ah," I said.

Drifting off into another realm, Reverend Q added, "Darkness whispers pretty things. Inviting, desirable. It promises to kiss away your loneliness." He shook his head, and his expression reminded me of Ma looking down at Dad's grave. "The loneliness digs into you, digs deep, never leaves…and so you listen to the whispers." He went silent.

"Pffft," Rong said dismissively, ushering us out the door of the lockup and over to the parking lot. "Let's get you checked out."

Within the hour, we were back at Gillian's sprawling estate. I was fascinated by my first look at the medical facility Nitro had described earlier. It had all the gadgets I expected in a clinic—autoclave, scale, supply cabinet, stomach-churning wall charts of people minus their skin—tucked away in a few basement rooms. This time, a doctor was in attendance, looking Q up and down.

"It hurts when I pee, Doc," Q told the doctor, who was older, neatly groomed, and unsurprisingly, Chinese.

The doctor said, "It's nothing to be worried about. It's your body telling you you're not used to such…exertions. You need to rest in a clean bed and eat some good food."

"Same thing Rong told me," Nitro whispered to me.

"And how do you feel?" I asked him.

"The worst of the pain has gone away," Nitro said.

"Good to know." The pinching sensation behind my balls was fading as well. It gave me some hope. I still made a mental note to get myself checked by my own doctor.

Rong walked over to us. I worried that he had heard us. If he had, he offered no sign of it. He said, "We'll take care of this man. We'll get him fully sober and find him a place to stay."

"Why are you doing all—" I started to ask, but Rong cut me off with a quick smile and walked back to the doctor and Reverend Q.

That evening, five of us had dinner at *McCormick and Schmick's* downtown, across Marietta Street from Atlanta Centennial Olympic Park. It felt odd to wear a jacket and tie again after so long. The restaurant's brass and fern decor included glass-partitioned booths, which was good, considering the nature of our conversation. Jing, Nitro, and I walked in and found Gillian and Rong already seated.

We made small talk and ordered drinks and food. I had the steak and iced tea. The ladies each indulged in the restaurant's signature oysters, accompanied by colorful beverages. Nitro had a burger well done, and water. Rong ordered a pitcher of Tsing Tao beer to go with his plate of charred octopus, a suckered limb that looked ready to reach up from the plate and fight back. The women owned the conversation, speaking mostly in Mandarin. Rong said little although I could gather that he filled them in on Q's status.

The steak came out a perfect medium-rare, a hint of red in the center and bloody enough to satisfy my Cro-Magnon tastes. I was enjoying it when I spotted Nitro looking at me in a certain way, then looking at Gillian, then at Jing, then back at me. Then for the briefest of moments, both women looked at me… and broke into girlish laughter. That's when it hit me. This was the first time I'd been together with both of these women…and it was less than twenty-four hours after I'd *been* with both of these women. The steak lost all flavor in my mouth.

The waitress brought both coffee and after-dinner liqueurs for Jing and Gillian.

"Jing Jing is to tell me you be making big statement, Mr. Zebulon," Gillian said, smiling up from her coffee.

Jing nudged me. "Go ahead. You were so full of fire at breakfast. Go ahead and tell her."

I looked to Nitro and took a breath. "Well, as president of our new company, I have decided to head up a mission to China." If I could have been two people at that moment, one would have slapped the other. It actually took me until that second to realize I didn't know what the hell I was saying. Go to

China? Why? Gillian had all the contacts. She didn't need me messing things up. I should wait until she either invited me on a trip or called me over to her house to be the white face of the company for visiting dignitaries.

"You are very bold," she said. I noted that sometimes she remembered the verb, sometimes not. Or maybe it was that she sometimes remembered to omit the verb. "You will leave in ten days." She looked over at Rong.

"Yes, I can make that work." He saw the curiosity on my face. Rong was in charge of the arrangements? I hope this didn't interfere with his online classes.

"You all going to China? You better take me along!" Nitro piped in.

Rong looked at him and said, "Yes, the three of us will go, a small group to avoid attracting attention."

The waitress came over, and Jing won the "grab the check" contest. She insisted we finish our conversation outside. "I have a fun surprise for us."

We stepped out of the restaurant into the muggy night. Even with the sun down, Atlanta was a sauna. Jing held her phone aloft, its screen flashing orange. I thought we were going to step into yet another Uber, but what arrived at the curb was more suited for Cinderella.

We piled into the horse-drawn carriage and began to circle the park. The horse looked bored pulling a gaudy white pumpkin-shaped framework on wheels festooned with faerie lights. The carriage had no doors or windows, allowing the city's noise and a mix of gas and food smell to flow through its skeleton. Cars pulled around us, their drivers never looking over. Oddly enough, it felt private. We took off onto Marietta Street, turning left to circle Centennial Olympic Park, where a local band was on a stage, playing an REM tune with more gusto than talent.

As the SkyView Ferris wheel on our right hauled tourists up for a treetop look at the city, Jing smiled and said, "It's fine, Zee. Gillian and I discussed it...among other things." *Great.* "She should give you a bigger role in things. You can be the face of the company for the benefit of our superior in Xi'an."

"Xi'an?" my question burst out. I was expecting Beijing, where many people spoke English and menus had pictures. I could find Beijing on a map. Xi'an, on the other hand...

"Rong will fill you in on the details along the way. Basically, you are going to deliver our data." With this, Jing pulled a phone from her purse. It wasn't the one she ordinarily used. She would never carry a phone in a rugged military-looking black case. "For you," she said, proffering the device to me. "Before you go, I will load it up with my data from the lab."

"The lab in our basement."

"Yes, baby."

"About that..."

"Through my own networking, I've tracked down talented freelancers who have been walking me through refining and field-testing our product," Jing said. I was picking up on the undertones in this conversation. Despite the outward sisterly act, Jing and Gillian were definitely in competition. In fact, it felt uncomfortable. Jing continued, "Kevin tried to get that data, but the encryption stopped him. Now it's time to move it all into this little phone."

Kevin did that? What freelancers? For that matter, I still didn't know who our superiors were. How many people knew that we kept happy monkeys in our rumpus room? Also—"Those trials included human testing like with Nitro and Reverend Q...and me."

Rong jumped in. "You don't have to get permission from the American government to test a natural dietary supplement."

"They taught you that in prelaw, did they?" I asked.

Rong has the most enchanting smile sometimes, like a shark. "As long as we don't label it as a drug, we're fine. We can say it's good, fun, wonderful, the best, but we cannot say that it cures or treats erectile dysfunction or anything else."

He could be right. I had no idea what US law considered "natural" or whether Jing had crossed a line with her work, which still left another question, "Hang on, why is Nitro coming?"

"Zebulon! Don't cut me out of this!" he protested.

Gillian said, "Mr. Marqus, he important man. He is to be proving the concept." *Okay, that was definitely too many verb tenses spooning in one sentence.*

This tickled Nitro. "Rong and I talked. I'm not just a company man. I'm also a customer. These superiors of theirs want to poke their guinea pig a little. For the money they're paying us, Zebulon, they can poke me high and low." He squealed in delight. Gillian seemed to like the display.

Our enchanted pumpkin turned past a half-completed pyramid of glass: the National Center for Civil and Human Rights, home to a reproduced "Whites Only" lunch counter, an emotional multimedia presentation on the 1963 church bombing that killed four Black girls and Dr. Martin Luther King Jr.'s personal papers. I started to point out the significance…

Jing kicked my leg. "Pay attention. I'll give you a special code later. You will have to memorize it. I will have the computer generate the code, and *you* and only you will *memorize* that code. I won't even look at that code. The computer will generate it and then immediately erase all memory of it. You are the only person in the world who will know that code." Jing said all this with great deliberation. I glanced over at Gillian and Rong, who were listening closely. Jing's speech was as much for their benefit as it was for mine, maybe more so.

The Georgia Aquarium with its whale sharks in a million-gallon tank slid by our carriage as Rong took up the thread. Clearly, he, Gillian, and Jing were on the same page. "The phone will allow you to transfer *our* company's data out to *our* superiors and their payment to our account simultaneously. It cannot go through networks. CCP monitors China's servers and can probably track any phone, VPN or no. This phone is set up for a direct exchange." I got the sense this phone with the rugged black case didn't come from the Apple Store.

"Can I see that?" Nitro asked. Jing started to pull back the phone from his reach, but I insisted she let him look at it. He took it in his fingers, turning it over several times and examining the ports closely. "Interesting." Nitro handed the phone back to Jing, who returned it to her purse. "And where did you say we're going? Sean?"

"Xi'an," said Gillian. "Ancient capital."

"And home of the Terracotta Warriors," I threw out because it was literally all I knew about Xi'an. I'd never been, though Jing promised to take me one day.

"Oh yeah, those big clay dudes," said Nitro. "Cool!"

CHAPTER 15

TEN DAYS LATER, NITRO, Rong, and I were at the airport's Maynard Jackson International Terminal, waiting to board a Delta flight to Shanghai. The Three Musketeers.

I grabbed a snack—a Coke and a bag of Trail Mix, $14.57, thank you very much—and sat down with the others, checking to see that my beloved Martin was still there. I had big plans to distill fresh exotic vistas and experiences into song.

"I think your missus is happy to see me gone," Nitro said.

"It's not so much you as your guests," I lied. It was both. Jing had made it clear that a "No Vacancy" sign would be shining bright red on the cottage when we got back.

"She doesn't seem to like Black folk." That blow landed. I fumbled for a comeback but couldn't think of one. Jing was *not* racist. I mean, mostly not.

I looked around the crowd at the gate and found a mix of Chinese and Americans. I scanned again. Aside from Nitro and the lady at the counter, there were no Black people in this group. I might have missed this fact, except that two young Chinese men kept looking over at Nitro then looking away. I met their eyes and started to get up. Both men, who had no carry-on bags, hastily left the gate area.

I considered alerting Rong, who sat there with loud jangly music leaking from his earbuds. I nudged his arm to get him to take them out and, changing my mind, struck out on a different tack. "So Atlanta is a prime location, thanks to the airport. Easy to get things in and out. Is that why your…superiors…like it?" The late-afternoon sun streaming through the concourse windows revealed fine lines in his face. He seemed far older than an average Tech student, certainly past his midtwenties.

As he looked up from his phone and yanking out one bud, his eye momentarily fixed on the two men watching Nitro. "Atlanta has strategic value for our interests, yes."

"What about the TSA?" Nitro whispered. "What do they think about all your strategizin'?"

We'd spent forty-five minutes going through the security lanes, getting x-rayed (Nitro looked even worse without clothes), groped, and prodded, but no one had even opened our carry-on luggage. In a bland dismissive tone, Rong said, "What about them? In America, we have to be careful, but it's no big deal. In China, things are different. We must *make sure* the right people are receptive to our doing business."

I took that to mean he was spreading bribes to the right officials. I wondered how much money was flying around this company that had me as its president and where that cash came from. Gillian may be loaded, but the rich are notoriously cheap. My suspicions had been growing since the day I met her. Now I wanted to know things.

"What does Jing contribute?" I asked softly. There were people everywhere, but they paid no attention to each other. Screaming children and teens in T-shirts that read "F——America" tended to drive people into their own bubble. We enjoyed the privacy of the crowd.

Rong took a moment to compose his answer. "She's our coordinator. My superiors arranged for contact between Dr. Angell and experts from all over North America. And she has apparently networked beyond those contacts." *Was that a note of annoyance?* "These experts have made certain she received enough training to conduct rudimentary experiments and to combine and refine our Tiger—"

"Tiger Pep," Nitro stuck in.

"Yes, our supplement. We have called its final form Tiger Pep, as you say. There are marketing reasons to maintain the 'tiger' part of the name. But the key ingredient comes from the fruit of one variety of longan tree that grows only in a small area of Xi'an. Longan means 'dragon eyes.'"

"Dragons, and tigers, and boners, oh my!" I said.

Rong actually laughed—well, a little. His voice took on an intimate tone, prompting Nitro and me to lean in. "Many years ago, farmers observed their animals eating the fruit of the tree. The beasts exhibited certain behaviors with which you must now be familiar. These men tried the fruit themselves with similar effect. They also tried to cultivate the fruit, but this prize proved elusive. Sometimes a grove would produce special fruit for generations and then fade. Other times, the fruit would offer its magic for only a season or two. A legend arose, and this eventually attracted the attention of my superiors.

"However, there are even more daunting problems in producing our supplements in large quantities. The fruit must be picked at the right time. It cannot be frozen, dried, or salted. Dr. Angell learned to create her candy without the need for cooking, but the current orchard's entire crop yields only a few pounds of candy, and even that has a short shelf life. Many of the batches have come back inert.

"My superiors arranged for Dr. Angell to take living cuttings of dragon eyes from a small stand of trees that currently yields powerful fruit and bring those clippings to her lab. She claims to have found a working refinement for mass production, something we had not been able to do in China."

"Why not?" I asked.

"There are great resources here in America as well as fewer entanglements. Attempting to incautiously tap Chinese assets would have drawn suspicion from Beijing." I wanted to ask why the Chinese government would be concerned about this fruity candy. "On our superiors' instructions, all information was compartmentalized. Again, Dr. Angell took that aspect of the plan one step further than expected, deciding what information to share. We have been tolerant up until now." That was the second time he had said "we" as if he was on a different team than Jing. "Now we have come to a crossroads. You may have noticed that your wife and my associate have a certain rivalry."

"Your associate? Gillian?" I both wanted to and feared to see the org chart.

"Mrs. Li, yes." There was something off about the way he said her name.

Nitro observed, "Lotsa smiles on the outside, but down deep, they like each other about as much as Angelina and Jessica."

"Angelina Jolie and *Jennifer* Aniston."

"Yeah, them two skinny gals both married to Chad Pitts." This time, I didn't even try to correct him. Then, to me, he added, "S'what happens when you double-dip, Zebulon." I couldn't argue that point.

Rong continued, "It did not start that way. The original plan called for both women to keep and share a complete set of files comprising all the work. However, Dr. Angell began making her reports verbally and withholding details. Mrs. Li grew concerned that she might be squeezed out of the arrangement. She struggled to understand the science, but there are so many pharmacological effects taking place in tandem, well—your wife seems to have solved a puzzle that's left laboratory teams the world over stumped for four years now. As I say, Mrs. Li tried to grasp the medical intricacies, but her fields of expertise do not include—"

"Botany," I said.

"And organic chemistry," Rong said with pride. I wondered why Gillian was running the show when it was Rong who had the bankable skills? I didn't ask.

"Yes, you mentioned that," I said. Not for the first time, I questioned the nature of this man. There was too much packed into this one package. On a whim, I decided to scratch one nagging question off my long list. "How old *are* you, Rong?"

Rong laughed loudly. "I am thirty-two," he said.

I went for it. "That's old enough to be a manager."

Rong didn't bite but rather continued with his previous line of thought. "I've been tutoring Mrs. Li's son, Kevin, but he seems less interested in learning how to manage a vast fortune than he does in spending it. However, Master Kevin has proven useful in providing Mrs. Li with…insurance." His eyes held mine, a snake mesmerizing its next meal.

My breath stopped. "What…are you talking about?" I got a glimmering of an answer in my mind and prayed I was wrong.

Phone in hand, Rong punched in a video call on WeChat. "This may come as a surprise to you, Mr. Angell." He said my name as if he had slipped it between my ribs and pressed its tip against my heart. "Your son does not have a girlfriend as he has told you. He is intimate but with someone you've already met."

A familiar face looked up from the screen. I had just seen him an hour ago, dropping us off and driving away with Zack. "Hi, Mr. Angell! Zack's with me," Kevin Li said. "I'm keeping an eye on him for you. We're having a great time."

"Hey, Dad. Did the plane crash already?" Zack called over from the passenger seat. Jokes. Maybe that was good. It meant that Zack didn't *feel* threatened.

My mind raced. Was Zack a hostage? At the very least, he was under some kind of influence from his boyfriend, Kevin, my asshat of a student.

I said, "We're fine. I wanted to say—"

Rong put his thumb on the red button, and my son's face vanished from the screen. "He is unharmed. He is in continual contact with Kevin and therefore within our reach at all times."

I was in the middle of a crowded airport. What came out came out quietly, but I wouldn't say calmly. "Don't you hurt him. Don't you touch my family." Then I spit out threats to kill Rong, Gillian, Kevin, and their mysterious bosses.

"Calm down, Zebulon! Zack's not in any danger right now." Nitro grabbed my sleeve and yanked, trying to let me know I was jumping into a flaming pit without a parachute.

It did no good. My ill-conceived threats raged on. "I'll go to China and find your goddamned superiors. I will kill them, their cronies, and every last panda if I have to. You understand me?"

"No one *wants* to hurt Zack or anyone else," Rong spoke so calmly it just made things worse. "This is business," he said. What a loaded phrase that was: *This is business.*

At that moment, the lady at the counter made the announcement. I grabbed my guitar, and we all took our carry-ons over to the boarding line for business class. It was time to go to China.

CHAPTER 16

AT THE EDGE OF panic, I considered running off to try to find Zack. Instead, I sent Jing a message using voice text while hauling my things down the slanted jet bridge and onto the plane. By the time I sat down and read back my words, the screen was a hot mess:

> *Ching whats going on check sack immediately hey christ scuse me I think this is 22 ayanbee puck whose crab is this is our overhead who crabs his stewardess im a flight attendant hose crab this and take that that mine snow it down my guitar chick sack wears sack ching.*

I spent ten minutes decoding and debugging my own text while the flight attendant (not stewardess) took the Martin four rows aft to another overhead compartment. I sent the corrected text but got nothing back from Jing before the pilot ordered us to turn off our cell phones and laptops.

I figured Jing knew about her son's choice of partners, though I wasn't certain she knew how Rong and Kevin had leveraged that choice into a threat. What was I involved in? We had a foul-tasting Chinese gummi that gave men a stiffy. How could that be worth threatening my son's life?

In all the confusion, Nitro had grabbed the window seat and taken his shoes off. I took the seat next to him on the aisle and Rong was on the opposite row, one back, meaning he could keep an eye on me while I had to twist around in an obvious manner if I wanted to look at him, Which I did. I needed to get a better read on this man. How could he be so polite, intelligent, and personable and still find room to be so cold-blooded?

I blamed Jing and Zack himself, for that matter. I kept thinking about when Zack was younger and was my little assistant, the boy who used to be there wherever I went, watching me, wanting to do the things I did. Work on the car, he was there. Curse and call the mechanic when I couldn't put the filter assembly back on, little Zack was looking on. When had we drifted so far apart? When did he get so big? When did he start liking boys? That can't have been an easy discovery in his life. Why hadn't I been there with support, understanding…a trip to the park or *something*? My drinking had stolen a huge chunk of our father-son time.

It was a long flight. I settled in. I watched two movies—one good (*Black Panther*—cool characters, cool special effects) and one sucko (*A Wrinkle in Time* pissed me off. I'd taught the book for years, but the film traded Madeleine L'Engle's warnings about authoritarianism for a cheap scary villain.). On the plus side, the earbuds blocked Nitro's snoring.

I played *Bejeweled* until my eyes watered, listened to a little music. We still had seven hours to go. I've never been able to sleep on a plane although the millionaire modules in first-class looked cozy enough. After an hour of trying to drop off, I surrendered to insomnia, took out a notepad, and set down a song.

I would have loved to play my Martin, but I doubted the other passengers would have loved me back. I should explain my process. Some songwriters get the melody first and carefully craft the lyrics to fit. I scratch out lyrics and strum the most generic chords known to man. *I need music theory lessons. Some day.*

My agent, Brendon Worley, said I should stick to love songs—the dumber, the better. "Teens love that crap. They get one, they play the hell out of it, then they dump it and move on to the next. For musicians, it's a river of cash." Brendon also liked to scold me. "For Chrissake, don't get political!" he'd say. "Don't get artsy-fartsy on me, either! I'll boot your ass to the curb. And whatever you do, don't write novelty songs. No one likes those. More importantly, no one buys those. And if you do strike a hit with a novelty song, audiences will demand you play that and nothing else until fifty years after you die." Brendon had pictures of all his clients on his wall; two wore steampunk top hats like Slash. I'd never heard of any of the people hanging there.

I flew over the Arctic, eating flavor-free meals, feeling my feet swell and my nasal membranes thin in the arid cabin air, and, with everything that was weaseling about in my mind, proceeded to write a novelty song.

> *Dark-eyed men with bad intentions*
> *Hidden in their tight blue denims*
> *Driving cars of deepest crimson*
> *Grab the gals and fire the pistons*
>
> *You'd better…*
> *Run for your life.*
> *The bad guys win tonight.*
>
> *Superman or Bats won't save you*
> *When these boys come to enslave you*
> *Plots from hearts like darkest night they*
> *Take you from your mama's bright day.*

Just you wait!
There's more to fate...
than
you
dream.

Sloe-eyed gals, sharp wit like talons
Making geldings out of stallions
Stomp your heart and drink your money
Come on, boy, ain't no free honey

You got to...
Run for your life.
The bad girls win tonight!

We landed in Shanghai just as I finished writing, and we began the slow process of collecting our things and exiting the plane. Nitro had been unusually quiet for the whole flight. I asked him what he thought about business class.

"I kept waiting for someone to tell me to go back to coach. I liked that one movie, though. 'Bout time Hollywood made a film about a forty-foot Oprah."

CHAPTER 17

"WE'RE ON CHINESE SOIL now, Mr. Angell, Mr. Blaine," Rong said as we collected our luggage in Shanghai's airport, which was so huge you could land a plane inside the main concourse. "CCP watches everything here, directly or indirectly." He gestured at cameras mounted high up in the overhead girders.

"CCP?" Nitro asked.

"The Chinese Communist Party," I said because I could, not because I knew much about the government. Jing was my tour guide, and I wished she were here for this trip. I jokingly said, "Jing likes to argue with police and security guards who get too nosy with our bags. One time, she stared down a guy who tried to seize a can of my shaving cream, travel size."

"That's fine for a Chinese woman if she has the balls," Rong said. "It won't work for you or me. You notice they are armed?" It was hard not to notice. "Those are QBZ-95 bullpup assault rifles. Standard for police, military, and common security."

Nitro mumbled something that sounded like alphabet soup to me. "Pfff. Gimme my old MK18 CQBR," he said.

"A fine choice, but make no mistake, these officers are proficient. They shoot, you fall, and they don't cry afterward like they do in the soap operas." Chinese soap operas were a hoot. Everyone cried, even uniformed men and women. I took Rong's word for it that these officers were less emotional than their TV counterparts...and very good at their jobs.

Rong continued, "We are watched. CCP controls the cameras and uses facial recognition. CCP controls and monitors internet service in most of the mainland, using the Great Fire Wall. You must use one of the state-run service providers. They block Google, Yahoo, and most western news services. I have set up a VPN. If you wish to check your e-mail, I suggest you do it now."

Getting out on the VPN took some practice. I wished I'd known about all this earlier. I wasn't sure whether I could use China Telecom to set up my own VPN *to get around* China Telecom. So taking Rong's advice, I turned on my phone and piggybacked my signal off his.

In came a text from Jing. "He'll be all right. Just do what Rong says." That was ominous but somewhat reassuring. Zack was in no immediate danger anyway. I could breathe.

I also got a batch of messages from Uber. Two customer complaints. My star rating was down to 4.72. Any lower and they'd…warn me some more, probably. Not that I gave a wet fart, but one of the complaints was from the same woman who'd stiffed me out of eleven dollars. I furiously typed in a new note resubmitting my appeal—which I had not heard back on. This was a matter of pride.

I also found an e-mail from my doctor. He'd gotten the lab results back from my exam the week before. The note began with two pages of numbers and Latin names I couldn't begin to understand. It concluded with a summary in simple, dumbed-down language. My triglycerides were high enough to kill a blue whale. I'd need to go back on the cholesterol pills. I hated those; taking pills every morning made me feel old. I'd asked Dr. Kenley about the pain behind my testicles, but he said there was nothing conclusive and to contact him if the pain persisted. There was also an odd notation: "Find a new fishmonger. Your blood has traces of mercury. There's no immediate cause for concern, but further exposure should be avoided as effects are cumulative and can lead to serious neurological disorders."

Even as I tried to digest the information, Rong's hands were on me, roughly pushing me toward a black van with military tags while also guiding a cart loaded with our bags. A soldier ran over, wearing a light-green short-sleeve shirt overloaded with ribbons, rank, and insignia, plus a cap with a red star. He began transferring our bags into the van, including my guitar case. He was fast; I tried to help but only managed to move one bag to his three. Nitro supervised.

"This is Officer Liu and his wife, Officer Zhang," Rong said, by way of introductions, as we took our seats in the vehicle. The woman wore a light-blue blouse with various doodads all over it. A police officer. Ah, thus "officer" and "officer" rather than naming them with their rank. Got it. The young couple squabbled nonstop but took a moment to look back at us and smile. Rong did not get in. "Stay close to them at all times."

Nitro made a face. "Why, you going someplace we ain't going to?"

"I have business to attend to. I will rejoin you soon. You may do as you wish, as long as you do not attract attention." He looked right at Nitro. "Don't spit. They are cracking down on spitting in Shanghai. And don't jaywalk, or else they'll post your picture on TV, and we don't need that!"

Rong slid the door shut with a clang, and the Chinese Communist Army drove us away from the Pudong Airport. Other drivers had to stop for tolls, but our driver kept going. "Our plates allow us through. Likewise, red lights are optional for the military," Officer Liu said in passable English.

We drove through traffic that made Atlanta's Downtown Connector look tame. The lanes were both wider and more numerous than in America, but the roads still lacked the capacity for the demand. If there were five lanes, there were eight cars riding abreast, with drivers choosing their own interpretations of the striping. To make it more interesting, the speeding cars changed lanes without signaling. *Okay, that was the same as in Atlanta.* Bicyclists kept a much slower pace, providing obstacles for the drivers. Once in a while, we'd pass a motored three-wheeler loaded eight feet high with goods and produce lashed down. These, too, made up their own rules of the road. I lost count of the times Officer Liu slammed on the brakes and screamed at jaywalkers. *See you on TV,* I thought.

Crazily shaped towers rose around us. On one side of the water, Shanghai looked like the city of the future envisioned by architects in the 1960s. Mirrored edifices rose alongside twisty spires and the iconic Oriental Pearl Tower, two melons impaled on a gargantuan bamboo chute. Officer Liu and Officer Zhang were chattering away. One or the other would glance back at us and break into giggles.

"What they laughing at?" Nitro asked, offended.

"We do not have Hēirén here," Officer Liu said, using a word I did not recognize but could guess at.

"You mean brothers?" Nitro asked graciously. To me, he said, "They aren't used to meeting the right people 'round here."

"Take a train. The Duke," said Officer Zhang, giggling like a fangirl meeting the star of her favorite sword and sorcery epic at DragonCon.

"Uh, sure," Nitro said politely adrift then perked up with, "Oh! Ellington. 'Take the A Train' by Duke Ellington." Now he was smiling. He even sang a few bars. Minutes later, he whispered to me, "You think they think I know Duke Ellington personally?"

"It's no big deal," I whispered to him. "They call me dabize." (It came out "dah-beetz-see.") The front seat erupted in laughter; apparently, I hadn't whispered softly enough. "It means 'big nose.' That's what they call westerners. After a while,

I got used to it. They aren't being mean. People like to laugh, and they laugh at anything new and different. That's us."

"I got no hurt feelings. I'm fine, all fine." In his situation, if I had said those words, it would have been a lie.

We crossed a bridge over the Chang Jiang River, the local stretch of the mighty Yangtze, and traded the dazzling architectural future for China's colonial past. Suddenly, the streets took on a western feel, specifically British, with stately courtyards outside homes of heavy stone, surrounded by wrought iron gates and guarded by stone lions. In fact, for every pair of fearsome British lions, we spotted a pair of Chinese lions looking back at them in inscrutable silence.

After twenty minutes, we came to a restaurant. The Red Army had good taste. It was a huge brightly lit space, filled with tables but not overly crowded. Through a hallway were private rooms for guests who so chose. While Officer Liu made the dinner arrangements, the rest of us stared at a giant fish tank where future meals were lazily swimming.

"What's all this over here?" Nitro asked.

One wall was set up like an old-style automat, with prepared dishes displayed in little windows. The guest could point, and someone on the other side would bring it out. The food looked wonderful: chicken cooked in a range of appealing spices atop a pile of vegetables, soups, snails, and a variety of beef, fish, and pork dishes. About waist level, there was one dish I wish I hadn't seen: a nine-inch cockroach or water bug on a bed of greens.

"Is that someone's dinner?" I asked.

"You want that?" Officer Zhang started to wave at a man behind the glass display wall, and I quickly had to stop her before someone served the big bug to me for dinner.

Officer Liu came back and led us to one of the rooms in the back. We sat down at a huge round table. Several other people, including a few more in uniform, joined us. One female officer had a little girl in tow, an adorable porcelain doll come to life. She became restless and began climbing the lattice that covered the walls. No one said anything. Her mother ordered her a bowl of noodles, and she settled down.

The staff fed the rest of us like emperors. The center of our table held a revolving platform. Onto it, they placed fungi and pork soup, tofu and chives, a kind of bacon that Nitro and I fought over, sushi, baked fish, duck, and chicken each reduced to bite-size chunks with the head propped in the middle of the plate, rolls stuffed with salty cabbage, seaweed soup, and, of course, tea. One platter, in particular, caught my attention. It was a hemisphere of pork, garnished with scorpions pinned on like cloves on a holiday ham. No one touched this dish, but our hosts did point out that one of the soups was the broth made from it. Bug soup. It looked harmless enough, so I slurped down a few spoonfuls. It was good, with a bit of a kick to it.

As the meal wore on, people wandered out and came back with bottles of baijiu. Lots of bottles. I wanted to be good, but it was a major insult to our hosts not to accept and join in the toasts. Nitro didn't say anything to me but told Officer Liu, "I'm sorry. I'm allergic to alcohol. It gives me acute incarceration."

I had a second bowl of scorpion soup and another round or two. The time flew.

CHAPTER 18

IT WAS TEN BY the time our married officers escorted us to the hotel, where the lobby gleamed a little too brightly for my baijiu-enhanced brain waves. A million crystals from a golden chandelier scattered rainbows across rich marbles, a lacquered baby grand piano, and burnished mirrored walls. A man in a short-sleeve shirt and high-water pants cinched tightly around his scrawny waist ignored the decor and instead focused on us. I smiled politely at him. He laughed, nodded, and grinned back at me and kept staring. I figured he hadn't seen many Americans and even fewer Black ones.

To our officers, I said, "I feel like I've been going for days." This was literally the case. "I could use something to take the edge off."

Officer Liu nodded and suggested Nitro and I drop off our things in our room then come back down. I wasn't sure what he had in mind. I was in a weird state. My body, having skipped one complete sleep cycle, was now trying to adjust to a twelve-hour time difference. In the end, my boozy mind decided an adventure was more important than sleep. I told him, "Give us half an hour," so we could shower away half a world's worth of sweat and fatigue.

We shared an elevator with an obviously drunken business-man in his fifties and a stone sober young woman who could have been his daughter except for the way he leered at her. The young lady struggled to hold him upright as he laughed off his own clumsiness. She marched him down the hall and bundled him into one of the rooms. Within seconds, we heard the sounds of raw unbridled commerce.

Opening the door to our room, I noticed a pile of glossy business cards on the floor. Each sported a picture of a beautiful Chinese girl and a phone number. I put one card in my front pocket, brushing Reverend Q's coin in the process. I didn't remember bringing it, but there it was. I didn't want to forget and lose it in the laundry, like so many of my past AA chips, so I slipped the coin inside my wallet and stuck it in my front pocket, safe from thieves.

I sat on the bed. The room was clean and pleasant aside from the garish decor: a male/female symbol mounted on the wall and a condom dispenser on the night table. Comfortable if not classy. I was tempted to lie down and forget about going back out. Water began running; Nitro was already in the shower. Turning my head, I sobered up instantly.

My bed stood next to an interior window. On the other side was the shower…and Nitro. All of him. I wondered why anyone would design a hotel room to make showering a spectator sport. I had answered my own question. This place was designed for couples on a fling or someone like the drunken businessman down the hall.

Nitro saw me through the glass and broke into a rousing rendition of "Take the A Train," complete with swinging hips and pantomime trumpet. Squinting my eyes tightly, I reached over and lowered the venetian blind that, small blessing, hung there. I showered next, ordering Nitro not to peek.

Thirty minutes later, Nitro, the Red Army, and I were on the street.

"You like to be having massage?" Officer Liu asked. I was about to ask questions when I noticed how many of the shops along the street were lit up for business. Restaurants and small food marts and electronic appliance stores were all ready for customers.

We walked on for a couple of blocks, passing a picture window filled with bored-looking young women in lingerie. They sat there in their provocative undies, some playing mahjong while others stared into their phones. "Look," said Nitro, "they got Fredrick's of China."

"That is barbershop," said Officer Liu, winking and grinning back at Nitro. He explained that prostitution was legal in Shanghai. At night, the local barbershops became brothels.

"I'm feelin' mighty scruffy," Nitro said. Actually, his hair hardly needed a trim. It was getting patchy.

Officer Zhang harangued and swatted at her husband and hastened us past the lingerie girls. We move to the next doorway, an unremarkable shop front. As we filed in, I noticed a skinny man in ill-fitting pants across the street, staring. I couldn't be sure it was the same man from the lobby, but he was smiling in the same way. That happened a lot in China. I was an object of curiosity. The man even took my picture with his phone.

Inside, the spa was a crudely decorated space. A few lights pushed back the gloom, the illumination barely reaching the plywood walls. There were adornments here and there, but I could have bought the whole place for what I earned driving in six months. A few men and women sat in the foyer, which led back to a hallway and a series of curtained-off booths.

A cigarette rode the old manager's lips, shedding ash as he called three middle-aged women to the front desk. The women then led Nitro, me, and both officers back to individual booths. Officer Liu and his wife together ducked into the first booth, which was the largest one. I could hear two masseuses inside waiting for them. Nitro went farther down the row and swept past a curtain. His attendant kept giggling, and as soon as he was inside, she called for another woman to come over. Both went in. Girlish tittering drifted over the fabric barrier. "Not so bad being the shiny new thing," I said to no one.

My attendant hustled me into a stall on the right, which was barely spacious enough to contain a massage table, a stand with a radio on it, and a chair. My masseuse had one milky white eye. Jing once mentioned that blindness was common in China and the blind took jobs like this to stay useful. The woman spoke no English. She motioned for me to strip down, so I got my things off and stood there in my shorts, wondering if I was overdressed. I felt sure Officer Zhang would not have taken us to a place of "happy endings," and I was kind of glad she hadn't done. A simple massage seemed like the right way to end a very long day.

The woman began by drawing a tub of hot water and adding Epsom salt. She carefully placed my feet in the steaming water. In fact, it was nearly scalding, and I winced but fought back the urge to pull myself out. She let me parboil for a bit, then dried my feet and ushered me to the massage table, where I lay face down. I was too tall, and my lobstered feet hung off the end.

She went to work, attacking my muscles with powerful fingers. She began on my feet, gripping them tightly, to the verge of pain, and I flinched more than once. This went on for a good twenty minutes. She was not rushing. She moved up my legs to my lower back, pummeling the deep tissue with her knuckles. It hurt so good.

Once I got used to being treated like raw meat in need of tenderizing, I relaxed. In the low lighting, I nodded off even as my masseuse continued her work. I had been up for a day and a half, after all.

My mind took a little trip. I was with Jessa and Zack. Following the logic of dreams, they were both their present selves and little kids at the same time. We were in a park of extraordinarily bright greens and blues…talking about them being themselves. I got it. My brain was saying it was important that I knew I was with my kids. We were together. For some reason, Jessa was all at once at the top of a tree, dangerously high up on a creaking limb. I started to climb, but Zack reminded me that I couldn't climb. Ever since I'd taken up drinking heavily, I'd developed paralyzing vertigo. The mere thought of heights sent electrical shocks through the nerves in my knees, causing them to buckle. Jessa was in danger, but I couldn't reach her. Then… she was standing beside me, handing me a drink. I took it and raised it to my mouth. Even as I swallowed the beer-wine-tequila in the glass, I felt my children's sadness pressing in on me. I looked, but they were gone. Gone. I was alone in the woods. Not alone. I turned to look, expecting that the wood spirit carving was looking at me from the belly of a tree. Instead, I saw hell. A word I could not read flamed as if it had been freshly branded into the bark of a broken and charred oak. My eyes refused to put meaning to the symbols because that is also in the nature of dreams, but I took its message, nonetheless. It was a warning, an omen. *There were noises and a sense of movement just out of sight.* Someone had made a joke and was laughing at the butt of that joke…and that butt was me. The blackened word was: shen. The word resolved into an image. The image was my face. *My face screamed in terror.*

Someone screamed in terror. All hell erupted around me. Ripped back into the real world, I flopped over on the table, so I was on my back. My milk-eyed masseuse went flying past me and slammed hard into the far wall. She cried out and crumpled to the floor, clutching the back of her head. There was blood on the wall and on her fingers—the same fingers that had been working on my body.

Rong was at the curtain—he'd thrown the woman from there. He was yelling at Officer Liu, who was busy pulling on his own uniform pants. Nitro appeared behind them.

"Get dressed! All of you!" Rong yelled at me. I noticed that his expensive eyeglasses were cracked…that he was handing me my pants…and that the pockets were turned out.

"Tell me where!" he demanded of the woman, who was now crying. She motioned to the chair I had sat in earlier. Rong ran over and pulled off the towel. My belongings were there: the hotel room card, the business card with the pretty girl on it, a pen, a comb, and a pack of breath mints. "Where is it?" I suddenly realized two things: he was yelling in English. My masseuse had no trouble understanding his meaning and his anger, but the words were for my benefit. The other thing that dawned on me was that my phone was not in the pile on the chair. As I finished pulling on my boots and stuffing things into my pants pockets, I grew alarmed by my missing phone, the one Jing had given me.

The parlor's manager came running back, holding the phone and my wallet out in front of him, frantically speaking Mandarin and kowtowing like I'd never seen before. Rong yelled at the old man, slapping a half-burned cigarette from his mouth. Not knowing what to say, I silently took back my phone and wallet and tucked them into my front pants pockets.

My head was finally clear. "I gave it to him," I said to Rong in as calm a tone as I could muster. "The manager locked it up for me while I was—"

Rong apishly pulled me to him so he was right in my face. "Never let it get away from you again," he hissed. "Without that phone…our customers will be upset with us. You don't want them upset, Mr. Angell. Bad things happen to those who upset these men."

"It's fine. I have it. I won't let go of it again. Not at all. I'll shower with it. I'll sleep with it." My words made little sense, even to me.

"Yes, you will," he said. By that point, Rong was shuffling all of us out the door and we were heading back to the hotel. Switching to Mandarin, Rong chastised Officer Liu while Officer Zhang attempted to apologize for her husband's lapse in judgment. I couldn't make out the specifics, but the threats and contrition were unmistakable. I wanted to tell Rong that going to the spa had been my idea, but he was angry at all of us, and there seemed little point in finessing the fury.

I checked my phone. It was past one in the morning. Rong kept glancing around to see if anyone was watching us. On the other side of the street, we passed a darkened building with a door wedged open. I cocked my head, trying to get a look inside. The last of the neon painted a coat of red over a pair of skinny legs, pant cuffs showing too much sock, stretched out in the entryway. Rong's beefy fingers were around my head in an instant, roughly twisting my view back the way we were going.

"Keep going. Don't stop to look."

"Hey! You're hurting me."

"Not as badly as others will."

I wanted to know why he attacked my poor milky-eyed masseuse, but Rong's smoldering eyes convinced me to keep my mouth shut. I looked to Nitro, who returned a bewildered expression.

Rong marched us back to our hotel and straight up to our room, warning us not to leave it until he came for us in the morning.

CHAPTER 19

DAWN LAGGED BEHIND THE city's noisy morning routine. China was perpetually under construction, and the crew call was at five-thirty sharp. Cranes groaned while men called out from the high girders. Big compressors rumbled and shook the thick dust on every windowsill. Drivers rudely blew their horns to clear slow-footed pedestrians. Near to our hotel, firecrackers competed for attention. There were always fireworks hissing, popping, and blasting, to keep demons away, to celebrate weddings, for good luck, whenever someone had too many fingers. Like a thoughtless roommate, the city was up.

Rong, sporting a new pair of glasses, appeared at our door early. Nitro and I were dragging, still jet-lagged, plus I was hungover. Even so, we managed to gather our things and head out after an elaborate breakfast in the hotel dining hall. It was self-serve, so we loaded our trays with bowls of hot congee, tea eggs, sticky rice, assorted vegetables, rolls, dragon fruit, and boba tea.

Properly fueled, we joined up with a becalmed Officer Zhang, who made no mention of her absent husband. She drove us through the busy streets of Shanghai to a warehouse. Officer Zhang parked in the street (illegally, taking advantage of the vehicle's military plates and her own police status) and stayed with the SUV. The building's exterior was nothing to look at. In the States, it would be a condemned property. Rong led us up some stairs, past offices decorated with lacquered cherry wood furniture, and into an office with an unfinished plywood door.

Two fiftyish gentlemen were there in work-casual attire. They'd traded their street shoes for slippers, giving the place a homey feel. One motioned for us to put on slippers as well. Both spoke only Chinese, and here, Rong was stingy with his translations. He didn't bother with introductions, so Nitro and I sat there, nodding and smiling politely. The office was piled with artwork waiting to be packed and shipped. Most were wall hangings made from cross sections of dark burled woods. The artist had glossed these, layering lacquer over images of mountain scenery, pandas, phoenixes, Mao, and a naked woman with a clock springing from her navel. There were also elaborate tea sets stacked all around.

One of the gentlemen served from a set finer than anything I'd seen in among their stock, its cups and pots done in a fishy motif. He lifted the lid, showing us the inside of the teapot. A fish smiled up from the tea. Rong explained fish and water together were considered good luck. After last night, I welcomed any help I could get.

Taking a large pot of boiling water in one hand and wooden tongs in the other, our host carefully rinsed the cups with steaming hot water, outside and in, allowing the excess to splash down the gutters in the deep tray. Only then did he fill each cup from the smaller pot of tea. The man pointed to a canister of tea on his shelf. Rong explained that it was a very expensive dark oolong, costing hundreds of dollars for a scant few servings. Collectors would pay in the millions of yuan (or "bucks") for a kilo; the Chinese took tea seriously, trading it like gold on their stock exchange. The man watched us as he tipped the fishy pot. Nothing happened, except that the man grinned. He repeated the motion and the tea poured. Rong pointed out that the man was covering the chimney vent hole with his thumb. Doing this, no tea came out. Being airtight meant the tea set was of high quality. The man released his thumb from the vent hole and the tea poured freely.

Once we realized he was honoring us, Nitro and I praised his fine tea set as best we could in English. I also thanked him for the western cookies (Nilla Wafers, just like Ma used to buy) he served with the tea, using one of the few Mandarin phrases I knew, "Xiè xie."

Both men bubbled with laughter. "Bú kè qì." ("You're welcome.") That was followed by more good-natured chuckling. The dabize was there for their amusement.

Rong conducted some brief business. One of the men slipped away but quickly returned with a thick silver briefcase. It had the same type of lock as Jing's monkey fridge. The man handed it to me, an, indeed, I found the case cool to the touch. The man handed Rong a folded piece of paper. We said our goodbyes and were off.

Back on the street, Officer Zhang drove us to Shanghai airport and dropped us off with a cursory farewell. I couldn't help wondering how much trouble we'd caused her and her husband. I wanted to express my regrets, but the wound was still fresh.

As we made our way inside the mammoth terminal, Rong flashed the paper the two gentlemen had given him, and we easily passed through security and boarded a small commuter jet. This time, Rong sat next to me, insisting I keep the case on my lap during the short flight. A trim attendant told us to stow the case in the overhead, but Rong brusquely spoke to her, and she immediately left us alone.

He didn't seem much interested in talking, but I had questions.

"What happened to Officer Liu?" I asked.

Rong offered something that wasn't quite an answer. "Officer Liu and Officer Zhang are loyal personnel. They work closely with CCP." Then a sharp left turn to throw me off, "The Party has had eyes on us for weeks now since before we left Atlanta."

"I noticed," I said, "at the airport and on a street the other night when we were handing out goodies." Rong looked amused but not surprised. "Friends of yours?" I asked.

"Most likely competitors. I couldn't say which ones."

"There are competitors?"

"Some people do business honorably. Others opt for expedience," Rong said.

Was the guy wearing high waters a competitor? Was he alive or dead? I had dark imaginings. What I said was "You don't shy away from expedience."

"I do what my superiors instruct me to do." There was a certain uneasiness there, maybe a guilty conscience, or just a dislike of having to follow orders no matter what. In any case, it was another peek behind the mask Rong wore.

From across the aisle, Nitro leaned over and whispered, "I thought we were here to make a delivery. Aren't we selling Tiger Pep to CCP?"

"No deals have been finalized. CCP is one possible customer or rather one faction within it is. CCP oversees eight other separate parties with a total membership of ninety million. Even when you think you know who you're dealing with, they can fool you. In any case, we are talking to several potential buyers. You had tea this morning with representatives of one such interested party."

"No wonder they smiled so much and broke out the oolong and Nillas."

Rong continued, "The decision on who gets Tiger Pep, and who does not, is not up to you or me. It will be settled in time by our superiors."

We were distracted by a tussle a few rows up. Two men were gesturing wildly and loudly arguing over a seat even though the flight was only half full. One of the men slapped the other squarely across the face and berated him for daring to question him. The slapped man went silent and found a different seat. We were the only ones on the plane who took notice of the disturbance. Even the cabin attendants ignored them. If this had happened on an American flight, we'd have been trending on Twitter by the time federal agents met us back at the gate. Jing said such displays were part of the Chinese language, a level of communication.

Jing. I couldn't make sense of her role in all this. There's no way she would have anything to do with CCP. Even back when we were dating, she'd bad-mouthed the Party as corrupt cheats and fake communists who preached austerity but lived like pooh-bahs. She felt it was fine to be cordial with the army. Jing had served two years, as did everyone here (Jing looked cute in her baggy green uniform, btw), but she would never help the Party. Gillian, on the other hand, might strike a deal with the Communists if there were enough bucks in it for her.

"So who gets this bad boy? What's inside?" I asked, tapping the metal container currently crushing my balls.

"You'll meet him…in a few days. We have business in Beijing first," Rong said with a tone that clipped off any further discussion. He did that a lot.

The flight was not what I was used to. It took off from a short runway, nosing up like a rocket. Minutes later, the cabin attendants served our drinks in open cups, even as the jet experienced pockets of serious turbulence. One sudden drop caused Rong to spill his hot tea all over his shirt. He cursed under his breath and got up to use the restroom.

While he was gone, Nitro leaned over again. "Zebulon, what's going on here?"

"What do you mean?"

"Why are we selling cooch candy to the Commies?" he asked with nice alliteration.

"They like to get lucky too, I guess. I mean there are like a billion them. More. They must have sex."

"That's what I mean. The Commies tried to stop people from having babies. One per family, right?"

"Yeah. That's right." The one-child policy had been a crashing failure and ended a few years earlier. Rural tradition held that if the first child were a girl, the couple could have a second. The policy also failed due to widespread bribery and a black market for documentation. Nobody accepted the government telling them how many kids to have. Even for true believers, that level of control crossed a line.

"So why do they want candy to help people to have *more* sex?"

My old AA buddy had a very good question. As Rong returned to his seat, I promised myself I would start getting real answers. I washed down that promise with a sip of scotch. Unlike Rong, I had skill enough to drink without spilling.

CHAPTER 20

I'D BEEN IN BEIJING a few times, so I was used to feeling hot, caustic air burning my skin. I was not used to seeing a piss-yellow sky this dense. The filth hung like the toxic fog it was, limiting visibility, so I saw only the first few blocks down the main avenue. Beyond that, solid buildings dissolved into the dun-colored void.

The trip across town took half an hour. While Rong got our bag from the Uber, I paid the driver. It was only a few bucks, a fraction of what I would have charged for the same trip in Atlanta. I felt sorry for him, which surprised me. I slipped him a two-dollar tip, which was more than the cost of the ride.

Rong gave me a dirty look, and I promptly grabbed the silver case that had been my pet since Shanghai. We handed our luggage—all except my silver case—to staffers outside the fabulous Sino-Swiss Hotel. It was a palace! Every imaginable amenity was there among the gleaming floors and the glass and brass decor. Beautiful people wandered in all directions.

"This is a five-star hotel, courtesy of our current hosts," Rong said. "They are also the latest potential clients of my superiors." He stressed the "my" this time to knock down any self-importance on my part.

We settled briefly in our plush room. The colors were a muted chocolate with tasteful gold trim. There were no condom dispensers. Our upper-floor window would have provided a fabulous view of Beijing, but today, it hung there like an unflushed toilet. Rong stayed with Nitro and me this time, checking his watch frequently. After fifteen minutes, he hustled us back to the elevator and hit one of the uppermost buttons.

Stepping onto a privately reserved floor in a luxury hotel is an experience that resets a man's earthly metrics. The walls were crammed with more silk screens, ancient artworks, and golden pheasants than I could count. Speckled koi nibbled the roots of lotus flowers floating in a stream that burbled from one end of the hall to the other. You had to cross a tiny red bridge to get into any of the rooms. I felt cheap inside my boots.

"I should have dressed up better," I said.

Rong answered, "There is no need. You are here to serve a purpose, and you are doing that."

Two trim-looking Asian men in flawlessly tailored suits came out of an ornately carved double doorway. "Welcome to Beijing. Thank you for coming to our hotel," one of the men said. "Takahashi kaichou will see you now, Angell san." He gestured toward the double doors. "And you, Baine san, will accompany us." The man held out a hand. Rong nodded at the case, and I handed it to the man.

"Nice place. The waiters have good manners," Nitro said, looking back as he followed the man now holding the case.

Rong told me to wait a minute then disappeared behind the doors. Indeed, it was only a minute or two before he reappeared and called me inside. I walked through a vestibule that contained an eight-foot-long ship of hand-carved jade on a spotlighted pedestal (someone had stuck a wallet-sized photo of Mao on its deck) and into the main room. The windows brought in a panoramic view, though again, it was blocked and wasted due to the current air quality. A desk sat off to one side. There were exquisite works of Oriental art positioned all over, but what dominated the room was a single dark-lacquered chair with mother-of-pearl inlay standing proudly on a riser in the precise center of the room, currently awaiting its occupant.

Chairwoman Takahashi made her entrance. She was, perhaps, seventy with a commanding presence in royal-yellow attire fit for an empress. Gems glinted about her neck, wrists, and fingers, and I had no doubt they were the genuine article. The only thing fake here was me. Another man flanked her, wearing a severe haircut and expression to match. He was dressed in a suit tailored to impress—or intimidate.

I didn't know what to say, so I followed Rong's lead. He said nothing, so the script was simple enough. Chairwoman Takahashi's right-hand man moved to stand by the power chair. He produced a silk cushion and set it down, making a sort of a curtsy in the process. Only when it was in place did Chairwoman Takahashi sit. The rest of us relaxed, slightly, and sat on a camelback couch opposite her throne. The furniture and its placement kept us at a respectful distance and forced us to look up to meet her eyes.

The minutes ticked by as we enjoyed essential formalities. Our hostess still had not spoken, but RHM (right-hand man) took care of the introductions while directing white-jacketed hotel staffers to serve tea (chrysanthemum, which tasted like pureed lawn mower clippings) and some gooey sweet snacks that helped get rid of the taste of the tea. I liked them and slipped a bunch in my pocket for later. Rong took the rest, which I thought seemed rude on our part, but RHM didn't protest, and they *were* good.

Finally, Chairwoman Takahashi spoke in a subdued voice only loud enough to reach her man's ears. As her tea-stained teeth flashed dark green, my ears could make out the earnest glottals that marked Japanese speech, but that was all.

RHM, who never did introduce himself so as not to upstage our host, said, "Takahashi kaichou hopes you are enjoying your visit. She suggests you take advantage of the sights while you are here although our business will be concluded tomorrow. You must visit the Great Wall or perhaps the Forbidden City."

"I've seen them," Rong and I said in unison although his tone was darker than mine. It did seem a touch condescending for them to play host in his backyard.

In any case, Rong immediately checked himself and added, "We have pressing business elsewhere. We will be leaving tomorrow night."

RHM said, "Business, then. Of course, Wei Rong." I thought I saw Rong's eyes flinch. What did it mean when a Japanese man omitted the "san" from a Chinese man's name? Generations of history and animosity hung in that one missing syllable. RHM continued, "We will review the information at hand and meet you tomorrow morning at the Ming Tombs. I will present our formal offer. It is nonnegotiable, of course."

"Your plan is acceptable," Rong said.

We all rose, the men watching Chairwoman Takahashi leave the room in a rustle of shiny saffron fabric. No smile, no frown. All business.

RHM saw us out to the elevator, where Nitro joined us. He patted his sleeve and said, "This keeps up, I'm gonna run dry. I should sell my blood and get rich that way." One of the men handed me back the silver case.

And we were done. The elevator took us back to our floor, where I told Rong we needed a nap before dinner. He grunted.

"You don't much like this bunch," I said.

"It's not for me to like or dislike prospective clients." As he was walking off to his own room down the hall, he called back, "Do not go out without me, Angell san."

Nitro and I ducked into our room. As I pulled off my boots, I asked, "That man is not a fan of the Japanese."

"They like you well enough, but they look down on him almost as much as they look down on me."

"Did they say something to you?"

"Not on purpose. I can't swim a note of Chinese, but I picked up a little *Nihongo*, Japanese, in the Navy. *Pātī wa dokoda, suu-ītī?*" he said with an evil chortle. "It means 'Where's the party?'" I could only guess where he'd use that phrase in Japan's ultra-polite society.

"I wish you'd been there for our part of the meeting with Takashima kuh-choo," I said.

"Kaichou. Chairwoman. Trust me. No one said anything in that room. That lady is big yen. Media on the books. Drugs under the table. They don't let on what they thinking," he said. Nitro surprised me with his insights.

"How do you know all this?"

"Research." He looked at me like I was a dumb schoolkid, which seemed fair at that moment. "Got the whole world right here on my buddy's phone." The phone I was supposed to keep on me at all times that I didn't remember letting him borrow. Of course, this was Nitro.

I let go of that issue. I had another question. Pulling out the phone we seemed to be sharing, I said, "I thought we were out of range to use Rong's VPN."

"You have your own. The app is right here!" He grabbed it and scrolled the screen to show me. Jing really had thought of everything. She always did.

"So you just googled it. The criminal parts and everything?"

"Zebulon, I spent twenty years of my life wearing dog tags. I learned a thing or two, and I have ways of finding out more."

"You were a spy?"

"Not a spy. But..." He heaved a deep sigh and looked at me with the eyes of an old man. "You really want to hear this?" I nodded. "Fine. I started in demolition. I was good. Went all over. All over, anywhere Uncle Sugar smelled oil or money, that's where we found enemies, and that's where I went to work. Took out ships, blew up an oil platform one time, lots of things. Ol' Marqus, he picked himself up a nickname and, after a while, a job offer to work in intelligence. Turns out those folks like to know a thing or two about someone before they blast him to hell."

I'd known Nitro for two years. This was the first time, in the rooms of AA or outside, that he'd talked about his service in any detail. "They taught you well," I said.

His eyes darkened, and his voice filled with country road gravel. "Fun Time Navy. One day, I got called into my commander's office. New game. They loaned me out to the spooks. And that shit I will never talk about. It made everything that came before seem like heavy petting. Ugly things. I did ugly things. I see faces at night, Zebulon, and they don't smile at Ol' Marqus. That's not even the bad part, though. You gotta understand. I was a young man. Smart, but stupid in ways that mattered most. Young men like to feel important, powerful. So when I was doing those things and collecting faces for my dreams, I...*enjoyed it*. Damn me, it felt *good*."

"I'm sorry."

"Pffft. So, anyway...I did that for twenty years. I learned how to hurt people, break things, and get drunk 'til I didn't feel any of it. That strong silent crap carries over, let me tell you. I drank myself out of jobs, money, marriages, a kid. Yeah, the Navy gave Nitro beaucoup drinking skills. If I could go back..." He shook his head. "If I had taken just one minute to think about it, I woulda skipped the whole ride."

He was silent for a long time. This confession was stirring up dark matter from down deep. I wanted to respect his emotional distance, so I changed the subject. "What about you today? They gave you another checkup?"

He took a swig from a bottle of water. "They poked me and looked into my eyes. Even did the rubber glove thing, BOHICA."

"Which is?"

"'Bend over, here it comes again.' They didn't say anything to my face, but they did seem interested in 'effects.' I heard one of them say they needed to get us a couple of *baishunpu*." He smirked as he said this last part.

"You know that term."

"Damn skippy! But then the other one got all agitated, sayin' they shouldn't be so obvious. I wish they'd been obvious, tell you the truth. Oh, and I think they were pissed about the case. I don't think they managed to open some inside part of it. I heard 'titanium,' which is the same in both English and Japanese, and then I heard some Japanese cussin'."

Nitro paced around the room. Fancy as it was, it was still a hotel room. The TV had a selection of Chinese soap operas and historical dramas, Chinese, of course. In the former, people cried. In the latter, a skinny young actor played a heroic version of Mao leading men into battle against the invading Japanese. Neither caught our interest.

"So what's in here?" I asked, tapping the locked silver case on my bed.

"Damned if I saw. They took it to another room to examine it. I heard them talking about samples and some kind of doctor's report. Sounded important."

I opened the minibar and pulled out a few tiny bottles. "Well, if we're gonna nap at this hour, we'll need some help."

"That's okay, Zebulon. I'll pass. I better keep a clear head." His face lit up. "Ha! Bet you never thought you'd hear me say that."

"You're serious? Okay," I said, pouring two little bottles into one plastic cup. *Fine, I was a lousy sponsor. I had earned this. I deserved it.*

Nitro stripped off the rest of his rumpled clothes and lay back, arm over his eyes. He was snoring within two minutes.

Nothing was going to wake him, so I hauled out my guitar to see if I could quiet my own brain. One of the strings had broken. I had spares with me but didn't feel like fooling with it.

Alone with my drink, I sat and played with my phone. Everything worked. In fact, this phone was much faster than my last one. I looked over at Nitro again. I knew I should follow his lead and take a nap to wash out the last of the jet lag, but...

I checked my messages. I could earn an extra ten dollars if I completed thirty trips this weekend. Screw Uber! Kevin had sent me an e-mail. "Mister Angell, could you check my ESL paper? It's due tomorrow! Thanks!" It was dated two days ago. Plus, since when did Kevin use a salutation...or actually write his own papers? A little virus detector icon thingy in the form of a red-horned devil popped up on the screen. I deleted the e-mail. *Nice try, Kevin.* If he weren't trying to hack this phone, I figured I could always tell him a satellite ate his homework.

I tried calling Jing. No answer. Taking a hard swig of the booze, I dialed Gillian's number. This time, I got voice mail. I gave up, fell back on the pillow, and stared at the ceiling for three hours.

We had a fine duck dinner, courtesy of Chairman Takahashi's largesse. The waitresses were wildly cute in their tight uniforms, but I got the feeling that I was being too obvious in my glances. They seemed to be staring at me. In fact, I felt a lot of eyes on me. I decided to focus all my attention on the duck. The restaurant served it the best way, sliced into feathers of succulent meat. As opposed to cleaving the bird into chunks loaded with choke hazard bone shards. It is unnerving to eat a duck while its bisected head sits upright on the platter staring back at you, but that didn't stop us. *Tough luck, Daffy, you're delicious!* I dipped the slices in Hoisin sauce, a soy-based brew conjured up with vinegar, chili peppers, and garlic, dropped on some celery slivers, and wrapped the whole thing in what Rong called "cake," though it was more like a tortilla or maybe a pancake. Nitro and Rong seemed to have lightened up. I had a few drinks and enjoyed the hell out of the meal.

Afterward, Rong again dropped us at our room. This time, Nitro skipped the shower and fell straight to sleep. I checked the time. It was morning in Atlanta. I tried both numbers with the same results.

Although I was exhausted, I needed to make contact with someone. I dialed one final number out of desperation. She answered.

"Zebulon! I was hoping to hear from you," Ma said. "We're about to head out to the Cracker Barrel," she beamed. She sounded happy as a pig in slop. Well, a pig at a Cracker Barrel anyway. I hadn't been to one of those in years.

"Who's *we*?" I asked.

"I got the kids. We're taking that trip you and I talked about, down the road a piece." She was in Zebulon, Georgia, my erstwhile hometown and source of my cursed name. She had Zack and Jessa. "Don't you worry about us. Your uncles are gonna take us shooting. It was their mama's idea. That Jenny sure is one smart cookie." (Jing, Ma. Jing.) That was too random. Ma may love her Canadian Club, but she was no fool. She was speaking as if someone might be listening.

I decided to take a chance. "Are you sure they have enough bullets?"

"Oh, don't you worry none about that. They got guns and ammo 'til Jesus comes back. If some rat looks at us funny, he'll catch a dozen rounds before he can blink. We're gonna stay here with the uncles for a while and practice shooting and enjoy ourselves."

"Can I speak to Jessa…or Zack?"

This took a moment. I heard her pass the request on to both of them. I did not hear either answer. I pulled some of the

Japanese snacks from earlier out of my pocket and began nibbling. Finally, with an audible sigh, Ma came back on. "I think they're going through a little thing, honey."

"What thing? I thought Jessa and I—"

"You two were doing better until you made your big announcement the other day. To tell you the truth, I think it hit her off guard seeing you so full of yourself. It brought back bad memories. Scared her…and Zack too. He's got other things to deal with, of course."

My mouth hung open. "Ma, thanks for taking them."

"Are you kidding? We're having a great time. Yesterday, we went to the County Fair."

"I touched a pig, Dad. MawMaw took us to see the pigs!" That was Zack. At least he still had some sense of indignant humor left. They were mad at me, but they were safe from Kevin and whoever else might show up. If anyone went to Zebulon to threaten my family, my family would give them a high-caliber Southern welcome. There wouldn't be enough left of the bad guys to fill a beer can.

"No one's blaming you, Zebulon," Ma said. "We wish you'd think things over is all. You could have backed out at any time. You still can. Maybe come home. Maybe that's not a bad idea, huh? You sound tired."

What a great Jewish mother my mother would make. I told her, "I've got commitments, Ma."

"Yes, you do. Remember the ones that matter."

"I'll be home before you know it, Ma." With that, I ended the call. My head was spinning from the long day and the drinks.

I tried pacing the room and poking around the minifridge. I could feel my anxiety rising. And that wasn't the only thing. I found the glossy business card I'd gotten in Shanghai and looked it over once or ten times. The woman was so damn pretty, perfect in fact. Her neckline plunged into heaven. I was trembling—I needed some relief. I was sure there were women available by phone. No, Rong was pissed enough at me. I looked over at Nitro. Sound sleeper or not, that snoring killed any notion of using the bathroom as a self-service station. These thoughts ran in circles until sometime after midnight when I stretched out on the bed and nodded off with a Toblerone box in my hand and my pants half off—and slept like crap. I dreamed about sex demons and woke up shaking and with a painful erection, plus the taste of blood in my mouth.

CHAPTER 21

NOT WANTING TO BE late for our meeting with a bunch of dead emperors, we rushed through the hotel's five-star breakfast, which was fine since I had little appetite on account of a low-grade toothache. The selection was western-style—omelets, bacon, sausage—with star fruit and sticky rice thrown in, and both Rong and Nitro did it justice.

At seven-thirty sharp, Driver Dong picked us up in a van. "Hello. Good. Morning." He worked very hard at pronouncing each word correctly. In Beijing, young people studied English. They were grateful for a chance to practice. At one point in my career transition, Jing pointed out that I could always move my tutoring business here. Government schools offered American teachers a place to live, a reasonable stipend, and two trips home per year. The capper was that you really didn't have to speak English well. You just had to sound like an American so the students could try to match the accent, idioms, and other nuances.

The trip north from the city took about forty-five minutes. It was hot, and I was grateful Driver Dong had packed a cooler with water bottles. He played the radio, songs that sounded like they were for children. Indeed, a number of them included a children's choir.

We rolled up to a huge pink pagoda with a tiled roof. A procession of nine mythical creatures commanded each ridgeline, including a dragon at the back and a phoenix in the lead, which indicated royalty. Driver Dong pointed out Tianshou Mountain looming over us. He said, "It means Heavenly Longevity." This was the Ding Ling Museum and Tomb, part of the vast Ming Dynasty Tombs.

As we moved toward the red brick entrance, Nitro asked Driver Dong, "You coming with us?"

He laughed and shook his head. "I. See. Many. Time. Many time. You. Enjoy." I figured that, for him, it was like living next door to Disney World—if Walt's corpse were part of the Country Bear Jamboree.

Crossing the baked mud paving stones of the Sacred Way, we passed between ancient generals who followed us with their petrified gaze while commanding an army of cedars and stony animals: a lion, a camel, an elephant, and a kind of unicorn called a xiezhi. After a good ways, we came to a literal treasure trove. Rong led us into the museum. "The gems are cut in the shape of the Chinese character for 'heart,'" he said. "That large vase over there once held lamp oil, and today is probably worth millions of yuan. That is if the government ever thought of selling it to a collector, which would never happen. CCP is very protective and possessive of China's antiquities."

"So you don't think they'd let me borrow one of those necklaces for Bessie?" Nitro joked.

"Not unless you want to spend the rest of your life in a reeducation camp out west." We took his warning seriously.

The museum was air-conditioned, and we moved through it too quickly before stepping back outside onto the griddle-hot stones of the sprawling Ming Tombs. The site was divided into numerous courtyards. Rong, who had also been here before, explained things, sounding like a seasoned tour guide. "Things are laid out according to the rules of feng shui to deflect evil winds and bad spirits from the north." For some reason, I looked around expecting to see...something. I wondered what an evil spirit looked like.

The sun was intense, making my head throb, as we moved through the first building arch and down a row of stone steps bordered by intricate carvings of lions, dragons, horses, and heroes. Their alert eyes checked us out as the beasts appeared ready to leap up in defense of their rulers. These characters were still on duty; this place was not some forgotten graveyard. This necropolis still functioned, still protected the men and women who once ruled China and who lay deep in the earth, keeping their secrets.

A harried-looking man ran past us into the Hall of Eminent Favor. We headed inside in time to see him run up to RHM. As we closed the distance, I could hear the man speaking frantically. I nudged Nitro.

"Can't understand it all," he whispered, "but he sure is apologizing a lot." Rong caught the comment and grinned at us as if to say, "Good for you." I think he grudgingly admired that we had a few surprises in us.

The frazzled man pressed an interoffice envelope into RHM's hands. RHM said something and tried to return the envelope, but the man pushed it back in the process bowing over and over like a frightened schoolboy trying to hand in a late term paper. My mind slipped into high gear. This had to be the test results on Nitro from yesterday. I assumed RHM wanted to look them over in private before he spoke to us, but the doctors were late in delivering the paperwork.

I waved at RHM. He responded with a slight bow in our direction. By the time we joined the two of them, a tour group closed in, and we were all swept along together. The tourists were speaking in German. Their guide, a teenager carrying a red pennant on a lightweight pole, switched easily from English to German to Chinese. RHM moved certain atrophied muscles in his face to simulate a smile. Whatever he wanted to say to us, he was obviously going to wait until he finished looking at his documents. He absorbed the information in furtive glances while we listened to our guide. She pointed out the massive cedar columns brought from distant lands via hand-dug canals, and the giant brass statue of the Yongle Emperor, third ruler of the Ming Dynasty, founder of these tombs, and ruler who ordered the construction of a new capital in Beijing six hundred years ago. There he sat, filling every inch of his throne, gazing out blankly as if lost in his own thoughts.

We headed outside once again and climbed a steep path. Our guide pointed down to a quarried sector off to one side. She said that was one of the tombs. In fact, thirteen of the sixteen Ming Dynasty emperors found their rest in this place. Twenty-three empresses and more than thirty high-class concubines joined them. I could only imagine how many thousands of workers slaved away at this site to service the final needs of these lucky few.

The grade of the path strained my legs, and for a moment, I felt a searingly familiar tug between them. I must have made a face because Nitro offered me a water bottle. Fortunately, the pain eased after a few more steps.

At the top of the hill, we came to a tall structure, the centerpiece of Ding Ling.

"They're in there, the emperors?" Nitro asked our guide.

She looked at him for a second, then, smirking, said, "Only one. And not in there, but under." I couldn't tell whether her amusement had to do with the question or the fact that Nitro was Black—the only Black man in our group and the only Black man I had seen in days. Or maybe she liked his Greek fisherman's cap.

"This is the entryway to the underground palace of Zhu Yijun, the Wanli Emperor. He died four hundred years ago after ruling for forty-eight years. He is remembered as a keen scholarly leader who kept peace and prosperity and rebuffed

Christian influences…but who became lazy and made decisions that weakened his dynasty. His is the only one of the tombs unearthed so far, and you'll see why." She ushered the group into the structure, through a constrictive passageway of stone to a high-arched atrium and a pair of cyclopean doors reinforced with brass studs. "If you count, you'll find eighty-one studs. That's nine columns of nine. This designates the highest social class and is used only for the emperor. That's because the number nine in Chinese is pronounced *jiǔ*, the same as the word for longevity eternal."

Nitro sniffed. "Didn't work. Old Wanli should get a refund." The guide giggled.

On we went. As soon as we stepped through the emperor's doorway, a chill went through me. It was more than the absence of sunlight. It felt like a loss of hope. I became increasingly anxious as we descended the stairs. There were a lot of them. We covered four flights of winding steps, passing antechambers of royal keepsakes: a throne, armor, vases by the dozen, each worth a fortune.

My knees felt like they were hooked to a car battery, each step sent a jolt of electricity through the joints. I put out my hand to ward off a touch of vertigo. I was starting to feel queasy and my vision blurred a little here and there. I looked at Rong and RHM to see if they noticed. They looked over occasionally but gave no indication that they saw my distress. It wasn't an illness so much as a feeling of dread. I was in a damned tomb after all. It might also be a palace, but it was no place for the living, and I didn't belong here. None of us belonged here.

The symptoms passed as quickly as they had come. RHM put his hands out and moved the five of us to one side, allowing the main group to step ahead. Despite the amplifying echoes of the stony acoustics, he managed to keep his voice intimate for our benefit. "I have reviewed the data on Baines san. You are in most excellent health. This is what we hoped for. Takahashi kaichou is now ready to present to you her offer."

I had wondered how RHM could stand wearing a jacket outside in that heat, but now in this cold space, I envied him. He reached in and pulled out a smaller envelope. Rong took it, opened it, withdrew a card, examined the writing on one side that he held so we couldn't see, replaced the card, and handed it back to RHM, who returned it to his jacket pocket.

"Thank you for your most generous offer. I will pass it to my superiors in the coming days."

"I believe the figure will negate the need for any further bids," RHM said.

"You will have to ask my superiors in person. I, of course, am far too lowly to…" Rong was spoon-feeding them their own poisonous racism, and I felt proud as hell of him.

"Very well, Mr. Wei," RHM said. Even I knew that phrasing of his name sounded funny, if not straight-up insulting. Rong kept his composure.

"And you, Angell san, I trust you are finding your visit to these tombs educational?" It was the first time this morning that he had addressed me directly.

"I'm feeling a little under the weather."

"That is too bad. Would you like to go back?" RHM looked genuinely concerned.

"No, I can keep going."

RHM's expression relaxed. "That is good. It is important to know how far one can be stressed." That was an odd way to say anything.

"I wonder if I might have a look at Nitro's chart." I looked RHM directly in the eye and held out my hand. In his expression, I had all the answers I needed. I knew I wasn't feeling right. And now I suddenly realized why I wasn't feeling right.

After a momentary hesitation, RHM motioned for us to catch up with the group while at the same time handing me the larger envelope he still carried. I pulled out the documents. Rong looked at me with a touch of exasperation. It was in Japanese, of course.

I scanned the page, which was set up vertically and in columns of symbols. At that moment, I couldn't remember whether to read it right to left or the other way, but of course, I couldn't read it at all. On the wild assumption that any of this corresponded to doctor charts I'd seen before at home, I picked out numbers that could have been blood pressure and heart rate and cholesterol. Could have been. On the back of the sheet, I saw only Japanese *kanji* and *kana* and a symbol made up of three interconnected triangles, plus there were two letters in English.

"H-g," I said.

RHM and Rong looked over and Nitro followed suit. "It's nothing to be concerned about," said Rong.

"Nitro, when Rong tested you before, did he say anything to you about mercury?" I asked.

"No," he answered.

"I wonder what my mercury level is like this morning."

"It's nothing to be concerned about," Rong repeated, keeping his voice low but adding greater emphasis. "I really think we should enjoy the rest of the tour." My vision was foggy, and I had an erection those stone lions couldn't scratch. I was not enjoying the tour.

RHM took back the document with a casual motion and returned it to its envelope.

Our group passed into the main chamber. To be honest, it was a bit of a letdown. Maybe in centuries past, this place held more decorations or something. The chamber had a cathedral-like ceiling but was not overly large considering the elaborate nature of the tomb up to this point. It held a series of red crypts, large wooden boxes that were stand-ins for the originals. Our guide said, "The first royal caskets were thrown out. Thinking themselves fortunate, farmers picked up the wood and took it home, only to discover the emperor was jealous of his property. Planning for the future, farmers fashioned pieces into caskets for themselves...and immediately dropped dead. Children died mysteriously around furniture newly built from the wood." This drew a muted gasp from the tomb visitors. My skin crawled at the thought of children falling victim to ghostly vengeance.

Our guide then changed her tone and let us in on a secret, "I hate to tell you, but you've come all this way, and the emperor is not here." Rong was amused while RHM remained inscrutable as ever. The guide continued, "Chinese archeologists unsealed this chamber in 1957. They quickly identified valuables throughout the tombs, exquisite jewelry and relics of incalculable worth. Here, the story gets messy. The archeologists failed to consider the effect the elements would have on the remains. They carelessly stored priceless silks and personal items in warehouses without proper climate control or any form of preservation. Pictures show remains and artifacts in an alarming condition.

"Then the situation got worse. Mao Zedong's Red Guard denounced the long-dead emperor and empresses and ultimately dragged their bones out to be burned. Since then, the Wanli Emperor's legacy has also come under close scrutiny. Modern experts suggest the emperor was addicted to opium, possibly taking it as *chunyao*, a sex formula. Some say he sought relief from maladies related to a congenital deformity, perhaps a curved spine. In any case, for the last twenty-five years of his reign, he holed up in the Forbidden City, refusing to appear at general audiences while waging a fifteen-year campaign to name as his successor his son by his beloved concubine, Zheng.

One official slandered Zheng as an 'evil fox' and ultimately court ministers installed the Wanli Emperor's eldest son, Zhu Changlou, whose mother was an empress. But the new emperor died only a month into his reign, plunging the Ming Dynasty into chaos."

Rough afterlife. One day, you're the emperor of China, the next you're dead, and four hundred years later, you're a smoking heap with a bad reputation.

I could almost feel his outrage. No. I *could* feel it. That fury was mine now. The Wanli Emperor was inside me somehow. There was one last emotion welling up from some hidden depth. I owned it but was not the source of it. Perhaps it was being in this ghastly collection of funereal excess, but I swear I could hear voices from the past. Wanli joined the other emperors who wandered these tombs, raising a spectral chorus of remorse. Being sure no one was looking, I allowed my lips to silently form the words they gave me.

"What has become of my empire?"

CHAPTER 22

RHM AND HIS CRONY split off as we returned to the surface and left the complex. He was an odd man. If this were a movie, he'd be a member of the yakuza. Rong, Nitro, and I walked in silence. I wasn't about to discuss what I'd just felt.

What did the unearthly chorus mean exactly? "What has become of my empire?" "*My* empire." There were many voices, but I could tell each thought of China as his sole property. Maybe the Wanli Emperor finally realized what his drug use cost him. What about the others? Were they upset with current affairs in China? Did ghosts hate Communism? *Please tell me we don't have to deal with politics through all eternity.* The spirits' words were tinged with a feeling of loss, the loss of stuff or worldly position and power. *Too bad! Happens to all of us, pal!* I tried to push away the memory. Once again sweating under the noon sun, any sense that I had been in touch with the dead faded like a nightmare chased off by an alarm clock.

Driver Dong took us to a snack bar obviously intended for tourists. While he sat with a group of other tour drivers, we ate our lunch from Styrofoam trays using plastic forks. It tasted like La Choy Chinese food from a can. A German couple at the table next to us put ketchup on their General Tso's chicken, which Jing blasted as fake Chinese.

I poked at my meal for a bit. Then, without looking up, I asked Rong, "Tiger Pep has mercury in it. Are you trying to poison us?"

"Try nothin'. It's workin'!" Nitro complained. "My hair's fallin' out in clumps. This morning, the shower drain looked like a poodle convention!" I'd noticed his hair was getting uneven. I remembered the taste of blood in my own mouth earlier.

Rong didn't seem surprised. "Trace amounts of…substances…exist in the final compound…causing minor random side effects…but I assure you, your lives are not in danger," he said. I wasn't sure I believed him.

"You put our candy inside the snacks the chairwoman served back in her suite."

"I didn't think we had any Tiger Pep with us, too risky," Nitro added.

"It was in my guitar. Thanks for breaking the string, by the way. And thanks for nearly getting me thrown in prison," I said to Rong.

"The Tiger Pep molded nicely to the inner shell of your guitar, like a fruit roll up," Rong said cheerily. "On an x-ray, it looks like part of the instrument."

"It doesn't smell like no guitar," Nitro said. He looked around to make sure no one was paying attention to us.

Rong said, "The supplement does not smell like any illegal drug, either. We saw no narcotics dogs, but even if there had been dogs and if they had found your supply—"

"Your stash."

"Our supply. Even if dogs had found our supply, it is a fruit-based dietary supplement."

"Hidden inside my guitar."

"That is why you carried it, Mr. Angell. If I had carried it and been discovered, even though I broke no law, US authorities could have thrown me out of the country. Had I been discovered carrying it here, Chinese authorities could have done far worse. You, however, would merely be returned to the US."

"You win a blue ribbon for being a smarty-pants," Nitro chuffed.

"So you got the Tiger Pep out of my guitar when we were out and what, layered it into the Japanese candy?" I patted a pocket on my cargo pants. I still had a few of the candies left, wrapped up in a napkin. I'd eaten a bunch last night, but I wasn't about to eat any more of them.

"I delivered the augmented snack to the Japanese…" And here, he tensed so visibly I thought he'd burst a blood vessel, "In time for you to consume the candies in front of that dowager bitch." Finally! Rong was showing genuine anger toward the Japanese for the way they treated him.

"You hate them, don't you?"

"These people have always acted superior to the Chinese. They have been invaders and monsters, doing unspeakable things because they see us as less than human. Nothing changes." He didn't go into the history of the two nations. We didn't have the time. I knew enough about twentieth-century China to know what the Empire of the Sun had done in places such as Nanjing, Shanghai, and Harbin. America's losses in World War II paled next to the horrors inflicted by the Japanese upon the Chinese.

"What about how you treat us? Nitro and me?" I looked at the man and saw a change, like a layer of a smoke clearing. "Don't tell me you were only following Gillian's orders."

"She's no better." That comment fouled the air. I wondered just what troubles he might have with Gillian. Then I thought about Gillian and I had my answer. There was a darkness behind her pretty eyes, an entitlement that pressed its Christian Louboutin stiletto heel into the throat of the unworthy. Rong continued, "I made a choice, and it became a long course of action that grew more…complex…than I perhaps anticipated. Mr. Angell, I like you and Mr. Baine. I promise I will tell you everything I can, but not here. Not before—you will know the rest when we get to Xi'an. I will also say that I would rather not have brought you both into this."

"So why did you?" I asked.

"The Chinese prefer to see your American face. *These* Japanese prefer not to do business with a Chinese face. It was better you did not know, so as to keep your reactions natural and at ease." That made as much sense as anything else right now.

"That still leaves one question."

"Really, Zebulon? One? 'Cause I still got a few left," Nitro said.

I said, "One question for now. Why did the chairwoman want me to eat more Tiger Pep."

"It's part of the ongoing tests. There will be more."

"Wonderful. Fine, what was this *test* for?"

"She planned our meeting. My superior told me to follow her instructions. She hoped you would eat several of the doctored snacks, which you did, though not until later." Obviously, she had spotted me pocketing the damn things. "If you hadn't taken a large amount, I was instructed to find a way to slip the supplement into your food. This morning, it was obvious from your flushed complexion and unsteadiness that you had taken several of the snacks." He said "taken" as in drugs, not "eaten" like with candy snacks.

"So I took more of the stuff than usual and didn't die."

"You did not die," Rong confirmed, as did my breathing. "The ill effects you're feeling now should pass. My colleagues are still mapping out the safe upper limits. The Japanese are sharing data with us as well, though I don't fully trust their reports. This test was part of that effort."

I wasn't done yet. "What if I'd pigged out and…by accident…keeled over?"

143

"There was not enough of the supplement to cause a fatal overdose," Rong said calmly.

"And how do you know that?" I asked.

At this, Rong brought his hands together, templed his fingers, and lowered his eyes. "Admittedly, a guess. The tests are ongoing. That is another reason you both are here. You knew this before you agreed, did you not?"

"I…guess so."

In truth, I had known Nitro was a lab rat. He had even joked about it, and that was fine. Now for the first time, it sunk in that *I* was somebody's lab rat too.

CHAPTER 23

RONG SAID HE WAS feeling bad about how Nitro and I had been treated, so he wanted to make it up to us with a home-cooked meal before we boarded our train to Xi'an.

We got on the highway south and drove through patch-work farmland to Tianjin, a city in the process of transforming itself from an ugly industrial port of thirteen million into a world-class city filled with a mix of modern and old European architecture and dazzling surprises. Tour boats plied the Haihe River, passing under the city's magnificently mismatched bridges. These ranged from a bridge done up in fairy-tale princess frippery to an imposing colonial-era span guarded by lions to one sleek bridge someone must have beamed in from the twenty-third century. At night, Rong said, the river walk came alive with dancers, musicians, fishermen, strolling lovers, and magicians.

Along the way, the tension eased in Rong's demeanor, which I assumed was the effect of coming home. He dropped the defensive mask we'd seen in Shanghai and Beijing. His conversation brightened. He even challenged me to see if I could make our latest driver, Mr. Lu, laugh. This was no small challenge since Mr. Lu spoke no English.

I thought for a moment and stole a joke from the master. "I came home last night and found a man in bed with my wife. I said, 'Hey! Who told you you could sleep with my wife?' He said, 'Everyone!'" I did not try to do my Dangerfield impression, and I had no idea whether my timing was anywhere as funny as Rodney's. I waited while Rong repeated the joke in Mandarin. The two spoke back and forth (over each other, really) and then went silent. A second later, Mr. Lu burst out laughing.

Rong said, "That's good. Funny. He liked that. I had to tell him a few times that it was about sex, but he got it." *Okay, good enough. Rodney plays in China.*

Oddly, though, Nitro looked lemon sour. "What's the problem?" I asked.

"Nuthin'!" he said, which was somethin'—something— but I could tell he wasn't in the mood to discuss it.

We drove to a five-story apartment complex. The city was in the process of ripping out these Mao-era cinderblock slums and replacing them with modern high-rises and shopping centers. For now, people lived in the dingy past. Laundry hung from jerry-rigged electrical wires, sex worker phone numbers covered the walls, awnings rotted in the polluted air, and pipes leaked onto shoulder-high piles of refuse. Pickers kept an eye on these heaps to check for anything useful. Drivers parked in the alleys and leaned plywood panels against their wheels to discourage dogs from whizzing on their tires. Around the corner, on the same sullied pavement, merchants set out their blankets and sold cherries, toothbrushes, hats, genuine Rolex watches, tea eggs, and kiddie toys.

We found a parking spot and got out. Mr. Lu waved and took off on foot. Rong led us up a side alley, past a small park where seniors were performing tai chi exercises to music from a boom box, and around a corner. "Home," he said.

His parents lived in a ground-floor apartment. I didn't get their names but heard Rong say Baba and Mama, so I went with that. As we walked up, Baba, with his bushy eyebrows and ears tufted in Maine Coon fashion, was tending his potted crops by the door. He and Rong exchanged animated greetings. Baba then led us inside, through a closet-sized porch loaded with precious junk. The main room dominated the home's submarine floorplan. Everything ran fore and aft, no left or right, no upstairs or basement. The hall incorporated a kitchenette and bathroom and led back to the bedroom. There were no closets, so there were boxes of clothes and assorted belongings piled everywhere. The front room contained two TVs (a broken one supported a working set that showed a musical variety show), a rickety chifforobe, a mismatched sofa and chairs, a table, a desk, and a quilt-covered *kang*, a big block for sleeping or sitting. Rong said his aunties lived in the countryside, where the *kang* was also the stove and dining table. A bare bulb hanging from the ceiling added to the meager light.

In the middle of this, Mama stood waiting in her drab tunic, her lined face a record of a life lived for her family. Baba suspended making introductions while Mama used tears to beckon her wayward son. Rong rushed over, hugged her, and kissed her thinning hair. She said something, though it came out more emotion than words, and continued to cry.

Nitro and I stood smiling and looking stupid. I felt especially dumb carrying my guitar and the silver case. Baba grabbed them out of my hands. Rong nodded to let me know this was acceptable. We didn't get the chance to sit down. Mama immediately ordered us to go to the market to pick up more food for dinner.

"Rule of the house. Everybody eats, but first, everybody works," Rong said.

Baba joined us on our errand to the market, which sported bins heaped high with fresh produce and mongers of marinated beef, tripe, toothsome fish, and spiced pork and lamb. We picked up some of everything.

By the time we got back, there were four more adults in the apartment as well as three children moving in all directions.

One of Rong's sisters was on the phone with a friend in New York. The sister yelled into the device, and I could hear a mix of Mandarin and English yelled back from Manhattan. They used their phones like a pair of tin cans connected by a seven-thousand-mile string. The children came up to us and stared or laughed. Their parents looked over and laughed as well. Nitro and I were a novelty act. It was all in good fun, though I could see Nitro flinch from time to time.

Rong took over the introductions, but no way could Nitro and I register all the names. Rong's brother smoked heavily and kept asking me in halting English about American politics. I did my best not to express my real feelings. As we talked, the women and Baba set up a huge pot of water over a can of cooking gel in the center of the table and began preparing plates of meats shaved tissue-thin and vegetables, including bunches of enoki mushrooms that looked like pearl pendulums. Mama scanned the inventory and then kvetched at Rong, who smiled and pulled a bag of spices from his pocket. Appeased, she and the others returned to their work.

I excused myself to use the bathroom. It was lit by a bare twenty-five-watt bulb, which was a minor blessing. The concrete walls had not a blush of paint anywhere. Laundry hung on a line strung between exposed pipes. After tending business over a bowl with no seat, I discovered that flushing this Rube Goldberg creation was a process. I had to use the sink to fill a bucket, take the lid off the tank and pour the water into it, then reach up to pull a chain to flush. That done, I went back to the sink and ran lukewarm water over my hands but decided against using the gray-streaked soap. Eyeing the stiff washrags hanging about me, I opted to leave the room with hands dripping. I won't mention the smell.

Nitro was talking to Rong. "You grew up here? Six of you?"

"Seven. I have a brother in Harbin." I could only imagine how that must have been. "Papa had eight brothers and sisters, and they lived in a hut."

Conversation moved the work along with two or three people speaking at any one time.

"What are they talking about now?" I asked.

"They went out to my uncles' graves to offer them a drink," Rong said.

"Um…"

"It's something we do. The graves are out in the country, on land they used to own before Mao took it." I didn't know what to say to this.

Next, the women began bickering—by the looks of it, about how to prepare the sauce for the hot pot they were working on. Mama pointed to some leafy greens while one of her daughters held up a bowl, indicating she had already gotten the sauce ready. The chatter grew quite loud. Mama slapped her daughter's hand as she took charge of preparing the serving bowls with blended sesame sauce, preserved tofu, and green chives seed.

"I am right here!" Nitro shouted. He looked upset, and I tried to ask him why, but he ducked out the door.

I followed him to the alley. Rong came out behind us. "My family is a lot, I know. The food's good, though. Here." He handed us each a drink with a picture of a smiling red fruit of some kind on the can. It was warm, but I gulped it down. It was good in the heat and extra good after being in a room choked with cigarette smoke.

Nitro stood silently.

"You gonna tell us what's bothering you?"

"I don't appreciate that word, in Chinese or English neither."

"What word?" I asked.

"You heard it!" Nitro insisted.

Comprehension dawned on Rong's face. "I think I know," he said. "Don't worry. They're not saying anything bad. When they're talking that fast, sometimes someone says, 'That that, I get it!' Except they say, '*Nega, nega. That, that.*' It's a filler word in Mandarin. It can mean '*that* thing there' or 'That! That! I understand.' You'll hear it in the north, Tianjin, Beijing. It's not the bad word."

Nitro narrowed his eyes and looked Rong up and down.

He continued, "Mama is almost seventy. She doesn't speak a word of English…certainly not that word. She and Baba were teenagers during the Cultural Revolution. They faced things. Baba lost two brothers to starvation. That's whose graves they visited today. Mama also lost a sister, and her nephew disappeared at Tiananmen. She's not making fun of you, Mr. Baine. They don't look down on other people."

"I'm sorry. I guess I heard something that wasn't there," Nitro said meekly.

"I hear things all the time in Atlanta, and I know what people mean when they say them," offered Rong.

I looked back in the doorway. The frenzy of activity continued as did the nonstop gabbing. Nitro collected himself, and we went back inside and had an incredible hot pot meal. I accepted enough alcohol to be sociable while Nitro nursed his soft drink.

The eating went on and on. Americans liked to set speed records with their consumption. Here, the moment mattered. People allowed time for talk, loud and confusing as it was. The general volume around the table tended to be a few decibels high, somewhere between the flight deck of the USS *Nimitz* and a kiddie party at Chuck E. Cheese.

When Rong's family wasn't eyeballing Nitro and chattering to each other about him, the women at the table were taking my measure. Occasionally, someone would gesture in my direction with tofu-laden chopsticks and comment.

"I guess they don't see many Americans," I said to Rong.

He answered, "It's not that. It's that you hold your chopsticks with your left hand. They find that hilarious."

"Zuǒ shǒu!" said one of the amused sisters.

Rong explained, "We don't have many lefties here. Schools teach all children to write characters with their right hand only."

I grinned back at his sister and hoisted some enoki mushrooms into my face.

The women tittered again. *Apparently, it was still my turn.* "What now?"

"They say you eat like a bird," Rong told me.

"I'm eating! I'm eating!" I didn't want to be rude to my hosts, plus the hot pot was wonderful, but in my mind, I was making a pig of myself. Maybe I wasn't showing the proper enthusiasm. Mama and Baba were of a generation that demonstrated appreciation for a meal by slurping and burping and otherwise emitting noises, which, along with the overlapping conversation, blended very nicely with the percolating of the hot pot.

"My sister wonders how you can eat so little and still have a big belly." Rong smirked as he said it. The words came out lightly with no malice attached.

I could not follow the table conversation, of course. I gathered that it was mostly family gossip anyway. At one point, Rong's brother handed him a packet of train tickets. Rong looked them over and said in English, "You're kidding me! You said we had our own first-class compartment."

"That's what I reserved," his brother said. "But when I went to pick up the tickets today, this was all they had. Someone must have bought our tickets."

Rong pursed his lips in disgust. "*Juigui*," he muttered, and his brother's face fell a mile. "It's okay, I guess." Noticing our concern, he said. "We got bumped by somebody richer. If I had known, I could have made a call or offered a few bucks to the agent. I should have put us on a bullet train instead. It's just that I thought one of the older, slower trains would be…more fun." That part came out like a confession. Rong was being too tough on himself. "We're leaving at eleven tonight, booked in a sleeper."

"It's okay. It's fine. We'll have fun."

I asked Rong what he said that hurt his brother's feelings.

"I said he was jingui. Literally, it means 'alcohol ghost.' He drinks too much and isn't all there." Alcohol ghost. Jingui. I had to remember that.

After dinner, Mama cried some more. Rong hugged her again and whispered things in her ear. He also handed her some money, which caused her to get flustered. She handed it back, using motherly strength to push the colorful bills into his hands. Rong stashed the money in a desk drawer and quickly moved away. Mama yammered but left the cash in place.

We took our things and piled into Mr. Lu's car. Somehow, he was waiting for us. How this all worked, I had no clue. Rong said we had a little time before we had to get on the train, so we decided to walk along the river.

We parked at the rail station, near the giant Century Clock with its gears-out, steampunk design celebrating the city's industrial heritage. I gawped as gargantuan fish swam across the faces of nearby office towers in a show of fanciful lighting tech. We hurried on, dodging drivers who ignored the crossing lights and made our way down the stone steps to the water near the brightly lit Jiefang Bridge.

The promenade at night was all that Rong had promised and more. Despite being stuffed, we indulged in street snacks of candied jujubes on a stick. We passed several groups enjoying

ZEBULON ANGELL AND THE SHADOW ARMY

the sultry night air. The Eye of Tianjin Ferris Wheel glowed in the middle distance, changing color every few seconds. Tianjin at night was a child's idea of what urban life could be, using shapes and rainbow lightings like so many blocks and crayons. We passed troupes of dancers moving about in spirited fashion. Nitro and I exchanged schoolboy comments about the women and their flouncy costumes.

Rong heard us but didn't join in the locker-room talk. He seemed to have reverted to his super-serious mode, too focused on the work at hand. It occurred to me that I'd never heard him talk about women or even caught him sneaking a peek at Gillian's keister. I was forming a theory that he was focusing all his energies on his future, sublimating his sexual urges. Or maybe he was like Thoreau, a celibate counting beans at the edge of some pond and looking for ways to "Simplify! Simplify!" Or maybe, like Thoreau, he was thinking about "two sturdy oaks… their roots…intertwined insep'rably." Or maybe I had read too many books.

We found a spot to sit and watch the fishermen try their luck amid the noise and light and passing tour boats. Nitro pointed over at two people lighting incense and throwing sheets of paper onto a small fire. "I saw that earlier. Folks burning shiny paper right on the sidewalk."

"It's August the twenty-fifth, I think. On the Chinese Lunar Calendar, this is the fifteenth night of the seventh month. Ghost Day."

"What, like Halloween?" I asked.

"Not really. No one gives out candy. People burn gifts for their loved ones who have passed on. It's part of *Zhongyuan Jie*, the Hungry Ghost Festival, when the spirits of our ancestors come out of the lower realm and pay a visit.

"And what exactly do these hungry ghosts wanna eat?" Nitro sounded a little nervous.

"Not you. You see the gold sheets with the little circles cut into them?"

"Yes."

"That's cash heading to the afterlife."

"Cool," I said.

Rong continued, "It's Taoist and Hindu tradition. You see it all over Hong Kong and other places. Families bring their ancestors' real alcohol and also gifts made of joss paper. Some of it looks like real money. It's known as Hell Bank Notes. You see it a lot at funerals, but joss paper can be made to represent all sorts of things, like apartments, cars, clothes, or washing machines."

"Ghost gotta keep his sheet clean," Nitro joked.

"Why do the dead need stuff?" I asked.

Rong answered, "It's more a matter of the living pleasing their loved ones."

I was stunned. Magic was all around us, literally at street level. This was magic at its most banal, and it was wonderful. I was tired to my core of the false church of money and power that grew spidery roots into each other, endlessly demanding more in life and, after death, seeking cloud-based mansions of gold. This was *want* beyond need or joy. It gathered ever inward until the addiction of getting and the fear of losing and the anger at those who might take…plunged the spirit into a black hole of self. Here along the Haihe River, I saw another way. I saw people burning paper to bridge the cosmic divide between life and death…and all they wanted to do was to please their lost loved ones with a washing machine or a stiff drink.

"There's a joke," Rong said, brightening. "A guy goes into the store to get something for his departed mother. The store owner holds up a piece of joss paper and says, 'How about a new iPhone?' The guy says, 'My mother wouldn't know how to use it.' The store owner says, 'No problem. Steve Jobs will show her.'"

"Can I send my father a new car?" I asked.

"You'd need to consult a feng shui master. If you set the fire in the wrong place, some other ghost will steal the offering."

I laughed. "That would be just Dad's luck." We watched mourners use the flames to send gifts on their way.

"Maybe your dad would like a hooker," Rong suggested.

"Seriously?"

"People burn all sorts of things for their loved ones."

Nitro snarked, "I hope someone sends me some scratch when I get to the other side. A hooker would be good too. I mean, until my Bessie shows up."

"I'm not sure my kids will be burning paper anythings for me," I said. It hurt to tell the truth.

"At least you still talk to your kids. I haven't seen my son in forever. I got work to do when I get home," Nitro said. "My man Rong here has it right. Be good to your family."

"I want to be good to them. You saw that apartment. I am saving to buy them a nicer place." (I remembered the toilet bowl with no seat.) "Another million bucks should do it. Then I will be worthwhile in their eyes. I want to help them now, not after they're gone. I would have done it already if Mrs. Li and people like her in the organization would stop treating me as nothing more than a cheap servant." His dislike of his situation was obviously eating at him.

"People are takers. It's true. Somebody owns you until the day you stand tall and change your own damn luck," Nitro said.

I took a hard look at him then said, "I'm willing to change mine. And I'm going to do it."

Rong reached in his shirt and pulled out a wolf's tooth. *Had I noticed the necklace on him before?* Its silver wolf's head fitting held a serious canine pendant. Rong clutched the curved tooth and pledged, "I am willing. I will change my luck."

CHAPTER 24

WE FOUND MR. LU with all our bags standing in a tightly packed line outside the train station. The line wasn't moving. It was ten thirty, and by quarter 'til eleven, we were concerned about making it to our train on time. The reason for the delay was obvious: two soldiers with what I now recognized as QBZ-95 bullpup assault rifles.

"Will they hold the train?" I asked Rong.

"I doubt it. They clamp down whenever there are protests anywhere. Around the country, students are supporting Hong Kong's right to autonomy, so these soldiers make a show of force." Rong stepped ahead of the others in line. "Keep up!" he called back to us.

What happened next felt as though we were daring the soldiers to shoot us. Rong said something to them in rapid-fire Mandarin. They argued for a heart-pounding moment, but Rong won out, and he slipped through the soldiers' checkpoint to the metal detectors, not looking back. Loaded down with our bags, me with my two bags, the haversack, plus the silver case and my guitar, we elbowed our way past the other waiting passengers. I wondered whether I'd get a bullet in the back for doing it, but no one stopped us. Rong took the silver case from me and walked around while our other bags passed along the scanning conveyor, and we stepped through the metal detector. As we gathered everything together on the other side, Rong jammed the silver case back into my hands. ("I told them you were a doctor and this is someone's heart!" *That worked?*) He led us up an enormous escalator to the even more enormous terminal area. In keeping with the Chinese love of large interior spaces, it was the size of Mercedes-Benz Stadium. The station clock indicated we had only minutes remaining. Even so, Rong stopped at one of the many kiosks lining the terminal and bought food and drinks. We then raced across the gleaming marble floor to the gate, down another huge escalator to the tracks, and onto our train. Immediately, we felt the floor lurch under our feet. We were off!

The three of us squeezed past several passengers. Most traveled with less luggage than we had, but a few appeared to be carrying their life's belongings. "Farmers," Rong said. They were migrant workers going from crop to crop like the Joad family. Two men with sun-leathered faces struggled to find a place in their compartment for bags of seed that had to weigh a hundred pounds each. We stepped over the burlap sacks blocking the aisle and kept going.

At last, we found our racks. There were half a dozen sleeping racks. Only the lower ones offered enough space to allow a person to sit up. A family of five was sitting in these, eating a dinner of pungent fish soup and rice.

Rong didn't say anything but began roughly moving their belongings up to the top racks or underneath to make way for our bags. The family simply finished eating. The mother then climbed to one of the middle racks with her twin babies, wedging them in against the bulkhead so she could protect them with her body. The father and an older child took the two coffin-like upper bunks. The clearance was so shallow, the father could not turn his shoulders sideways and had to lay on his back.

"I'll take the other middle bunk," Rong offered, then said to me, "You sleep with your phone in your pocket and the case against the wall."

The bunk came with a mattress, clean blanket, and pillow. We stripped off our shoes and stretched out. There was nowhere to change into nightclothes, nor did I want to go digging through my luggage.

Nitro made himself comfortable. "Just like the Navy."

Minutes later, the train's interior lights clicked off. Outside the windows, utility lights flew by at odd intervals. I felt myself drifting off until someone cut loose with the loudest snore I'd ever heard. It was a six-cylinder diesel engine misfiring on cams two and five.

"Nitro, turn to the wall!" I hissed into the dark.

"It ain't me. It's Poppa Bear in the top rack," he said.

Nitro's snoring soon joined the chorus. No one else seemed disturbed by it, so I lay in the dark, listening to the heavy breathing and the sound of the tracks clattering underneath us.

I checked my phone. The charge was low, but I had enough to read a message from Jing. "Be careful. Gillian is not answering." Why was she telling me to be careful? Was Gillian coming to China after all? What had changed? I messaged her back. She sent: "I don't know. Just be careful." I typed out "I love you." The letters turned into a red heart emoji, which was fine. I slid my thumb down to the send button, and…we went into a tunnel, and the text went away. The phone clicked into conservation mode, basically hibernating. I couldn't tell if my last text made it out.

The only nearby electrical outlet was a single plug mounted beneath the aisle window. A young man sat there in the drop seat using the plug to play a game on his device. I could hear the explosions and gunfire through his earbuds. They were nothing compared to the snore opera all around me, which had now been joined by the mother. Someone farted *con fuoco* in their sleep.

In the morning, the food cart came around. I understood why Rong had taken a risk to stock up back in the train terminal. These meals were sealed in plastic pouches. The family we shared our compartment with bought some. They cut the ends open and squeezed out semiliquified meat and fish that looked as though it had been run over by a tractor. The mother poured steaming hot water into tubs of Ramen noodles and the meal actually smelled appealing.

Rong broke out our wrapped provision, which included tempting slices of duck and lychees with leaves still clinging to them. Family farms slid by outside while the seven of us pooled our food, ate off the crowded central counter, and talked. Not that I understood much of what was said. The father lit a cigarette, and the mother changed the twins' diapers, adding a certain note to the meal's aroma.

"They speak Cantonese," Rong explained. "They're heading west to look for work so they can make more money. The mother wants more children." I looked at the father. He looked back.

Nitro said, "That is true love right there."

Outside, a nascent city flew by. There were clusters of apartment buildings, perhaps thirty or forty stories high. The morning sun winked through these skeletons, gleaming into the far windows and out the near ones. No interior walls. Lower buildings surrounded the high-rises, with plenty of parks and other green space, but the whole thing sat there, failing to ignite into a vibrant urban center. I didn't expect to make out people at this distance, but I should have been able to see smog engulfing the buildings. In fact, I could not pick out cars or trucks or movement of any kind on the roads. It was as if a boy had created a diorama, forgetting to include the functional details.

I asked, "What's with the empty buildings everywhere?

Rong said, "Politicians tried to will cities into existence all at once. It made for bad planning. It looked like a good idea ten years ago, no doubt. CCP built dozens of these cities, creating a nice economic growth bubble, but no one moved in. The government played too many games trying to tighten loose financial policies. It killed the market. Most of these places are still empty."

"Ghost cities," Nitro said.

"Exactly. CCP is spending a mountain of bucks to build modern highways and electronic infrastructure, but so far, very few people have taken the bait. They'll figure it all out eventually." Rong leaned in grinning and added, "Communists are like everyone else. They love money."

After breakfast, I took out my guitar. I'd come up with a line to finish a song I'd been working on. I found a sheet of notes in the guitar case and jotted down my brilliance. Plucking a few chords, I took the song out for a spin. What the hell? I had a captive audience.

John's got Mary in a dream home
Mortgage, babies, and a puppy or two
Under skies so blue
You think you've found your little whoop-a-doo

Work and fun-time make you run time
Wears you through and through
Where'd your years go runnin' to?
One fine day...your mind strays where it oughtn't go to
And Little John shouts, "Hey, let me go there with ya too!"
Down to whoop-a-doo

Your head's a mess
Boss yells, "You're through!"
Money's tight
You're down and out and screwed
What will ole Johnny do?

You're running fast
Aww Aww, life is faster
You chase the night, lose the "ever after"
So true
When you live for whoop-a-doo
One fine day…your mind strays in ways minds
ought not do
And Little John sings, "Hey, you know I'm going
too!"
Get me some whoop-a-doo

The choice you make, the things you do
Mary's gone, John is blue
It's true—in his little whoop-a-doo
John is you—in your little whoop-a-doo

Our bunkmates applauded along with a small crowd that had gathered 'round. One man smiled, nodded vigorously, and motioned with both hands as if lifting something. *Up, up? No. Duh! He wanted more, more. Fine.* I figured this crowd would dig some good Southern rock. I strummed the opening chords for "Statesboro Blues." The father and mother smiled and bobbed their heads in time to the music. I was about to hit 'em with a sweltering "Wake up Momma!" but they beat me to it. They began singing. Loudly. I kept playing, surrendering the vocals.

I listened to their voices. The accent was thick, but there was something familiar. They were singing Taylor Swift's latest song. Soon the rest of the crowd was clapping and singing along. What the hell! The audience is always right.

After a few more tunes, the miniconcert finished up, and people went on their way to smoke and chat. I was feeling good about myself when Rong became agitated. He leaned over me and ruffled through the blankets. Cursing in Mandarin, he looked under the bunk then checked the upper racks.

"It was your job, Mr. Angell! Where the hell is it?"

"What? What are you so excited about?"

"The case!"

My hide went walk-in-beer-cooler-in-shorts cold. The silver case had been with me like herpes since Shanghai. It was gone.

Nitro was gone too.

Rong was furious. "This is serious. That case is very important to our superiors. They will not like it if Mr. Baine disturbs the contents."

"He can't have gone anywhere. He didn't jump off a train going thirty miles an hour. Maybe he went looking for some coffee."

"They don't have coffee."

"Maybe he's developed a taste for tea."

"I'll check the dining car. Don't you go anywhere, Mr. Angell."

As soon as Rong stepped through the door, I got up to make my own search. I found Nitro at the sink area at the opposite end of the car. Other passengers were busy shaving and brushing their teeth in cloudy tap water.

He pulled me across the narrow aisle into one of the water closets. It made me nostalgic for Mama and Baba's bathroom. Despite efforts to westernize, water closets were still common throughout China. They literally consisted of a hole. No seat.

No handles. Balance was everything. Here, too, was a hole in the floor of the train through which I could see the tracks speeding by underneath us. The train's rocking motion had caused someone to miss. Nitro and I did our best to avoid that spot and also to not breathe any more than absolutely necessary.

"What the hell are we doing here?" I demanded.

Nitro said, "Well, I ain't going potty. I'll hold it until we're back in Georgia, thanks."

"Why did you run off with the case?"

"I hoped you had a few more tunes in you. I tried to signal, but you were going full Elvis. Anyway, I've got it open."

"How?"

He smirked. Nitro. He flipped up the lid of the case. The open left side held blood samples and some paper files, but there was a compartment with a coded lock. "Look, a dragon! There, out the window!"

"Right." I looked out the tiny window to humor him.

A moment later, Nitro let fly a terrible scream. "Those bastards! Oh, dammit, Zebulon. They're all the same. They're all the damn same, every one of 'em. Those bastards!"

I took the silver case from his hands and turned it to face me. Nitro released it and began pounding his fists on the filthy walls. The interior of the case was cold to the touch—some kind of built-in refrigeration. Nitro had managed to unlock the inner titanium lid on the right half. I lifted it and looked inside. Two ice-crusted brown eyes stared back from a vacuum-sealed plastic bag. There were three other packets containing biopsied tissue. One the color of spoiled raw steak was probably a liver while the gray-pink bits had to be from someone's brain and the third was…mystery meat. They'd chopped someone up into portable bits to check the effects of Tiger Pep.

It wasn't hard to see who it was. The inner lid of the titanium compartment had a small glowing screen. On it was the toothless face of a Black man with patches of thin white hair and bits of beard. The picture was a postmortem, taken before they harvested his eyes. This was Reverend Q.

There was another clue inside the case. On the sample bags, branded on the inside of the case, and even on the small screen: a triple triangle. I'd seen it recently.

The door to the water closet flew open, and Rong's angry face was there glaring at us. He reached over and grabbed the case, carefully shutting and locking the inner section and then the lid to the case itself.

"Quit standing around in someone else's shit. Get back to our compartment. We've got real trouble!"

CHAPTER 25

SCENERY ROLLED BY AT a modest rate as the train climbed an incline through the mountains. The yellow-gray skies of Tianjin had given way to brilliant blues and sunshine that warmed terraced farms. Villages and mining towns clung within forbidding crags. Tunnels blackened the train's windows for long minutes as we pierced the leviathan's heart, reemerging just as abruptly into the sunlit world.

Nitro stopped crying. "This was a good man once. I know he made mistakes. I'm not the man to judge him for those failings. He was a good man, a powerful and inspiring preacher."

"I'm sorry," I said.

"I am sorry also," Rong said. "Your friend was already in a failing condition when my colleagues took up his care. I assure you they would have saved him if they could have."

"So they couldn't save him. That doesn't mean they had to carve him up and stick him in a box!"

"I'm sorry," Rong said again.

I lost it. "I'm tired of you being sorry then being threatening. Tell us what's going on. All of it!"

The other family was on the lower bunk with us but didn't seem to give a damn about what we were saying. The father was smoking again, oblivious to the fact that his wife was nursing their twin babies. A young man took his video game and charger off the one and only outlet, and I jumped on it, plugging in my phone.

"Don't lose that either!" Rong hissed. "We are in enough trouble."

"Start talking," I said with as much menace as I could muster against Rong, whom I had no doubt could finish any fight I started.

He blinked. "You are the couriers for the formula and also the guinea pigs."

"Tiger Pep does *what* exactly?"

"It comes from Xi'an. There are trees that grow only there. The fruit is the basis of Tiger Pep. You know the first part. It offers a euphoria and increases desire…but there is a more significant effect. Over time, a fairly brief period, it leaves the male sterile."

"Lord help me!" Nitro said.

"Why would anyone want this?" I asked.

"We had it all wrong, Zebulon," Nitro said. "The buyer doesn't take it. He gives it away."

"He's right," said Rong. "There are parties all over the world who will pay a fortune for a product such as this…which uses pleasure to extract a terrible price."

Nitro elaborated, "You put it out there in the right communities, and poof! People you don't like stop having babies."

"Genocide," I whispered as if the universe were listening. *Did the universe care? I had my doubts.*

"Imperfect. Spotty. But yes, it would leave large numbers of males sterile," Rong said. "The interested parties believe they can use this herbal supplement in communities they wish to cull. The CCP, for instance, has long had a desire to sterilize the Uygur separatists, not to mention paring Tibetans down to a more manageable number. The Turks have expressed an interest in this product, no doubt as a solution to their Kurdish difficulties. Certain parties within America would like to see the Black community downsized. Global arms merchants would like to add Tiger Pep to their arsenals. The list is as long as hate itself.

"Some of our potential customers are unwilling to rely solely on fair bidding, however. They would like to steal the formula, or at least as much information as possible. I saw our friend from Beijing in the dining compartment." He meant RHM. "I pulled back and watched him through the door. Fortunately, the man was facing the other way. He was with two women. You can't miss them. They're big."

"Like fat?"

"No, not fat. Sumos."

"Huh?" said Nitro. "There ain't no women sumos. I've been to Japan. A woman can't even touch the *dohyō*. It's bad luck."

"Things change. These are female sumos."

"I'll be…"

Rong continued, "I think our friend brought them with him for two reasons. They are strong, and they are women."

Nitro and I looked at each other. The beginnings of a thought tickled the back of my brain, not in a fun way.

"Are you sayin' those sumos are for us?" Nitro asked.

"The Japanese would like further samples from you, Mr. Baine. You as well, Mr. Angell. I'm sure they'd also like the case."

"Samples?" Nitro and I asked together.

"Samples," Rong said.

We spent the day eating and sitting around without saying much more.

Finally, Nitro asked, "Can we trust you, Rong? How do we know you're a good guy?"

"I have been debating that question for myself. I have come up with a plan of insurance, and I ask you to trust me one more time. Show me your phone." I did. He took the wolf tooth from around his neck…and snapped the tooth part from the silver mounting. Inside was a small metal plug. "A flash drive," Rong said.

"It's too small to be a flash drive," I said.

"I don't shop at Best Buy." Rong lifted a flap of rubber on the phone's rugged case and fit the drive into an extra port I had not even noticed. On the small screen, a list came up—names, places. "It's what I've been able to gather in my travels during the past months. This list has a certain value all its own. When the time is right, when it is safe to do so, I will sell it. I will move my parents to a new home. I will also share some of the profits with you two, but just so you know, my superiors would kill me for creating a record of this information, and you as well."

"I'm sure they would," I said.

Rong carefully removed the flash drive and made sure the phone retained no trace of the data. He then snapped it back in place inside the wolf's head and tucked the pendant into his shirt.

He was just in time. A door slid open at the far end of our car. RHM stepped in, followed by two distinct-looking women. I don't mean that as body shaming because, although they were large, they were not flabby. They were...dense. I utterly respected the power in their frames.

"Time to go!" Rong said.

I grabbed the silver case, and we took off just as the train plunged into the latest tunnel. We were out the opposite end of the car in seconds and onto the platform in between cars. Inside the stone roots of the mountain, the temperature dropped noticeably. I shivered as we moved to the next car. I looked back and saw RHM's two women closing the distance rapidly.

Nitro and Rong reached the next car and opened the dividing door. I was about to follow them through it when a beefy hand caught my arm. I might as well have been a puppy tugging at its leash. The lady sumo pulled me into the nearest sleeper compartment and sat me down on one of the lower racks. RHM and the other sumo went barreling past us.

There was only one occupant in this compartment: a lanky old man who was somewhere between his mideighties and late three hundreds stretched out in a top rack listening to music through a pair of headphones.

"Hello," she said to me. "I am Tatsuo. You are Zebulon? (It came out *Zeh-BOO'-ron*.) I like that name." She spoke passable English, her *l*'s drifting ever so slightly to *r*'s. It was kinda sexy. I gave her credit for learning my language. I felt stupid by comparison. There's an old joke: What do you call someone who speaks two languages? Bilingual. What do you call someone who speaks three languages? Trilingual. What do you call someone who speaks one language? American.

"Hi," I stammered. Tatsuo was quite pleasant, though her sizable presence made me nervous. "Um, nice to meet you?" I had no clue what to say to this woman. In desperation, I blurted out, "So you're a sumo wrestler. What's that like?" My brain had slipped into junior prom mode.

"I work hard at it. It's still a new idea for many of the fans, including my father. *Touchan* is traditional. He cannot accept women fighting in the ring. I am working hard to make him understand, but it is not easy. Perhaps if he sees me win some bouts, he will change his mind. Such competitions require money."

"I guess that's why you took this job." She was holding my hand like we were on a first date.

"Yes. You are helping me earn enough to pay the entry fees in the upcoming Dragon Tournament. I'm going to win!"

"I would never bet against you. So…what exactly are your plans now?"

Tatsuo had the most delightful little girl whoop of a laugh. I was charmed and terrified. "I think you know. Would you like to go back to our compartment? It's more private." *The private compartment we were supposed to have gotten.* "I need a little something from you." High school sex ed taught me that sperm stayed viable inside a woman's body for days. It also taught me to use a condom, but clearly, that wasn't an option in this particular encounter.

"Um. If I say no, are you going to hurt me?"

Another whoop. The old guy in the upper rack was in his own world. One or two people passed by in the aisle, but no one looked over. I had the feeling they'd seen it all on these trains. Regardless, I wasn't ready for them to see *me* seeing it all.

"We can stay here. That can be fun too." She reached over and spread a blanket over the front of us then pulled me closer to her and leaned us back against the wall of the rack. It was getting warmer.

"Oh gosh! I hate to disappoint you, but I'm a married man…"

"That's fine, Zebulon. You're cute. I'll send you back to your wife in one piece." Her hands were moving very quickly at this point. She had my belt and zipper open in seconds. I really did try to stop her, but as I fumbled at putting my pants back together, she slapped my hand hard enough to let me know she meant business. "Wouldn't you like to play with Tatsuo?"

"Not with everyone looking!"

"No one cares. Fine, have it your own way. You'll never know what you missed!"

She turned her head. Her hands moved off me, and for a second, I felt a flush of relief, but it was not a withdrawal. She turned back to face me, holding up a plastic cup with the screw lid off. Plan B. One of her arms wrapped around me, and the other hand headed south.

"What?"

"What, what? What you think. I need a tiny sample." *Tiny?* She was making her move. "We can kiss if you like. I'd like you to kiss me." I don't know why it surprised me to discover that a sumo lady wore perfume or that her small mouth was so appealing. "You can feel my boobies if you like."

I tried to think of something. Anything. I had a wife. And she had a name. And that name probably started with… *I want to say J?* I couldn't focus. All I could think about was… Well, I only did what any healthy male would do in my situation.

At that moment, Nitro came rushing back into the car and spotted us. "I honestly did not know there were lady sumos," he said, out of breath.

I had whiplash looking at Nitro then back to Tatsuo. She was busy capping up her sample cup and stowing it in her pocket.

"Don't you two look awful cozy now? What have you been up to? I only left you alone for a minute." *It was at least three minutes!*

The end door opened loudly again, and RHM came back into the car and looked over at us. Tatsuo gave him a proud smile, and he nodded but otherwise showed no expression. "Come with us," RHM said.

I rose, adjusting myself as gracefully as I could, thankful I was wearing dark pants. I looked up at the old man in the top bunk. For a second, he did nothing, then he looked me square in the eye, and gave me the old Flying Tigers thumbs-up.

I followed RHM and Tatsuo, who was coquettishly licking her fingers, onto the platform between cars. Rong was already in the crowded space, his back against a door mounted in a flimsy armature of plastic and panels. The plates below our feet shook as if they'd work themselves loose and send us flying at any moment.

"From this point on, I will call to the shooting," RHM said.

"'I'll be *calling* the shots.' Please try not to be a walking cliché." I wasn't in the mood for his crap.

"Very well. I see that we have some of what we need anyway. My other associate will now escort Baine san so that he can contribute."

"Contribute?" Nitro seemed oblivious, then realized the sumo lady was eyeing him. "Oh! You don't want me, mama san. I'm fragile." He edged away, but the sumo lady, who was even larger than Tatsuo, took Nitro's arm and started to pull him back toward the car.

"We'll also need that case, of course." The case? I looked down. I was indeed holding the silver case as always, despite recent distractions.

"No. Not until I get the word from my superiors," Rong said. He was definitely angry. This was the part where I expected everyone to pull out a gun. That's what would have happened in America. Here, the duel ran a different way.

"I have been in touch with someone of your acquaintance. There is another avenue of opportunity to consider," RHM said.

For a split second, this caught Rong off his guard. Both of us wondered whether Gillian had made a side deal to betray us, one that depended on who got the case. It was impossible to know whether RHM was bluffing or Gillian was being Gillian. Rong parried. "I've seen soldiers on this train," he said. I hadn't. They were all over the train station, but I hadn't spotted any onboard. "I don't think even *the yakuza* wants to tangle with Chinese soldiers out in the open," Rong said, his lip quivering into a snarl.

"We prefer to the term *ninkyō dantai*, 'chivalrous organizations.' And we will do whatever the soldiers say…assuming they show up."

RHM reached down to grab the case out of my hand. Rong swung a fist over his head and struck him, using his other hand to pull RHM off his center of gravity. Things quickly went sideways.

Tatsuo stepped in to try to take the case while the other sumo lady grabbed hold of Nitro and Rong. Rong's glasses flew off his face and were quickly trampled on the floor plates. Nitro tried to trip Tatsuo, which forced her attention onto him and allowed Rong to break free. He then launched himself against RHM, sending both of them crashing full weight against the flimsy side door. I pictured them tumbling out onto the raw terrain, and my heart skipped two beats.

I felt like the least valuable player on my team, roughly equivalent in skills to RHM. Nitro was no longer young, but his hand-to-hand combat training held up fairly well. Rong, meanwhile, managed to land most of his blows even without his glasses. At this point, our blocking was as confusing as a Michael Bay movie, and I couldn't keep track of much except that everyone kept grabbing at my silver case.

I managed to swing my body free and twist around just in time to feel Tatsuo's weight—all of it!—land against me. I went careening against the same side doorway. I heard something metallic snap inside its frame. Worse, I felt the case pulled from my hand.

The second sumo had it. Then Nitro had it. He tried to get into the next car, but Tatsuo cartoonishly yanked him back by the belt. As RHM tried to grab the case, Rong ducked in, taking hold of it and poking viciously at RHM's eyes. RHM flinched and fell off his feet. The larger sumo lady went to help him. Rong had the case. A dragon's determination blazed in Tatsuo's eyes. She charged Rong. He tossed the case over both their heads to me. I caught it, smiling and suddenly feeling pretty good about my role in this tussle—but not for long.

Tatsuo had already set her well-trained mass in motion to crush Rong. She did, pinning him against the side door. With a tortured whine and pop, the door snapped its lock and flew open. I saw the feet of Tatsuo and Rong flying out into the open air.

That was the last I ever saw of either of them.

WHOOP-A-DOO

LOSS IS STRANGE. YOU don't appreciate the person at the center of your life until you stare at the hole she leaves behind. I lost Jing chasing something imaginary. Call it middle-aged craziness or delusion. I could accept my actions now and their cost. With everything so churned up, another sunken memory floated to the surface, and there is nothing meaner than a conscience waking up after a long booze-soaked snooze.

This was late last year, around Halloween, I think. I was drinking daily at that point. Stupid things happen to me when I drink. Sometimes the phone finds my hand and an old high school classmate hears what I really thought of him. Sometimes the garage gets smaller when I'm trying to park. This time, I'd decided to build a birdhouse for Jessa. It was the focus of all my attention and creative energy. It would attract finches and parakeets. If it didn't, I'd stop by the pet store and buy a few dozen parakeets and release them in the yard so they would use the birdhouse. If they didn't survive the winter, I'd get more in the spring. I had thoughts. The sugar in the alcohol raced my brain to an impressive level.

I was smart enough to picture in my mind how much stronger my birdhouse would be if I used both glue and nails. I took a swig of brain booster and picked up the hammer and a nail. I wanted to join the first wall to the second. There was a vise clamp mounted on the counter, but I figured that was too much work. Instead, I tried bracing the two flat pieces of wood in my lap. It took at least one hand to hold the wooden pieces at a ninety-degree angle, and that only left one hand for both hammer and nail. Not a problem. The nail gun was hooked to the compressor, stored not far from the vise-clamp I wasn't using. I turned it on—it was loud!—and once again braced the wood in my lap. I took another slug and got to work.

I fired the nail gun.

Jing had some painkillers stashed away. I needed them.

The injury wasn't too bad. The worst part was pulling out the nail. I probably should have called 911, but…I got the bandages on and threw out my ruined pants. They were old anyway. By that time, the painkillers were working great. I took a little nap.

The next day, my leg was still throbbing. Jing was off on one of her trips, so I made another little withdrawal from her supplies. After a week, I'd depleted her stock of pills and decided to replenish it. This entailed a trip downtown at two in the morning. It was something I'd never done before, but it went better than I could have hoped. Soon I was on a first-name basis with the salesman at the Five Points Marta station near Underground Atlanta.

I had it all under control until Jing ruined my system by complaining that the new pills didn't match the old ones. Also, the lock on her desk drawer had gotten mangled.

"I'm sorry," I said. I meant it. At that moment, I felt bad.

"Zee, this isn't something I can overlook," she said, tears racing down her face. "It's not bad enough you're screwing your blond junkie girlfriend, but you're supplying her with pills. *My* pills."

"Um…"

Until that exact moment, I had forgotten the girl. Even now, I only remember she was young, probably twenty. Maybe nineteen. And that's all. Jing accused *her* of suggesting the drug swap out. She said the girl—Marcie or Marnie or…—was using me to get the good stuff.

"The pills were there…"

"No, Zee! First, you went to a street dealer. Then you started using my account to order the painkillers."

It was as if the book in my head was rewriting itself, as Jing told me about things I had done it was as though I were living them for the first time. Everything she said made sense once she said it. The girl—Mattie?—convinced me to find Jing's passcodes and use her accounts to get the drugs. We'd been doing it for months, long before the stupid birdhouse shot me in the leg. The one thing I found difficult to grasp was that I couldn't remember the girl. How had we met? Was she a former student? I tried to remember, but all I got was flashes of blond hair, bad teeth, and tits. Beyond that, nothing. I couldn't even recall the conversation we must have had afterward to "end it." Maybe there were texts. I don't know.

I had lost an entire human being.

I lost Jing in the process. She kicked me out of the house and ordered me to live in the cottage.

All this went through my mind in about two seconds.

Loss is a strange thing. I felt Jing's words acutely but only after a delay. The loss of Rong struck me immediately, but the overwhelming feeling was that I had failed to truly appreciate him as a friend.

I would lose Jing completely unless I did the right thing to win her back.

CHAPTER 26

NITRO PRESSED HIS FACE against the glass door to our car. "I see soldiers coming this way." He turned to RHM. "I wonder if they'll run faster if I yell."

RHM growled something guttural. I was afraid he'd make one last try for the case, so I stepped over to the ruined door, extended my arm, and hung the case out in the breeze. The lights went out for a second. We were in another tunnel. It occurred to me that if my hand got too close to the stone wall, it would snap off my arm like a dry twig. By the time our eyes adjusted, RHM and the other sumo lady were gone.

"They've got the right idea. We should go too," said Nitro, pulling me back inside. We quickly made our way to our racks, several cars down. Some of the passengers seemed agitated, but I wasn't sure what they might have seen because, of course, my translator had stepped out. I assumed someone would at least discover the broken door. How they handled situations like this, I did not know, but we did *not* see any soldiers. Nitro was my favorite liar.

I didn't feel like talking, so I let Nitro fiddle on my phone. "This thing's got all sorts of gizmos, Zebulon. There's a shopping app here. Point the camera at something, and the app tells you how much and where to get one. Look. Push the button. Your boots are worth fourteen dollars at Goodwill." I wasn't in the mood for jokes. I made him promise to keep it fully charged. That meant chasing off two fat kids with an Xbox, but we secured the outlet like it was Omaha Beach.

I had met Rong's family yesterday. I should tell them, and yet I had no hope of finding my way back through the streets of Tianjin or tracking down their phone number. I didn't relish the idea of trying to find the right "Wei" in a Chinese phone book.

Nitro and I packed up Rong's belongings as well as our own. As we pulled into the station in Xi'an, I had no clue what came next. That was Rong's department, and he had not briefed us on the particulars from that point on. There was nothing else to do but get off the train and call Jing.

"Maybe there's a nice hotel," Nitro offered.

Stepping onto the platform with all our luggage, I looked both ways. I didn't see RHM or his remaining sumo gal. This was not his element. I imagined he'd slip back into the shadows for now.

Nitro and I began walking toward the exit stairs. The crowd poured out of the train lugging their belongings and creating insistent currents all around. A group of men in casual wear spotted us and moved in fast to intercept. Nitro and I doubled our pace, but we were overburdened, outmatched, and outflanked. Two of the men got in front of us and two behind. Stepping up from a safe distance came their boss.

"Hi, Mr. Angell," said Kevin.

CHAPTER 27

MY WORST STUDENT EVER stood there with his four henchmen. They weren't sumo-sized, but they'd do.

"Yo momma know you're playing hooky from school, kid?" Nitro asked.

Kevin grinned. I don't think school was a top priority for him. "She's waiting for us along with Herr Fuchs." That name was new to me. Kevin looked forward and then back along the tracks. "Where's Wei Rong?"

"He had an accident," I said with as much emotional control as I could manage. Had Kevin been a human being, I would have offered him my sympathy. He'd known Rong longer than I had. Kevin was Kevin, however.

He let my words sink in and after a moment's reflection said, "Anything to say before my men beat the snot out of you?"

"You'd be prettier if you'd smile." You had to say something to the bad guys who were about to kill you. No one laughed. The men roughly took hold of me and Nitro.

This day was not going well. I'd been milked by a hard-bodied geisha, lost a friend, and now I was going to die at the hands of a pimply-faced creep who was too lazy to read *To Kill a Mockingbird*.

"Hold on now!" Nitro said. "You might want to look back over there." With his head, he motioned at the train. Six cars down from where we were standing on the platform, a man in maintenance clothes was examining the damage to one side door. He was showing the problem to two heavily armed soldiers.

"We'll continue this fun later," Kevin said. His men grabbed our belongings, including the silver case, and quick-marched us toward the stairs leading to street level. I had a feeling Kevin was taking us to the case's rightful owner, so I stopped worrying about him and started worrying about my immediate future. We walked through the mammoth terminal, which gleamed like it had been built five minutes earlier, and then stepped through the main doors to a waiting van. It held our bags and the seven of us. It should have held eight. Kevin sat up front with his first henchman, who drove with alarming speed. Number four kept a close watch on Nitro in the back seat while I sat squeezed between numbers two and three.

No one spoke at first. Then Henchman Number Three said, "Xi'an is a beautiful city. It is the capital of Shaanxi Province, as well as the starting point of the Silk Road." One of the other men groaned, and we drove on. Henchman Number Three continued, "Xi'an was one of China's four great ancient capitals under the great dynasties of Western Zhou, Qin, Western Han, Sui, and Tang."

The driver began complaining and arguing in Chinese with Henchman Number Three.

"What's he saying?" Nitro asked.

Kevin answered, "He says he wishes this were for him so he wouldn't have to listen to Nianzu bore us with his old docent scripts."

"Wishes *what* was for him?" I asked. As an answer, something sharp pricked my arm.

"Praise Jesus!" Nitro shouted as he too received a shot.

Number four was grinning at him. Number two was grinning at me.

And then the world got fuzzy around the edges, and I took a little nap.

CHAPTER 28

A MURKY NUMBER OF hours later, Kevin, backed by two of his apes, rousted us with a vicious poking stick. I had the worst hangover ever, and I hadn't even enjoyed a good drunk, plus I was starving. My muscles ached from being left in a cool draft in my stocking feet. My boots were gone. Meanwhile, someone had put a mask over my nose and mouth. I noticed the others wore masks as well. As my senses cleared, I realized we were in an earthy-smelling cell built of large bricks chipped at the edges. A dungeon Poe would have loved!

"Watch it! I ain't no T-bone!" Nitro yelled. "Get away from me with that damn spear."

"It is a *Ji*," Henchman Number Three informed us. "While the handle is, of course, a reproduction, the dagger-ax head and tip are original Qin manufacture, displaying early Chinese metallurgical mastery. The surface is coated in ten microns of chromium to preserve its edge. It is one of nearly forty-thousand—"

"Shut up," said Henchman Number One, this time in English.

Kevin finally spoke, "Get them cleaned up." He pulled my phone from his pocket. "Oh, this is yours."

I took the phone and examined it. It was on, but there was no service. "I assume you tried to hack into it…" I looked the little turd muffin straight in the eye. "And failed. Otherwise, Nitro and I would have gone on dreaming forever. Am I right?"

"Come on," was his only answer.

The two guards manhandled us roughly from the drafty cell and into…another world. A very old world. Millennia old. We stepped out among numerous stone structures, laid out in a yawning expanse of black. My senses groped, aching for sunlight but taking in heavy nothingness. I got little sense of the borders of this underground space because only a dozen stand-alone lighting instruments on industrial tripods revealed the immediate area. I guessed there were more of these little work lights waiting in the dark.

From what I could see, it was as if someone had scooped up a city and encased it in stone. There were also large modern machines with fans and compressors, plus thick hoses running in all directions. Some ran through the perimeter wall into a dark tunnel. The appliances droned on steadily, blowing out the chill sigh of some forlorn giant.

Silvery pathways wound in all directions, reflecting weak light upward onto brickwork storage rooms and temples. Workers had placed temporary flooring over some of these pathways, as well as setting up platforms. This allowed visitors mobility while protecting the ancient floors from modern feet. The largest of these platforms stood near a giant structure at the shallow end of a basin situated high enough to feed the pathways. They were rivers. The structure that rose farther than I could see was, in fact, a cistern, though what it contained was not water. A faucet jutted out, sporting a black demonic face with bulging eyes and a cruel gaping mouth. Someone had shut off the tap. The riverbeds were shiny but dry.

These channels and the general layout of the place suggested a great map whose central point was a blocky stone edifice several hundred yards away.

"Welcome to the Qin necropolis. He rests there," Kevin said with a dramatic flourish, pointing to the burial chamber.

"Few mortals have seen this place and lived." This was some kind of game to him.

"Qin? As in the name China?" I prodded.

"First emperor of a united China," said our eager docent, Henchman Number Three, with a deep note of pride. "Traditional geomancy suggests that a dragon straddles the area between the Lishan Mountains and Mount Hua. You are at Mount Li, the dragon's eye, inside the imperial tomb of Qin Shi Huang."

"Your honor!" Nitro said, bowing in the direction of the sepulcher.

"I read they hadn't excavated this site yet," I said.

"*They* haven't. *We* have," said a confident voice with crisp Teutonic shadings. Stepping from behind one of the lights was a tall man in a double-breasted suit, its pitch-black fabric bleeding into the shadows. His eyes were two blue sparks from Völundr's hammer while severely styled platinum hair framed his angular face. On his lapel, he wore a gold pin in a design of three interlocked triangles. "Good morning. I am Franz Fuchs, president and CEO of ValKnut Pharma and Holistics, GmbH. Please call me Frank."

Frank. He of the wagyu steaks and jet-set lifestyle. *Jing's boss, Frank, and the face of Rong's superiors.*

"You may remove your mask. The air is safe for short-term exposure, thanks to our ventilation system." He removed his own mask and pocketed it. "Your wife has been quite an asset to me, Mr. Angell. May I call you Zee?" *Finally, a second human being wanted to call me Zee, and look who I got.* "I believe you also know…"

Kevin had spoiled this surprise. His mother moved to Frank's side and took his arm. She seemed unconcerned with making a public display of affection in front of her teenaged son.

"Gillian," I said, "how fun to run into you here. Visit a lot of tombs, do you?"

"Mr. Zebulon. You to be looking well." Gillian was over-dressed for grave robbing, in an eye-catching red-and-black qipao that coordinated perfectly with Frank's suit and tie. She was maybe five-four, fully a foot shorter than her Aryan companion, for a pair they certainly were. "I to feel to be best my being—"

"Just speak in the clear!" I said flatly. I'd had enough of her wide-eyed China girl routine.

Even Frank chuckled.

"As you wish," Gillian continued. "I felt it best I be here for tomorrow's auction. I am not pleased that your wife has chosen to complicate our part of the transaction."

"Good English. Good honest contempt," I said.

"Jing and I enjoy a friendly rivalry." She chuffed like a tigress munching on an antelope.

"If you're talking about you and me…forget it. That ended when you sent your son to threaten mine."

"*Das reicht, Kinder.* Let us leave," Frank said. Two henchmen moved to escort us. "*Ach*! Put that thing away, boy!" He hissed at Kevin, who casually set his ancient dagger-ax against a wall. It wasn't the kind of thing one should carry out in the open. Frank's tone was a bit rough, probably because Kevin had come up empty in his attempt to get into my phone. Gillian never flinched at the treatment of her son.

Our group moved to the tunnel. Frank stayed close to me while ignoring Nitro. Part of the inclined passageway was finished in stone while some stretches appeared hewn from raw earth buttressed by steel framing. The rough walls flattened sounds and absorbed echoes, giving it the soundscape of an attic. My socks provided little protection from jabbing pebbles or the deep chill of the stone. Frank aimed an LED penlight at large sconces set near a set of enormous doors. "Be careful! There are booby traps!" He said it as if trying to scare children.

"Really?" My mind played a John Williams score complete with bullwhip snaps.

As if listening in, Frank said, "No rolling boulders to chase us, but we've had to bring in experts to disarm fearsome-looking crossbows." He indicated the dark recesses. "These sentinels have guarded the emperor since antiquity but are safely in storage at present. Nothing ruined, as per our promise to the Party. We also catalogued and stored away the skeletal remains of several dozen workers trapped inside. Someone closed the doors on them when they sealed this place. We found some near the doors, and others scattered about. They had their run of the place for a time, though I do not think they enjoyed it. Evidence suggests they resorted to extreme measures at the end, turning on one another for food."

"Cool!" cried Kevin.

Ignoring him, Frank continued, "Then there is the great centerpiece, the emperor's burial chamber, which remains off-limits even to us." Looking around to make sure only Gillian, Nitro, and I could hear, he whispered, "Officially. My teams are under constant observation, but…there is time yet. I have my eye on a lovely ring of jade. You can't come so far and not take home a souvenir or two, *ja?*" A sideways glance from Gillian told me this part of the plan was news to her.

When at last we reached sunlight, an open-air tram was waiting to take us to the main complex. I got in, looking back at the tree-covered hill from which we'd emerged. As we got some distance, the "hill" revealed its obviously man-made pyramidal contours.

Frank spoke as if he were making a presentation to the stockholders. "It's hard to believe, but local farmers let their beasts graze up there. Among those trees are a handful of longans. Every once in a while, they play their trick! They deliver the quintessence of our dreams. Not long after we arrived, we discovered a grove of super longan trees several kilometers from here, with especially high concentrations.

"For many years, farmers kept this secret, using the Tiger Penis for their enjoyment, while bemoaning a drop in livestock fertility. They failed to put the two together. Whole family lines dwindled and died out. This went unnoticed, however, as misery seems engrained in rural Chinese life.

"Then in 1974, farmers discovered the first of the Terracotta Soldiers and archeologists soon confirmed the nearby burial mound for what it is. Now people remembered the stories of childless families. They concocted this curse, saying Emperor Qin Shi Huang was exacting revenge on those who dared disturb his slumbers. Nonsense, of course, but persistent talk drew scientific inquiries.

"In time, ValKnut heard of it. I took on the project personally in 2013 and forged an agreement with a certain faction within CCP. We brought to bear ValKnut's network of resources to properly exploit the find. That has since entailed major expenditures, including bringing in German engineers to get through the durable, hard-packed earthen shell and open the hermetically sealed mausoleum. It took nine weeks just to excavate the outer gate without damaging it.

"Anyway, we had indeed identified the fruit, but we needed a formula to make it profitable. We hoped the emperor kept records. Every good curse should be written down after all. It's basic storybook protocol. We have searched, but so far…pffft!" He laughed. "So even as we dug and brushed away spiders, we also shone the light of science. Only to hit another obstacle.

"CCP insisted Chinese scientists work on unlocking this secret of the emperor's curse. That is where your wife came in, some four years ago." I swear she'd never mentioned ValKnut by name—or had she? Maybe I was drinking at the time. "Jing has American citizenship now, but she was born in China and is acceptable to our associates. And now my faith in her has paid off."

A duck blind of sorts blocked the open mouth of the tunnel from general view. We drove around it and on through make-shift but sturdy fencing. Visitors were unable to stroll around this part of the park for now. Curious uninvited guests to the tomb could well find themselves staying there and embracing eternity.

The tram took us west to an enormous complex. One of the henchmen handed us a bag full of Shaanxi sandwiches, sea-soned braised pork on a toasted flatbread. Nitro and I sloppily inhaled the fragrant eats nonstop until we reached the hangar.

We made our way in through a side entrance and then to the staff showers, where we shaved, cleaned up, and got into fresh clothes from our own luggage. Pulling on my boots—*finally!*—I spotted the Martin's case among our bags, and an odd feeling came over me. I picked it up and set it on a counter.

"I intended to throw a tight cordon of security around our activities, but our hosts are adamant about limiting personnel. Circumstances dictate I utilize what I have and choose func-tionaries from the local talent pool," Frank side-eyed Kevin. "Their actions exceeded my instructions, I assure you."

The sound of the latches snapping back bounced off the tile walls like gunshots. There sat my poor Martin, her feminine curves violated. They'd torn off her pretty face to get inside.

"Did you find more of your herbal product?" Nitro asked.

Frank answered tersely, "A small amount of Dr. Angell's refined product. Enough to be useful."

"You didn't have to break the man's guitar," Nitro said. Frank stepped between the two of us and turned his back to Nitro.

To me, he said, "Again, my apologies. Allow me to make it up to you in some small measure. I will take you on a guided tour of the Terracotta Army, a view from the pits that no tourist ever sees."

We followed him out through the museum and into an enormous space, bigger even than airports we had visited, containing several pits, occupied by battalions of stony men. The site drew thousands of visitors each day, mostly Chinese but many from around the world as well. The latest group thronged in a slow circuit around the largest pit and then on to the smaller ones. We slipped into line, then at one point along a long side stretch, we simply did the unthinkable. With a jaunty wave to several sets of guards around the perimeter, Frank led us down a short ladder and into the pit itself!

"Don't make eye contact with the tourists. They're jealous," Frank joked. "It was a simple matter to isolate the emperor's burial mound. Most people skip that part of the tour since, to them anyway, it is merely a hill covered in scrappy trees. For this part of our tour, boldness is key. Proceed as if we are alone among this magnificence." Frank swept his arm back, drawing our attention to the massive pit, which had numerous trenches dug into its floor. These contained hauntingly lifelike statues beyond counting. "Extending the size of several football pitches, American or European, these excavations hold a formidable army of the dead."

He turned back to us. A cavernous modern superstructure contained this field and two other pits, allowing in a minimum of natural sunlight. Even the overhead floodlights only brought the interior brightness to the equivalent of dusk. Spreading his arms wide, Frank said, "Behold, evidence of one man's ambition." And then smiling to himself, he motioned Henchman Number Three over to the front of our group. "You may tell the story."

I've never seen a man puff out his chest quite so much. *Hench*, as I now thought of him, began the presentation of a lifetime, "You see armed soldiers from the dawn of China's history as a unified nation." We walked among the workshop area, where carefully tagged bits were coming together slowly. These life-size statues lay in shards after more than twenty-two centuries in the earth, but scientists had painstakingly restored them. Imagine a chocolate Easter bunny smashed with a hammer then lovingly reassembled.

The experts had recreated a parade ground flash-frozen in time. "Ordered by the great Qin, who also ordered construction begun on the Great Wall, this was a massive undertaking. More than 8,000 soldiers have been discovered, along with 130 chariots and 520 horses as well as 150 cavalry horses." Hench led us down another ladder and into one groove that held a tight formation of fighters from another era. "This is the Terracotta Army or Shadow Army. Other pits have been found containing officials, acrobats, and musicians.

"The existence was an open secret for centuries, but no one dared disturb the site until a farmer digging a well found the first of the soldiers by accident. You may have heard rumors of a mass grave of artisans killed to keep the secret of this place. Do not believe such lies." Hench was a good little actor as it turned out. "Countless thousands of workers and master craftsman labored for thirty-eight years to create the emperor's burial palace and these figures around you. Such numbers made any secrecy impossible.

"Notice that each statue is unique. So much so, those long-ago artists signed many of the individual pieces." I looked around. Some of the figures were in robes while others wore plated armor. Some were clean-shaven while their brothers in arms had a mustache or full beard. The faces showed a great range of age and character. The detail was exquisite: laces holding together the squares that made up their armor and intricate patterns on the sandals of those on horseback. Each clay man represented a person who lived and played a role in Qin's army. Each figure breathed, laughed, complained, ate, had a family, and dreamed of conquest and glory…or perhaps he wished for a quiet life.

Hench continued, "Notice that they are of differing heights and weights. The lower officers have adorable pot bellies while the generals are the tallest and the fattest. *Jing's brother would do well in this army.*

"You'll notice, many of the men stand as if holding bows or spears, but there are none to be seen. This whole field was once inside a structure, buried in the earth. A later emperor coveted its armory of very real weapons and broke in to loot the site. His men set the roofing beams on fire, causing wide-spread collapses. So far, only one soldier, a crouching archer, has been found intact. These around you are three-dimensional jigsaw puzzles. The work to reassemble them stretches ahead for decades. Many must stand without heads on their shoulders. We can only imagine walking among these columns what it must have looked like when the crypt was pristine."

Yes, I could imagine it. The sense of wonder swept over me like—

"Two thousand years and no women?" Nitro said. "I'll pass."

"Of course. There are those, however, who do not fear eternity," Frank said, never making eye contact with Nitro.

Hench said, "You can see that the figures are standing on roads. Early on, farmers quietly hauled off these paving bricks for use in pigsties. The government moved three villages and bought back the bricks for thirty yuan each, a lot of money at the time. Today, each brick is valued at half-a-million yuan, about eight thousand US dollars." Trying to sound funny, he said, "If you are caught with one, you will pay a higher price! We honor our ancestors by protecting what is theirs."

We climbed back up and made our way over to one of the other two pits. This time, we walked around the edges of the excavations, looking at angular stone walls where petrified men stood holding invisible reins. "There's also a full-size chariot drawn by four horses, all done in bronze, recovered from outside the tomb," our chatty guide informed us. Some of the excavations held shattered troops, still awaiting a good sorting out, others showed only the early stages of recovery work.

"I can see bits of faded color on some of the statues. Were they painted?" Kevin asked. At least he showed some curiosity. He was fingering something in one hand. It was…a finger. The little peckerwood slipped it into his pocket when he thought no one was looking.

Hench went on. "They were crafted to be lifelike. However, once the archeologists exposed them to air and light after more than two thousand years, pigments began to vanish. Within days, mere traces remained. There was nothing they could do. This is one reason the government has not opened the First Qin Emperor's Tomb. Not *officially*."

Here, Frank stepped in to explain. "Beijing patiently awaits the development of technology to protect the treasures under that hill. I have brought such technology to bear. In fact, we have barely touched the artifacts. We explore with German-made instruments rather than breaking through ancient walls with pick and shovel. When we are finished…when I have learned the emperor's secrets…we will rebury his city of repose. Then we will turn over our equipment and leave. At a future time, Chinese archeologists will 'discover' the tomb and grin proudly at the world, ja?"

Gillian squeezed Frank's arm. "The People's Party will own the glory," she said for the benefit of the Chinese in the room.

CHAPTER 29

WALKING ON ANCIENT ROADS wore out our feet while building up an appetite. Frank took Gillian and me to dinner, pointedly leaving Kevin with the Chinese contingent and sending Nitro back to the stone cell inside the spectral city.

Our chosen nightspot, Shang Palace, shone like a jewel in the elegant Shangri-la Golden Flower Hotel. Crystal chandeliers lit red-carpeted rooms accented by ornate dark wood furnishing. Staffers in spotless uniforms scurried in and out of our private dining room, bringing us serving after serving of the sous-chef's best Cantonese, Sichuan, and Shaanxi dishes. We tore into the beef ribs in red wine and pine nuts like a trio of sophisticated velociraptors. I had eaten roasted duck already on this trip, but not like this. Here, the succulent meat drew an accent from Shaanxi spices, kiwi, and sweet flour sauces. Bowls of cherry sauce and honey melon competed with sinus-clearing wasabi.

Tea and liquor appeared as if by magic and continued to flow, as did the conversation. I wanted to talk about Rong, but I did not want to darken the pleasant mood. My status was in question, and I needed these two to like me. It did strike me odd that Gillian never mentioned her colleague, but then perhaps Rong had been merely her errand boy. I knew he was worth more than that.

After a time, Gillian excused herself to the lady's room, and I would swear she sashayed on her way out, for the benefit of her boys at the table.

Frank waited until she was almost out of earshot before commenting, "She is quite…how would you put it?"

"A hottie," I suggested

"I might have said 'beguiling,' but a noun is more efficient. *Hottie*. Pity she is not of better stock. Still, the Chinese have their…charms. I am grateful to Gillian for introducing me to your wife, who is possessed of both charm and scientific acumen." I felt like I'd missed a turn somewhere. "Jing attacks each problem with a fierce curiosity and allows her intuition to flourish in a way not encouraged by many research centers." Even as he mentioned Jing, my mind flashed an image of them together. Then my mind flashed on him and Gillian. *Wait. Was I jealous on behalf of my wife because her lover was also boning her business partner?*

"Thank you," I said, not feeling grateful.

"She has told me about you, your love of music, of cowboy boots, and your sense of humor. I feel we could be friends, you and I."

"I hope Jing hasn't told you…everything." If nothing else, marriage was a devout prayer for discretion.

"No, no. She speaks highly of you. So we must add loyalty to her list of attributes. Fealty is important in a woman. Or a man. Don't you agree?"

"I don't know what to say." No, really. I had no idea what he was getting at. It felt like an attempt to bring me into his confidence, but I couldn't deal with the ookiness factor.

Frank sipped his Courvoisier and changed tack. "Again, I must apologize for the loss of your instrument. You will allow me to replace it," he said, pointing his steepled hands toward me to indicate sincerity. "Still, it did yield a measure of Tiger Penis—I can never say that name and not snigger like a boy." I thought about pitching the name change, but he was ahead of me. "We will rebrand. Tiger Gummi, perhaps. In any case, we have a supply and…" He nodded in the direction Gillian had gone. "Someone to use it with. We should split this bounty, should we not?"

What flashed through my mind caused puckering lower down.

"Ummm…actually, the stuff gives me a pain."

"Indeed, no pleasure without pain, eh? Fortunately, I have pills for that." He leaned in and whispered conspiratorially, "It so happens, I am the head of a major pharmaceutical company. I know the *best* drug pushers." If I'm being honest, Frank did have a disarming self-assuredness I envied. He reminded me of Dad before the stroke. Anyway, I thought I could come to like Frank.

I should have shut up at that point, but that's not really my thing. "And the mercury?"

"Ja, this is a concern. In the tomb as well. We had to shut down the mercury flow and scrub the air. However, there is no need for worry." It was a curiously ambivalent answer coming from a medical man. Frank brightened. "Consider the benefits. Great sex! And, for myself, sterility is no curse. I already have three fine children, two boys, Garold and Odie, and a girl, Malkyn. *Mein Schatzi*." He slipped in German phrases from time to time but avoided most of the clichés, such as saying "und" for "and." Frank was in perfect control of himself at all times. "So now with this product of ours, I am out of the 'Kinder Biz' as it were. I take this as a plus as it spares me certain repercussions involving my social life." I got it. He was doing his wife a favor by not getting his mistresses pregnant. I went back to hating him.

Gillian returned from the powder room. Frank repeated his idea in efficient terminology. Lots of consonants. I stared at her but did not see Gillian. For a split second, I felt myself sliding back to a day at Jones Beach and a smile that would find its way into a driftwood frame. The image changed again. I saw a different face in leaf-dappled light, backed by Sope Creek.

"Mr. Zebulon?" Gillian inquired.

I sputtered an objection through nervous laughter, "Look at the time!"

"It's eight o'clock," said Frank, extending his wrist to display an Audemars Piguet Royal Oak Offshore Automatic Tourbillon Men's Chronograph. (My nifty app said it was $249,670 retail. *Holy crap!*)

"Still," I said. "We've all got a big morning ahead. I should head back to my little dungeon…" It struck me how much things had changed from the last time Gillian had seduced me. I desperately wanted to be with Jing and only Jing. Plus, I was pretty sure Gillian wanted to kill me…possibly as foreplay for Frank.

Gillian patted my knee and said, "It's no big deal."

"Indeed," Frank said. "You Americans are so…what is the word?"

"Traditional?" I ventured.

"*Constipated*…in your sexual mores." He took another sip of his Courvoisier and leaned back, spreading his arms over the seat like an emperor on his throne. "It is, of course, your choice. I merely wish to deepen our level of cooperation. Fealty, even."

Here it comes, I thought. "Meaning?"

"It would be simpler if I were the one to key in the passcode tomorrow. It confuses the clients to have too many actors on the stage during a presentation."

"Sorry. I'll have to pass on passing…the passcode." Lord, I sounded like such a nerd. Worse, I'd just cut off my best options for making nice with these two. Frank and Gillian both looked at me sternly. I lifted my rice-flavored beer to my lips and spoke into the mug, "For now, I mean. Let me sleep on it."

Frank looked unconvinced. He wanted what he wanted now. "As you choose. I've reserved a room for you here at the hotel. You'll sleep soundly…*alone*."

"Actually, I should keep Marqus company."

"That cell was an expedient only. Mere cots and—"

"Good enough for lab rats."

"Again, I must apologize for certain decisions that I now see should have—"

"You did get the samples you wanted?" I hated to think about how they got them. I figured it wasn't as much fun as getting squeezed by a sumo lady.

"We took the liberty while you were sleeping. By the way, you won't be making babies anymore, either."

"Good to know."

"Mr. Zebulon would do well to cultivate a sense of priorities in the business world," Gillian volunteered. Frank put his hand firmly on top of hers, and she stopped talking.

Frank spoke in a monotone, "We are in the final inning, as Americans say. If we all play ball, we can make a great deal of money. By this time tomorrow, you will have a hefty bank account and be on your way…home."

"That sounds…" *Ominous? Threatening?* "…great."

"Until tomorrow then," Frank said.

CHAPTER 30

AS I'D REQUESTED, THEY threw me back into the stone cell, along with Nitro. Seriously, a dungeon, albeit one with a curtain for a door. It may have once been an ancient storage area or workers' water closet. There was a hole in the floor that no doubt tied into the elaborate drainage system Frank had talked about over dinner. It connected to the sea and kept the place from flooding, at the same time conveying a unique substance to a nearby longan grove. In any case, the frigging cell was just as cold as I remembered. This was not helped by the fact that they took away my boots again. They gave Nitro and me paper shoes, so as to ensure we didn't leave twenty-first-century footprints anywhere in the tomb. That prissiness didn't extend to trash management, apparently. In one corner sat a McDonald's bag, the remains of Nitro's dinner provided by the guards. *Seriously, is there anywhere McDonald's won't sling its awful food?*

A self-contained LED stuck on the wall lit the cell. They'd also given us a battery-powered charging cradle for my phone. The generators must have been maxed out with the air circulation and filtration systems. Nitro inspected the light and the charger. He said there were no listening devices. He also said the phone needed Wi-Fi. "I've seen our guards make calls once or twice. Maybe we'll get lucky and they'll turn it on before the big show."

"The auction in the morning."

"Yeah," he said that in a funny way that made me worry.

Nitro told me he had gotten a message out. "Back on the train, after Rong's death, I texted one of my Navy intelligence contacts. I told them we were headed to Xi'an." I had mixed feelings. I didn't trust our situation, but I also didn't want to piss off Frank. Jing wanted me to be careful but to do my part. Nitro said, "The bad news is the cavalry's not coming into the Lost City."

"So? What are they doing?"

"They're monitoring the situation."

"Terrific."

"Zebulon, we really stepped in it," Nitro said, sounding more sober and focused than I'd ever heard him. "My contact says this operation has tripped alarms all over the world. Interpol is involved, and I don't know how many other agencies. Some that don't have names. My contact says our guys can probably help us, but we have to get to *them*."

"Probably? You didn't pin them down?"

"This is no time to demand favors. They'll be able to do more if we come up with something they want."

"Like what?" I asked.

Nitro said, "Well…I been thinking. There are a lot of badasses coming, sketchy types with big connections all over the world. They're all waiting for you to work your mojo with that phone, right?"

"Yes. I key in the code—"

He was about to continue when his eyes narrowed. "You remember the code, right?"

"Of course I—Yes."

"Good. Fine. *Right*?"

"Yes, I remember!" My voice rang off the walls.

"Okay," Nitro said. "So maybe while you're fiddling with your phone, you could take a few pictures. These Tony Maneros could smile for the birdie."

"Uh—rrrgh! Tony Manero is *Saturday Night Fever*. I think you mean Tony Montana from *Scarface*, and yes, I think I could make that work."

"I also got word out…don't get pissed…to some old friends in CCP."

I said, "Um, I thought we were trying *not* to get thrown into prison forever."

"It's cool. They have reason to make good with the less-bad CCP types."

I was lost but didn't feel like admitting it. "I hope so." It did sound like a plan…from Nitro. *Who'd have thunk?* "Wonderful! So all we have to do is survive and then get to the US embassy in Beijing?"

"It'll be watched. My Navy contact suggests the consulate in Guangzhou."

"That's all very complicated," I said. "Maybe Frank is being straight with us. Maybe I should just do what Jing told me to do…and nothing else."

"You can't play with these people, Zebulon. You know what they're gonna do."

"Yes, what *they* will do. I'm not hurting anyone. You're not. *They* are. All we're doing is meeting them in the middle."

Nitro looked at me for a moment then lay back on his cot. In a sleepy voice, he said, "My grandma used to tell me something just before she took a switch and tore the seat out of my breeches. She'd say, 'Marqus, when you meet the devil in the middle, you're halfway to hell.'"

Nitro's snores felt reassuring, adding a familiar element to the otherworldly surroundings. As hoped, the Wi-Fi blinked on. I sat up for hours, clutching a blanket around my shoulders and checking things on my phone. I tried shopping, just in case everything ran according to plan, and I got rich. I might retire my Corolla and get something a man actually should drive.

A notion needled my curiosity. I surfed around, trying to learn what I could about the tomb we were in. The information was speculative, some of it contradictory. All I was sure of was this place was huge, about a quarter the size of the Forbidden City in Beijing, which Jing and I had exhausted ourselves exploring. If these websites were right, the land beyond the edge of our lights was a marvel for the ages.

I don't know what time it was when I heard the sound—almost musical, some half-heard chord but like nothing I could identify. I got up and peeked out from behind the curtain. There was no sign of our guards. That was odd, but I wasn't going to miss my chance to explore. I was in an ancient tomb, possibly held captive or possibly as an honored guest. As part of the new, more decisive Zee, I decided to look around.

I followed the walkway, but it only extended a few dozen yards. So in my paper-clad feet, I stepped off…more than twenty-two centuries into the past—and met the Son of Heaven.

CHAPTER 31

EVEN IN THIS LIGHTING, Emperor Qin Shi Huang cut a startling figure, with a cruel snarl fixed on his lip, a dramatic dark mustache, and a beard that streamed down from his chin like noodles. On his head balanced a hat that resembled Jessa's graduation mortarboard, only narrower and with wispy tassels in front and back. Layer upon layer of sumptuous silk sheathed his belly in saffron and black with a dragon design on the flowing lower gown. Poking out from its hem, I saw two elaborately embroidered boots, toes jutting upward. I wouldn't have put those on for all the tea in…but on him, they looked good. A broad belt girded his middle and from it hung a magnificent scabbard holding a sword that no doubt had separated more than one head from its body.

There was one other detail I couldn't help but notice. He was as big as a pagoda. His eyes twinkled at me in the half-light like a hungry creature considering whether I was food or not. Seriously, this guy hadn't missed a meal since the third century BCE.

His words came out in a guttural tone with plenty of juice in his delivery. "I am your emperor. You dare stand?"

"I'm American. We don't bow to royalty. It's a long story. Anyhoo, American, *měi guó ren.*" That meant nothing to him.

"*Yangguizi!*" I knew "foreign devil"—thought it was funny when someone called me that; however, I doubted it was the same word people used so long ago. He shouldn't have been speaking modern Mandarin…or English for that matter. I was in the presence of magic—or something.

"You're looking well for someone who's—"

"Silence, worm," he rumbled. "You and these other invaders have come to my night city. Why?"

"To learn from the greatest emperor China has ever known." He liked that part. *Phew*! There were probably a million supplications I should be making, signs of respect. I knew nary a one. I did know how to kiss ass, and this guy presented a big target. "You slept long, my emperor. Many years have passed."

He looked straight at my phone. "It is 2018 as you mark the years." *Okay, so magic likes to cut straight to the chase.* "Come, witness the wonders around you and tremble."

He led me through a doorless gate shaped like the moon, carved with sensual phoenixes, tempting fruit, plus the ancient symbol for eternity. We passed into a court garden dominated by a longan tree of solid silver. Unlike the silver tree outside Gillian's mansion, the dragon eye fruit on this one was done in precious jade. As we stood there, the gleaming tree (which, as I thought about it, should have been heavily oxidized and black) glowed with a blue-white light that spread into the space around us, revealing details I could never have imagined. Above was a heavenly constellation of stars worked in gems in the vaulted ceiling. It was impossibly beautiful. I found it inconceivable that only one guy got to enjoy all this. Sure, he was dead, but still…

The emp led me up flights of steps bordered by stone carvings, followed by a strenuous climb inside a scenic tower. He moved fast for a dead man his size. My vertigo remained under control even as my mind struggled to understand how all this could still be underground. Had we left the mausoleum? At least some of this had to be beyond the perimeter. Or not.

From the highest level of the tower, we could see more courtyards, storage buildings, fanciful homes populated by clay courtiers of the highest order still bearing their colorful paint jobs. I could see…everything. Against all logic, the totality of this place showed its face, pristine and exuding a blue-white miasma. There was food everywhere. Row upon row of chest-tall clay vessels held vinegar for the jars of fresh fish. My eyes thought they saw livestock and fowl of every description. Could these be descendants of animals sealed in here so long ago? What did they eat? How had they survived the poisoned air? It made no sense. All this was meant to pump up the overpumped ego of the man standing beside me.

I had barely caught my breath before we were hauling ourselves back down into the streets, over lovely nine-arched bridges, and into new spaces. Here were excesses to make the most avaricious billionaire blush. Walls and fixtures glinted with hints of precious metals. Porcelains worth all a man could raise in a lifetime lay about the place like cast-off underwear. We stuck our heads inside storehouses filled to bursting with a king's ransom in fine silks. Imaginative geometric configurations of glossy rosewood cabinets clutched private memories within their 9,999 drawers. Bronze cranes dotted the landscape. Surely, these aged things would collapse at my slightest touch. Emp pointed to a number of multitiered palaces and regaled me with a detailed list of the treasures within. He rushed to show me his favorite kitchens, complete with rows of knives and terracotta cooks ready to prepare freshly killed game that hung from hooks. Clay or meat, I could no longer tell. We got to see Emp's plush bedchamber, followed by his sumptuous morning napping salon and his snazzy afternoon reclining palace. Continuing, we visited a cool spot where he sometimes went for a change of scenery and to doze.

Again, I wondered, how much did a man need? Did he use this city in life before they sealed in his bloated carcass? Or was it all a diorama to be admired but never enjoyed? I questioned the idea that his shen had been hanging out for two millennia. Time on that order would crush any sentient mind. And so again…how many toys could a dead man's ego play with?

He casually led me through ornately decorated rooms dedicated to gluttony and lust. "With each annual event, the feasting and pleasuring stretched on for eight days, involving one thousand dishes and forty of my youngest concubines."

"Lucky girls," I said to stroke his male ego.

"Their fathers paid me to take them into my palace. I gained both ways." He gave me a wink. "Sometimes, I would take women on horseback!" *And then eat the horse? I'm telling ya, this guy was fat.*

It felt smarter to keep him talking. I asked, "Any favorites?" He made a face of dismissal: no one's picture in a frame. Did he even remember any of their names? "No empress?"

"Ha! To what gain? My women gave me fifty children! Who needs a wife?" He then pointed out his personal stockpile of jade, silver, and ivory sex toys, plus his gigantic collection of pornographic pottery with explicit scenes glazed in flagrante. Bulky, this bachelor stash filled two warehouses. Tubby owned an unquenchable thirst for pleasure.

We stood outside the imperial burial chamber, a mammoth sarcophagus of bronze—again, strangely showing no signs of age and reflecting the light of slow-burning manfish candles (blubber, I figured) and guarded by nine-foot earthen soldiers. "Tell your children, American, that I allowed you to see and touch *this*." He guided my hand to a green doughnut mounted on a near wall. "The Heirloom Seal of the Realm, symbol of my power and my great unification of China."

I used my phone app. "The real one disappeared sometime in the tenth century. Oh! You can get a nice reproduction for thirty thousand yuan at a shop in Hotan."

"This is my sacred seal!" stormed his terrible majesty. "I brought it to my night city before my death and commissioned a reproduction for my successors. This object is unique in all the world, made from the sacred He Shi Bi jade. There is a story—"

"Got it. A guy finds this sacred rock and takes it to his king," I said, reading from the screen. "The king thinks the guy's lying about it...and cuts off his left foot. Later, the guy goes to the new king...who chops off his other foot. Nice bedtime story for the kiddies."

"I care nothing for that pathetic man. The Son of Heaven has no need to trouble himself with the plight of those who crawl."

"Naturally. And the artisans who made your soldiers? Did you have them killed?"

"Their fate is of no importance either." *What a heartless prick.*

Our tour continued. With his sleeves sweeping about him like the fins of a tropical fish, Emp would have been a natural on the catwalks of Milan or Paris. He was entertaining himself as he showed his realm to me, his first visitor in a while. He proudly pointed out the hundred rivers, including the Yangtze and Yellow, and the man-made sea, all designed to run on and on thanks to a great reservoir of mercury. Boats cast in solid silver floated atop the heavier liquid metal. Silver on silvery waters, whim upon fancy, these wraith models navigated past ports and topographical features both grand and fine. Emp's final resting place reflected the world he once ruled.

He stopped and regarded me with concern. "Tell me, American, how fares my China? Has my empire conquered

206

your world of smartphones and paper shoes?"

Now I felt self-conscious in my stupid slippers. "The Chinese are working hard at it. Actually, America is number one, but China is breathing down our neck and manufactures most of our phones and shoes." He seemed pleased enough by this news.

"And my great works. What of my roads and my canals and my Wall?"

"Still in use. The Great Wall of China totals thirteen thousand miles. Ten million tourists visit every year." *And a million dead workers are buried under it*, I didn't say.

Other matters dominated his curiosity. "My bloodline?"

I typed furiously, but even with the VPN, I couldn't find a site that answered his questions directly. Chinese history streams off in all directions like a delta. I did find one tidbit and—*Oooooh. Not good.*

Emp saw it in my eyes. He grabbed my wrist and read from the screen…because spooky ghost powers let him read English or something. I didn't know how this worked. The site said that after Qin Shi Huang's death, his advisers put an heir on the throne, then rounded up all those eager-to-please concubines and chopped them up to avoid any legal claims to power from their children. "They died for their emperor." What an odd thing to say. The heir didn't last long, and the brief Qin Dynasty was over and done.

I quickly pointed out another line, "You, Emperor Qin Shi Huang, set the standard for a dynastic system that ruled China into the twentieth century."

"And in all that time, have others found my elixir of virility and immortality?" I was getting punch-drunk from the flow of information, and I'll confess to not knowing which possibility made me less comfortable, standing next to a shen or to a fat immortal. Was he a spirit who thought he was still alive or a really old butthole who thought he was a god? "Answer me, American."

"Call me Zee."

We began walking again and soon stepped back onto the platform, though I remembered it being farther away.

"I spared no effort in my search. I sent my apothecaries to all reaches of my empire and beyond. I sent some into the great sea to the east."

"The Pacific Ocean."

"As you call it. My emissaries settled a new kingdom of islands there."

"We call that Japan," I was just guessing at this point, but it seemed to fit. I wondered if any historians would believe me if I told them my source.

"So, answer me," he demanded, regarding me as a predator would do while lulling its victim into submission. "Have you found my secret?"

"We have not. I mean, no one has. Yet." *Damn me*!

"Yet?" Emp slapped both sides of my face with the bejeweled fingers of his meaty paws and held me fast. "You and your fellow bandits dare to search my private sanctum? You will find your death!"

I giggled. "Sorry. It's just when you talk like that... Actually, we didn't even know you had Gatorade of the gods."

"The gods alone may drink." He meant himself, of course. "It brings ruin to the unworthy."

"Yeah, we actually know that part. The sterility."

"It is my greatest weapon. From my throne, I will extend China's grasp and make kingdoms across the earth tremble. I have noted the presence of invaders who would steal this weapon from me. They have yet to find it." He glanced over my shoulder, making me turn around to look. What I saw in that direction was a fairly simple structure, all black. The spectral ruler continued, "My Onyx Pagoda. Misfortune will consume anyone who enters to steal my secret. I alone, the Great Dragon, shall swallow the world. My elixir will smite all who stand against me."

"You seem too dead to be smiting anyone."

"Irreverence. Good. It will serve you well when you die." He smiled the absolute, bar none, butt-ugliest smile I've ever seen. His worn and cracked teeth glowed green—a tribute to his love of green tea, no doubt—in the ghostly light of the silver longan tree. I won't mention Emp's breath or his gassiness or his attempt to cover his body odor with spices Popeye would have thrown overboard. Won't say a word.

I did say, "I was hoping to not die, actually."

"Then prove yourself worthy. Serve me by serving my China!" His sword flashed from its scabbard, swept upward, and hung above my head as if to strike. "Be prepared!"

"For what?" Nitro asked, standing there next to me on the platform surrounded by our guards.

CHAPTER 32

OKAY, THERE'S A THING about magic that I've never been comfortable about. It doesn't come when you call it, doesn't seem to remember its own rules, and it tends to drop you in the deep end.

"Prepared for what?" Nitro repeated. "What are you talking about, Zebulon?"

I took another bite of my Jianbean. I was eating a greasy delicious Jianbean that someone had gotten me, and I had already taken several bites out of it that I couldn't remember taking. I was wearing a nice suit and brand-new dress boots. I had even shaved. I had no memory of the last few hours.

"Just be ready for anything," I said, wondering where my spirit buddy had disappeared to.

"I'm always ready."

Our guards stood on either side of us, holding ancient weapons. Hench took the trash from our breakfast and stuffed it into a large plastic bag. He was showing respect for the tomb after all. I looked around. It appeared the same as yesterday but not the same as last night. Nothing glinted, nothing glowed. The spheres of man-made illumination revealed extreme age on their near surfaces.

"Did you see anything unusual last night?" I asked Hench.

"No. Why?" he said.

"Do you believe in shen?"

"Which kind? Demons, the spirits of the dead, gods? The word can mean many things. It all depends on the context and the four tones."

"I think shen invented Mandarin."

He chuckled at my frustration. "Cantonese has six tones."

I kept going. "In any case, shen, *ghosts*, roam when they're uneasy, right?"

"In the movies," he said, enjoying this conversation more than I was. "Who'd you see?"

Fine. I figured it was harmless to make it a game. "I saw the big guy." I nodded toward the burial chamber. "Why do you suppose he's out and about? Didn't he die quietly in bed at a ripe old age?" It was a taunt.

Hench bit on the hook. "No! He was on a campaign to visit the seven kingdoms, including his own and the six he conquered, but he died suddenly. The dynasty went to crap a few years after that."

"Funny, he was supposed to be immortal. Had an elixir and everything."

"Sure he did. That's what killed him."

"The immortality elixir?"

Hench gestured all around, at the silvered riverbeds. "The elixir was made of mercury. That stuff is poison. That's why we spent months draining these channels and blowing out the bad air."

The guests arrived by tram, and a lovely group they were too. They chattered as they made their way through the tunnel. As best I could identify some of the accents, they were from Russia, Turkey, Germany, the US, Israel, China, and Japan. I recognized RHM immediately. These then were the finalists in the bid for our formula.

Gillian and Kevin came in as well. She wore a breathtaking gold D&G gown. (She name-checked it to everyone who'd listen.) The four guards, including Hench, formed a perimeter. As the guests settled into a cluster of a dozen or so chairs on the main platform, a thick, guttural, operatic music swelled from the darkness. Das Rheingold seemed strangely appropriate under the circumstances.

Along with this, the tomb's heart came alive with light. As I'd suspected, Frank's teams had set up more lighting instruments throughout the underground city. Laser rainbows darted onto and around the structures, hinting at forms but flickering too quickly to allow the eye to resolve this mystical puzzle. Scattered beams hit a pearl moon and pearl stars, creating fiery novas in the expansive ceiling. The guests *oooh'd* and *ahhh'd* like teenagers at a fireworks display. I, too, found it bedazzling, though not so enchanting as the blue-white light of the royal longan tree.

Frank took a moment to speak with me, as Nitro hung back almost out of earshot. "I hope you will play your part without hesitation?"

"I wonder who this is going to hurt."

"A conscience is for the loser, Zee, the one who tells himself, 'I didn't seize the moment because somebody might get hurt.' You and I are winners." He looked over at Nitro. "We represent a superior level of mankind, ja?" Frank said, "Tiger Pep works because the lower segments of society crave things beyond need or enjoyment."

"That's addiction," I said.

"That…is…opportunity," said Frank emphatically and with gusto. "For us. Pharmaceuticals enjoy sales of one trillion US dollars annually. Opportunity."

I let the moment breathe. It seemed my hesitation last night hadn't rattled him too much. Frank was willing to have me involved in the big transaction. That started me thinking. I said, "True. As long as I get out of this with my skin… and some money. What do I care what happens to a bunch of losers?"

"Just so."

I moved to where Nitro was standing stone-faced. He said nothing.

The music faded a little as Frank took his place behind the little podium. Its plexiglass frame looked cheap among the emperor's opulent night palace. Behind and to one side, someone had set up a jumbo screen. It flared and came on, showing the symbol of Frank's company. "Friends, for years, you have known me as the face of ValKnut Pharma and Holistics, GmbH. I am your doctor with sweets." This got a laugh. I kinda suspected Frank had served them mimosas with breakfast. They looked loose, ready to take on the world and kill part of it.

He began in earnest, "The ValKnut itself possesses an interesting history. Some say it symbolizes Odin's power to bind the minds of men. It is no coincidence, I think, that the ValKnut resembles another symbol." And there it was, on the screen as large as life: a fucking swastika. It was a close match with some of the carvings on the Moon Gate, but while those symbolized eternities, this one had been jerked off true and hung at a malevolent tilt.

I would have thought someone in this audience would have taken offense, but there they sat calmly, taking it all in. Frank continued, "We are all aware of the dangers of dreaming of power. Wielding real power requires many things. Vision, determination"—and again, he looked directly at Nitro—"a willingness to free ourselves of impurities." I could feel Nitro's discomfort, like heat coming off him, but to his credit, he never let it show on his face.

I was about to say something, to try to calm him down, when I sensed a change in the air pressure. The machines were humming along as usual. It was something else, some movement behind me in the shifting darkness.

Frank said, "As part of our demonstration today, I will need our honored test subject." One of the guards was at Nitro's side, pulling him forward.

"What the hell?" he protested.

A second guard took hold of Nitro and also produced a plum-sized chunk of our candy, which he held up to Nitro's face.

"If you would be so kind as to bite down, Mr. Baine," Frank said blandly.

Nitro was helpless. I was his friend, his former sponsor. I had gotten him into this mess. Jing and Gillian tracked Nitro down and then tracked down Bessie all because of me. I wondered what our options were at this point. We could try to break away and run out of the tunnel. If we both fought…but that was stupid. It hit me that this was as much a demonstration of Tiger Pep for the buyers in the audience as it was a test of my loyalty to Frank. I tried to convey some of this with my eyes, which was hopeless. Nitro glared at me like I had just called him a "dumb n——."

Nitro pulled one hand free and took the candy chunk. He ate it without comment.

Frank gestured to another of the guards. This was Hench, who stepped away for a moment, going back to our cell and immediately returning with a young woman, rawboned and slack-mouthed, dressed in provocative clothes and a fake fur coat. She was little more than a girl. I could only imagine what her life had been like up to this point. The woman-child teetered on her heels as Hench led her forward.

The audience began to fidget, not with disgust but anticipation. They were going to get a show before they made their bid.

Out of the corner of my eye, I saw the shadows part. He was back, and he was not happy.

Hench took the girl closer to Nitro, who was sweating. She immediately dropped her coat on the platform flooring and began cuddling him, running her hand up and down his body, rubbing it close to his groin.

"I don't see anything happening," the Russian said with a leer on his face. The other buyers—all men, none of them Black—were making catcalls. Gillian seemed amused at Nitro's distress while Kevin's eyes followed the woman's hand along its course over Nitro's body with fascination and anticipation.

"Maybe he doesn't like women!" the Turk called.

"Hey, are you a *homosexuell*?" the German taunted.

"It takes a minute!" Nitro barked back.

Two men in the back row began a running duel to see which of them could call out the crudest sexual position for Nitro to try.

As this part of the entertainment dragged on, the final guest to this party stepped through the Moon Gate and came up onto the platform. No one reacted, which was odd because it was hard to ignore Emperor Qin Shi Huang.

Frank said, "As you wish, Mr. Baine. Perhaps this public venue is not inspirational." He motioned to Hench, who led Nitro and the drugged woman back to the cell. "We'll check in on them later, eh?"

There were boos from the crowd, but they accepted the decision. Meanwhile, Emp stepped over to Frank's side, looking at him long and hard as he continued his presentation.

"Shhhh," Frank told the buyers. "We'll keep an eye on things." On the big screen, Nitro appeared. *When had they put in a camera?* The woman was holding onto him, grinding slowly. Whatever she was on, it was even more stupefying than Tiger Pep. Nitro was clearly miserable and angry but kept his composure. He pushed the dazed woman back, gently but firmly.

"As you will shortly see demonstrated, ValKnut has provided the means to an end." Frank's hand played over a small device jacked into the podium. The big screen split. Side by side with Nitro's discomfort it now showed a dizzying array of scientific data. "Here is the real proof. Within weeks of taking Tiger Pep on a regular basis, the male is rendered sterile.

"The buyers of this formula will hold unique power over anyone who confounds their ambitions." With an irritated shen standing inches from him, he said, "It is a secret I have wrested from the hand of the emperor himself! And now I offer you the chance to secure your own empires…as a franchisee of ValKnut Pharma."

Emp looked at me. He did not speak. Instead, he thought at me, *What is this?*

I thought back, *He's screwing his customers. He's going to limit the supply. Make them buy it over and over. He's also kissing off the idea of exclusivity. He wants to sell it to all of them.*

There is no honor in this, Qin Shi Huang said. I agreed.

Frank held up his hands, and with his charming smile turned up full, he told the restless gathering, "Those who buy in will acquire the means to accomplish more than they ever dreamed possible."

"This was not the deal!" someone shouted. RHM reached for something in his suit jacket.

"The deal is what I say it is," Frank responded in a tone as chill as the air in the mausoleum.

He turned his back on his buyers, but I could see his face. A wink was for my benefit. Frank was telling me he knew his customers, that if the prize were big enough, he could treat them like dirt, and they would love him all the more for it. These men had come from all over the face of the earth expecting to buy the cow. Frank would make more money by selling them the milk. He waited a beat and sprung his trap, "Unless one of you wishes to impress me with a bid of sufficient value to secure a higher tier of participation."

The crowd quieted down. They understood the rules now: simple greed. They got that.

I took my cue, "If you want the Platinum Plan, a big supply, then open your wallets wide. Piddly little bids will get you the 'fun size.'" My analogy could have been better, but what mattered was they paid attention—to me. I was Frank's partner.

"Understand what I offer, friends," Frank continued. "We can ship Tiger Pep anywhere in the world, using a traveling exhibition of the Terracotta Soldiers. These figures from antiquity are both magnificent…and hollow." Nervous laughter. He was reeling them in. "With the formula in hand, we are prepared to produce mass quantities of Tiger Pep in a variety of forms. In addition to distributing it as sex candy, you will be able to introduce it into food, or water supplies, even use it in aerosol form. You may wish to focus your efforts on bars or sex clubs or schools and homes. One hundred percent saturation in targeted communities will be possible and practical."

The Great Dragon's eyes grew as wide as his jade seal. He stepped away from Frank and took a seat in the audience next to Gillian. He ogled her as the folding chair bifurcating his cheeks moaned in metallic distress. *Didn't anyone else hear that?*

Frank continued, "Gentlemen, in this product, the past meets the future. Those of you in this room have expressed frustration at the intractability of your neighbors or with subcultures within your homeland. You have tried political solutions. You have tried intimidation. And still, your problem remains. Tiger Pep is a *strategic* weapon, providing," and he pronounced the next words with the crispness of a starched uniform bearing a silver skull, "a *final solution*. Those who plague you may do so for a generation or two longer, but you will write their history's ending. A new dawn of freedom will shine. Tomorrow belongs to those of us enlightened enough to seize it." The screen went back to a picture of a longan tree over the ValKnut symbol.

"Now, my partner, Mr. Zebulon Angell, will bring in the formula." Again, Frank touched the device on the podium. Now the screen split into three slices. One was Nitro, barely keeping the woman at bay but looking as though the Tiger Pep was grinding down his will. The second part of the screen left a spot for the formula to pop up as soon as it arrived via satellite, blurred, of course. The third part of the screen showed a lovely face.

"Hello, everyone," she said. "Hello, Zee." Even bouncing off orbiting links and feeding in on Wi-Fi, her expression shone a certain expectation and concern.

"Jing. Hey, babe!" I said. "Frank's here. And Gillian. They've gotten really close."

"She told me all about it. That's not important now. You just need to key in the code so we can all get what's coming." Jing's jaw muscles clenched. She was definitely stressed. I hated to think what she must be feeling, being shoved aside by her former friend. *God, how I wanted to comfort her.*

"Your turn, Zee," Frank said, looking at me. At that moment, I felt his gravity. I was in his orbit, and it was…right. I could please Jing and Frank both with a few taps on my phone's screen.

Emp had other ideas. He stood up, drawing my gaze back to himself. He drew his magnificent sword, holding it high in the same fashion as he had the night before. It was a military command, a call to action. *Prove yourself. Serve my China.*

I wondered…

"Zee?" Frank urged.

I had feet colder than the sun-starved stones around us. I picked up the connector hooked to the podium and jacked the free end into my phone's secret port. Wagner's bombast dropped away, swallowed by a tinny chirp. I was in charge of this proceeding.

My mind rushed to process conflicting feelings. Right here and now, I was someone important. What I did mattered. I would have money and titles and awards. Recognition. My children would…

They would think I was *pathetic*. Pathetic like my father, who after his stroke slept in the dining room all day waiting for Ma and me to feed him and change his sheets and who made it impossible for me to have my friends over because of the smell and the shame.

This spiritual whiplash couldn't have lasted more than a second, but it was enough. I saw Zack and Jessa's faces and imagined them one day dismissing the memory of *me* as pathetic, no matter whether I was rich or poor. What I wanted most of all wasn't in this dark place. It was with them. I made my choice.

I decided…there was no use letting a captive audience go to waste. I nodded confidently at Frank and hit some buttons on my phone.

> *She's just a sex-EE maCHINE*
> *In her skintight blue JEANS*
> *Will you look at that girl*
> *Don't she rock my world!*
> *I think y'all know what I MEAN…*

My voice bounced off the eons-old walls, backed by my late great Martin. Emp pumped his fist and smiled his green smile, letting me know he approved of my audacity. I think he even liked my song. Others did not. I barely made it through the opening stanza when most of the men on the platform pulled their guns. It was a tough room.

"Oh, Zee," Jing sighed. "How I wish you would not think and just do as I ask."

"This is an American joke?" RHM screamed, even as Frank came over and turned off my song. The assembly grew restless.

Frank raised both hands to command attention. "Indeed, this is a jest on my associate's part, but now he will—"

I stood there shaking my head no. *Goodbye money, titles, fame.*

Gillian leaped to her feet. "It does not matter. Mr. Zebulon had his chance to do his part, but he has let opportunity slip away. Now I will do the honors." Gillian was ready to show her worth to the men in the room. She strode forward with purpose, as much as anyone can in stiletto heels. *She was stunning, by the way. Great calves.*

Reaching the podium, she blithely grabbed my phone, then coyly drew a slip of paper from its coveted place over her heart. "The code." To me, she whispered, "From inside your guitar, where your wife thoughtfully placed it in case you forgot!"

"That wasn't yours, Gillian," Jing said.

Something struck me odd. Jing had said not even she would know the code the computer showed me that day. I was the fail-safe. Was I confused? Yes, usually. In any case, things were moving rapidly.

Frank wasn't pleased. "You might have mentioned this last night," he said to Gillian. Emp was standing between them, grinning ear to ear.

Gillian wore Serge Lutens L'Étoffe du Mat lipstick on her rictus smile...which collapsed as men in windbreakers appeared behind Jing on the big screen. They wore sunglasses and had curly wires dangling from their ears. The feds were at our house.

"You were supposed to screw me *after* you got the goods, Gillian," Jing scolded her.

"I didn't send those agents. In any case, I'm sure you'll deal with them, dear. It doesn't matter in any case. I have the code."

Gillian stood facing the gathering and keyed in the numbers on the paper. The section of the big screen set aside for displaying the formula burst into light. Reds and oranges, then a dazzling montage of money, gold coins, yuan, rubles, lira, yen, dollars, euros showering down like something from a Busby Berkeley film from the 1930s. The buyers liked what they saw. Then fireworks. A dragon. Really, a cartoon dragon. Then a train wreck, an atom bomb explosion, flies buzzing around a dead animal. The buyers began to talk among themselves in unpleasant murmurs. The screen went on with a waterfall, a puppy, somebody's foot. It was nonsense.

The pictures stopped. The phone made a farting noise and died. The big screen switched to a double split, losing the display the buyers most wanted to see. It took a moment before the audience realized that their great hopes for world domination had just randomized into digital diarrhea along with all of Jing's research.

"Sorry, Gillian. It seems that was the wrong code, dear. That note in the guitar wasn't for Zee. It was for you," Jing said. The men in windbreakers behind her were watching as she spoke but made no move to put her in cuffs.

Frank spoke in a soft voice. "You disappoint me, Jing." He turned to his clients. "This is a setback only. Within weeks, we will reconstruct the formula."

Jing said, just as softly, "No, Frank. You won't." The crowd's grumbling tapered off while they listened to her lay it out. "I don't have a PowerPoint, so bear with me. The Terracotta Soldiers were discovered in 1974, but farmers have long known about the special longan trees. They fed the dragon eyes fruit, what we call Tiger Penis or Tiger Pep, to their animals, and even took it themselves. It gave them visions of grandeur and made them virile, or so they thought. While they indulged in a great deal of sex, these men fathered no children. Traditional medicine practitioners blamed guishen, demons. In fact, the Tiger Pep rendered the men sterile.

"The fruit in its natural state is too volatile to store. Freezing destroys the effect. Even the candy has a short shelf life, only a couple of weeks. Trees transplanted or grown from clippings or seed do not exhibit the same properties when cultivated away from the old city."

Frank grumbled, "I know all this."

"When I first visited the emperor's burial mound," Jing spoke over him. She'd been inside. Another interesting fact for me to learn this late in the game. "You told me it was hermetically sealed. Except that I found spiders inside—there's Coke in the fridge. Help yourself—sorry, not you. I have...guests." She motioned to the agents who were moving around her now. "Where was I? Little spiders that don't spin webs and eat God knows what, each other I think. Spiders got in, which means other things could get out.

"Soil samples confirmed high levels of mercury everywhere near the site. The Chinese were geniuses of engineering, but— check the lower shelf, behind the watermelon—sorry. Even the Chinese could not plan for two thousand years. The mercury rivers amused a dead man for many centuries, but they had to stop sometime. Things fall apart.

"I want to make sure your buyers know that I was able to identify a process, using the fruit. Under perfect laboratory conditions, I could stretch a modest supply into hundreds of thousands of dosages."

"Process? What of the formula?" Frank was clearly off his center of gravity.

"There is no formula, Frank. There can never be a formula. What I did was to isolate an element within the fruit. What it is or where it comes from, I can't say. As far as I know, no one's seen it in twenty-two centuries. ValKnut's other scientists tried to work around this mystery element to create a formula that, simply put, cannot work."

Frank's face went pale. He was desperate to keep his buyers happy. "All this means is that we have a limited supply of our product. Tiger Pep works! It works!"

"It won't work for long. You turned off the flow of the thing that made it work. I have samples of the fruit going back four years. The earliest are inert but indicate high concentrations of the active ingredients. The samples came from just after you opened the tomb and drained the mercury rivers." Jing's voice continued, but her image became a thrumming wall of orange fluff. "After that, the concentration drops quickly. You poured out the mercury you drained, didn't you? Let's just say 'yes' because I know you dumped it at some local farm or other. Bottom line, you created the newest super grove, but you also killed the goose that laid the golden eggs, Frank."

"*Quatsch!*" he said feebly.

"I got this, Mama!" Kevin yelled. He ran off the stage, brushing past Nitro, who was just stepping out of the cell.

Jing grabbed Damn Kitty Two and dropped him on the floor with an audible thud then continued, "I estimate those trees will revert to normal longans within a year. The current concentrations already make it difficult to create the Tiger Pep."

"You did this, Jing darling. You have made many enemies today," Gillian glowered.

"On the contrary, Gillian, *darling*, you are the one who destroyed the only record of a process that could have saved your skin." Jing wasn't kidding. Judging by the faces in the crowd, these men were ready to roast somebody alive. The only question was who. "By the time you reconstruct the process, if you ever do, nature will have restored balance. The fruit will be harmless. Whoever set this up had the knowledge we do not. Maybe it's all the work of shen. I don't know, but it's over. The curse is lifted from the land." *Nice Chinese Operatic ending there, Jing, my love!*

"This changes nothing!" Frank said, brightening. "We installed a regulator onto the cistern's faucet. An engineer will open it up once we are ready to leave."

Emp looked at me and shook his head. I said, "And how long will that last? That mercury evaporates. It seeps into the earth. That cistern has been dripping for more than twenty-two centuries. How much do you think's left in the tank?"

Kevin came running back, now carrying his favorite souvenir. Nitro tried to grab him, but he dodged around Nitro, and past the people at the podium, straight to the ancient faucet. The others stared dumbfounded.

"You little turd bird!" Nitro yelled. He was the first to realize Kevin's intentions and ran over to stop him. It was too late. The unmotivated teen had decided the one thing he wanted to do was to impress his mother by whacking away at the cistern. On his third swing with the dagger-ax, a crack opened behind the faucet.

As designed, mercury poured out into the channel that fed the artificial sea. The pour became a gush. The liquid metal splashed all over Kevin's clothes, though it did not soak in like water but rather beaded and fell off in huge droplets. By this point, I was there, helping Nitro save my star pupil from his own stupidity.

The mercury coursed toward the nearby "sea," which fed the pattern of rivers running throughout Emp's shen city. It would take hours to refill everything, but—

"The vapor!" Frank yelled. "Everyone out!" At this point, he pulled his own gun. I was expecting a vintage Luger, but it was a Bondesque Walther PPK. He wasn't supposed to have a gun at all. Of course, neither was anyone else. It's a terrible thing when a man who keeps himself under control all the time is pushed to the point of rage. I could see the fury in his eyes.

For a second, I thought Frank planned to shoot Kevin for smashing the faucet. No. He was gonna kill me instead. That made sense.

Nitro and I made a run for it. With armed men in the tunnel, there was only one direction to go. Emp grinned at me. *We will meet these fools together in my shadowlands.*

CHAPTER 33

AS SOON AS WE slipped beyond the work lights, my eyes protested, filling my vision with bouncing red suns. I hoped the same disorientation would slow the others and give us a chance to escape, not that there was anywhere to go.

Behind us, guys with guns were pulling on masks and screaming like homicidal toddlers. Most were moving toward the tunnel. "Get everyone out! We'll deal with this!" Frank yelled over the others.

Unconcerned about drawing fire with his voice, Nitro called back, "Somebody help the girl! She's passed out! Help her, you bastards!" Hench grabbed one of his fellow guards and anxiously told him to get the drugged girl, which the other man did. To my disappointment, Hench then joined the remaining guards in a chase after Nitro and me.

Between the three of them, I saw only one gun. That was something anyway.

We passed through the Moon Gate and saw…Emp. He had been on the platform a moment ago. *Okay. Shen trick. Got it.* He was pointing the way in the dark. The lasers were still strobing, making it easy to miss a step in the on-again, off-again darkness of the night city.

Hench called after us, "Please surrender. Please! I beg you to respect your surroundings. Don't make us fire. 'We are simply passing through history. This…this *is* history.'" *Oh my god, he even affected Belloq's accent…with Frank in earshot.*

He was serious. Hench and his buddies would never shoot if it meant damaging their great ancestor's domain. If he got a clear shot at meat, however…

We ducked around a number of sharp corners. Each time we took a turn, there was the emperor, using his sword like some homicidal traffic cop, directing our way.

"Where the hell are we going?" Nitro asked. When I didn't answer him, he added, "You forgot that damn code, didn't you, Zebulon?"

"Yep. Come on!"

I ran as fast as I could over the stones. I could hear Nitro falling behind, but Emp urged me ever onward. I couldn't tell where we were going since we weren't keeping to a straight line. He was waiting for me, having popped ahead once again. I bent forward, hands on knees, to catch my breath.

Another figure stepped from behind a black wall. It was RHM. In his hand, the well-dressed businessman held a lacquered wooden cylinder. He pulled the ends apart, unsheathing a small version of a katana. It was adorable! Also, I had no doubt RHM could slit my throat with it.

"I believe you have something of mine," he said. "I will not fail Chairwoman Takahashi again."

"Who is this man?" Emp asked indignantly.

"The right-hand man of a Japanese dowager who wants to steal your great elixir," I answered.

RHM looked at me and then at the emperor, or at least at the space the emperor filled. "Who are you talking to?" He could not see Emp.

I was out of breath and out of clever ideas. I gestured to Emp and told RHM, "This is the first emperor of China, Qin Shi Huang."

RHM smiled and narrowed his eyes. "You have succumbed to the rapture of this place."

"I'm serious."

"Very well, Angell san, ask the great emperor where I may find the formula you so recently lost."

I asked Emp the question. I was wondering where Nitro had gotten to. I hoped that maybe if I stretched this out, he'd show up and maybe the two of us together could overpower a man with a knife—or Nitro could while I cheered him on. Emp answered me, "Tell this man he will find his reward inside the Onyx Pagoda." It was the building next to us, the building Qin Shi Huang had led me to and RHM had tracked me to.

"He says your formula is inside this place," I dutifully told RHM.

We walked around to the front entryway. The structure was utterly bleak, made in part of onyx, but also of black alabaster. None of the laser lights found their way inside, and the ones that hit its side vanished into that event horizon.

"In here?" RHM asked, amused. I got it.

"Maybe you'd prefer it if I went in first," I said.

"I would very much prefer you to take the lead," RHM snickered.

I stepped gingerly inside. Two strides behind with his blade pointed at my spine, RHM followed, turning his phone light on in the process. It did little good, but it did show the only two objects in the room that were not pitch black in color. They were two stone tablets that held ancient Chinese glyphs.

"Two tablets. A puzzle?" RHM asked.

Emp was beside me now. He gave RHM steely regard. "I will tell you truthfully, American, a bad choice in my Onyx Pagoda always brings misfortune." That sounded nasty. I repeated it word for word to RHM. "Get this man to take the left-hand tablet," Emp added.

I knew what this dead monarch was doing. I considered how to phrase it just so, but it came out, "I think he wants you to take the left-hand tablet." I was an idiot.

"Is that what he wants?" RHM said sarcastically with a forced laugh.

"American, you are terrible at this game," Emp told me. "The tiger must use guile before he can feast. You have no skill, no heart for murder." This was true although after what RHM did to Rong, it came as a surprise to me.

RHM spoke again, "In that case, your emperor will now show you the right choice." For good measure, he flicked the blade toward my face, making me pull back instinctively.

Emp took my arm and led me forward. The space seemed infinite since I could not perceive the far wall. I took one step at a time, my footfalls clicking on the smooth onyx floor. Finally, I was within reach of the right-hand tablet. I moved to take it from its perch.

"No!" Emp said.

"He says, 'No.'" I told RHM. "Um, why not?" I asked Emp.

He replied, "The tablet and all that comes with it belongs to the man who first removes it from its home. You are not worthy, American."

"He says I'm not worthy to pick it up."

"Nonsense!" RHM grunted. He began to close the distance between us.

At that moment, I thought I heard Nitro's voice from the other side of the wall, calling in a stage whisper, "Zebulon! Where are you? Don't leave me alone, man!"

I started walking toward the entryway. The illumination on the other side was a welcome sight.

"Don't move, Angell san!" I froze where I was. "I will deal with your colored friend in a moment. First…" RHM kept his blade pointed at me. I had no doubt he could cut me before I could escape. He stepped toward the right-hand tablet, and when he came to the exact spot where I'd been standing…he vanished.

The chamber went black as RHM and his phone light dropped from sight. There was a brief cry of alarm, then a low rumbling transmitted up through the floor, and finally a muffled crackling sound, kind of like the sound a body makes when it's being crushed between two huge millstones hidden in the depths of an ancient Chinese deathtrap.

"Good to know that still works," Emp puffed with pride. "Now let us rejoin your friend." He led me out of the Pagoda.

"Shouldn't I take the tablet?" I asked, still clinging to hopes of appeasing Frank.

"Not unless you want to read my poetry. That is all that is written on either stone tablet. Birds and waterfalls and mountains. In truth, it is very bad." He laughed, "The Onyx Pagoda is a trap with no prize to protect."

We turned a corner and found Nitro. He was frazzled. "Lord, I'm glad to see you, Zebulon! I've been calling. I stopped to rest for just a minute over on that stoop. As soon as I stood up, the damn thing flew into the air then fell right back down." He pointed to a slab of onyx that seemed to serve no purpose unless, of course, it was to counterbalance an extension that ran under the wall of the pagoda and acted as a trapdoor. It was a simple seesaw weighted at one end by Nitro to keep me from taking the plunge. I had no idea how Emp had worked out the timing, but I was grateful to him.

A second onyx plank ran next to the first one. "What's that for?" I asked Emp while Nitro's head was turned.

"In case he chose the left-hand tablet," Emp said, pleased with himself.

He was already moving, motioning for me to follow. I decided not to tell Nitro his ass was a murder weapon—besides, I wasn't quite sure whether I felt bad or felt like laughing at

RHM's death. In any case, Nitro and I weren't free and clear yet. Hench and his buddies were still looking for us; I could hear them not far off.

This time, Nitro stayed close. More turns and switchbacks. I really wanted to see this place fully lit, with a map in my hand, when I had time to enjoy it.

Up some steps, we came to an open storehouse. It was full of weapons, a row of Nu, or crossbows, plus halberds, wicked-looking billhooks…and also ghosts. Three tall gray generals stood there with their big bellies facing each other. Their clay faces—how do I say it?—*un*baked enough for them to speak. Their features became molten, juicy even, like oversize chocolate Easter bunnies that had been left on the windowsill too long. They had not stopped off to get a fresh paint job, either, but rather come straight from the terracotta pits. They argued and shouted over each other. Occasionally, one would reach out and swat another across his muddy face.

With their emperor looking on, the ghastly commanders concocted a battle plan. It was brilliant. We would use their familiarity with the city to full advantage. They pinpointed the most defensible positions on the map table before them. Uh… there was a map table before them.

"We need force!" proclaimed one general in fish scale armor adorned with eight ribbons. "Call the soldiers from their slumber and let us fight!" As he spoke, the walls came alive with images of earthen fighters stirring from their long silence in the pits, ready to move stiffly yet steadfastly into action.

A fatter general disagreed, slapping the first one with a wet *kwapth!* that sprayed gritty droplets all over me. "It is cunning that kills, deviousness that buys victory. Call the soldiers but have them pull up the flagstones from the great courtyard." And so the figures toiled, obedient and resolute, as shown in the spectral diorama that now encircled us. "We will dig snare pits, fill them with vipers, and then drive our enemies to their doom!" In the images pulsing there, I could see the shock and hopelessness on the faces of the men who fell into these traps and hear their unanswered cries for mercy.

The third general, who wore a crown with a square plate backed by a twisted pheasant tail, kicked the second general's shin and said, "Be certain to leave some survivors. We will release them and track them back to whatever kingdom was foolish enough to invade this domain."

The first general jabbed a thumb into the third one's eye, but the third general persisted. "My emperor, give me six chariot teams and two thousand soldiers, no more, and I will raze their city walls and slaughter every man, woman, and child inside!" The carnage of his vision painted the indifferent walls of our meeting place, the view provided by some immaterial eye wandering the streets of a muted city while above, carrion eaters circled in no particular hurry.

I didn't have the heart to tell them we only had about a dozen men to defeat. I was pumped! The campaign would begin with us. Nitro and I were to pick up armloads of weapons and take them to a tower where we could hold off a siege for months if need be. I reached down for a weapon. If Hench and Frank wanted a fight, I'd lance them with this spear—

The one that broke in two in my hand because it was really, really old, and wood doesn't hold up forever, not even underground in a city-sized fridge. The metal bits were no longer fresh from the forge, either.

I stood there, looking at Nitro, who was looking at the three human guards now surrounding us, and the gun one of them pointed at my heart.

Nitro was less worried about our predicament than about me. "Zebulon. Who were you talking to? You weren't making any sense. Towers and guile and slaughtering babies. You didn't make no sense at all."

Arms folded in front of his chest, Emp looked on as the guards pulled us out of the warehouse. His generals had vanished like a draft of foul air into the cracks of the cold dark walls.

"Let's go," said Hench.

Trudging back to the platform, I checked my messages. Uber finally resolved my claim for eleven dollars. I would get four. *Rat bastards*! I started typing in my latest protest…

"Zebulon?"

My hands were empty. I was poking my palm with my finger. My phone was still on the podium, and it was *as dead as Qin Shi Huang's dick*, I thought. He stuck out his tongue at me. *Well, it's true*, I told him. He faded out before my eyes.

No more shen appeared as we made our way back through the Moon Gate. Hench and his men were around us. Still on the podium, Frank was livid. Gillian and Kevin were gone, presumably having rushed out in all the confusion.

"I am getting calls from the other end of the tunnel," Frank said as we reached the edge of the circle of light. "It seems CCP has sent troops to meet my guests."

"Couldn't happen to a nicer bunch of fellows," Nitro laughed.

"Those soldiers will be coming inside in a moment," Frank said. "An unplanned distraction."

He put his mask back on. I reached in my pocket for mine and motioned for Hench and his fellows to use theirs. Only Nitro was without. I had no idea how long it would take for the fumes to fill this place, but it wouldn't be long.

"We need to get out of here, Frank," I yelled. "I'm sure you can cut a deal with the Party."

"They'll force me to reseal this mausoleum with all its treasures and secrets." He was seriously pissed and didn't need any more prodding.

"Tough luck," Nitro prodded.

Frank held his gun at arm's length, taking careful aim at Nitro, and like some cartoon villain, announced, "At least, I can remove one piece of rubbish from this tomb."

I ducked down and plowed my full weight into Nitro's midsection, pushing us both toward cover. When Frank's finger tightened, we were really close to being safe. *So close.* In some imaginary photo of the moment, Nitro was behind the Moon Gate and I was a horizontal missile with my favorite parts hanging in midair. Frank was quickly adjusting his aim, but in his eagerness, his shot struck the gate, shattering the head of a lovely stone phoenix. The bullet ricocheted, hitting me in the groin area.

I landed hard and in pain. I reached down, fearful that the shot had severed an artery. Under these circumstances, I would bleed out faster than the cracked cistern. Thankfully, though, there was no blood, only pain.

The three henchmen were staring at the ruined carving on the Moon Gate. Hench raised his gun at Frank, but another henchman, our former driver whom I guessed was the senior man, pulled Hench's arm down. The two men exchanged an unspoken thought and Hench tossed his gun to where we were sheltering. Nitro snatched it up quickly. Frank, seeing the change in the situation, ducked behind the scant protection of the podium.

"I won't miss a second time. I'm rated an expert marksman by the *Deutschen Schützenbund.*" He stressed "Deutschen" through gritted teeth.

Even as Frank was finishing his threat, Nitro rolled out, keeping his body low to present a minimal target, and fired.

The sharp report filled the emperor's Candyland-lit tomb. The echoes lost out to Frank's screaming as he rolled from behind the podium, dropping his gun as he clutched his shattered knee with both hands. Nitro straightened up and called over, "US Navy, motherfucker!" We went over to Frank. Nitro grabbed his pistol, saying, "*We* don't shoot old birdies when we're aiming at Nazi kneecaps." I undid Frank's silk tie to use as a tourniquet.

In the glare of the lighting instruments, I got a better look at my wounded thigh, which was throbbing mightily but not bleeding through the hole in my new pants. I reached in my front left pocket and pulled out my wallet, and I understood. *Coincidence had gotten a boost.*

Jing was still on the video link. "Your two-timing Aryan boyfriend tried to shoot me in the dick!" I told her.

By this point, the Red Army was pouring through the tunnel and into our busy little monument. They had plenty of CCP types with them. I could tell by the red-starred lapels. One nicely tailored jacket lapel, worn by a serious-looking Black woman, sported an American flag. I got a good look at it as she came and stood over me.

They all wore respirators. A few carried spares and handed them to those of us already inside. We gladly traded our masks for the improved protection. Soldiers led Hench and his partners away. I liked Hench, even if he had, briefly, pointed a gun at me. I hoped he'd be okay. With luck, he and his friends were lowly enough to escape the coming CCP purge, a messy business, no doubt.

There was room for hope. Among the swarm of soldiers, Officer Zhang and Officer Liu smiled and waved at us like we were schoolyard pals! Nitro's message had gotten through. The fact that they were here meant these two had switched loyalties to the main Party faction. Nitro had given them the leverage they needed to make up for the incident at the massage parlor in Shanghai. I was happy for them.

I did wonder at the timing. Nitro had said he gave his contacts our location as somewhere in Xi'an, but he had not known the time of the auction. Maybe the authorities staked it out. We didn't get the chance to ask. They were too busy rounding up all of the sophisticated German equipment scattered around the mausoleum.

"Pretty good work, Uncle Marqus," the American agent said to Nitro.

"Thanks, Johnetta. How's your mom?"

"She's fine."

It took me a second. I said, "You said you had contacts."

"Johnetta's a contact."

"Uncle Marqus tried to talk me out of following in his footsteps, but I fell in love with his Navy stories."

"That's 'cause I skipped the ugly parts." Nitro sighed.

Agent Johnetta continued, "When I took your message to my boss, he nearly freaked, but…here we are!" She took a second to look around. "They're going to reseal this place. You two are with me unless you'd rather stay inside permanently."

A Party official with stern eyes and lots of thingies on his uniform appeared at her shoulder. He spoke to Frank, "Herr Fuchs, you have violated our agreement. This site represents the very heart of China's identity as a nation, and you have turned it into a shooting gallery. It is time for you to return to Germany." He spoke good English, knew his business, and got his meaning across. "The Party will indeed seal the mausoleum, and we will keep a close watch on the fruit trees outside."

There was definitely a reshuffling going on behind the scenes. I had no doubt the Party would take charge of the dwindling supply of Tiger Pep. I wondered whether people like that could get their kicks committing limited genocide. *Wait, was this what Emperor Qin Shi Huang had meant by "Serve my China"? Was I responsible?*

"Mr. Angell, Mr. Baine, we ask you to leave as well," the Party official said, nodding to the American agent.

"Can you give us a lift to Guangzhou?" Nitro asked.

"Yes, I think that's a good choice," said Agent Johnetta.

I looked over at the big screen. "First, let me talk to my wife."

Jing had her laptop camera facing into the kitchen now, where she was bringing trays of food over to her collection of men in windbreakers. She looked up as I waved to her. "What's the situation there?" she asked.

"The cistern is out of commission," I said through my respirator. "You called it. The crack behind the faucet drained it. There's a new pool at the low end of the great sea, but it's not too close to where we're standing. The level is nowhere near high enough to feed the spillways leading to the hundred rivers. After two millennia, the great big dispenser is out of secret sauce." Emperor Qin Shi Huang's fountain of youth...fountain of sex...fountain of a hopeless, childless future...was dry.

Jing rung her hands and said, "I wish you had done what I asked you to do instead of *thinking*." I would have expected her to be happy with me, at least a little bit.

As a medic led him off, Frank was babbling, though no longer dripping blood. "There must be a formula. It may take years, but we will figure it out! *Ich schwöre es!*" He was going to talk his way out of this mess with the Party, there was no doubt in my mind, but if CCP really wanted to punish him for shooting the head of a phoenix, they would send him home to face ValKnut Practical's shareholders. Like the CCP traitors, Frank was looking at early retirement.

"It's over, Jing. I'm coming home. We're free now. We can go back to our lives."

She was furious at losing the money. I knew that. I also knew our kids were safe and this adventure was behind us. We could make a fresh start. It was all going to be the way it was before. *Better!*

I had the best thought.

"Babe, when I get back, let's have a wedding. I want to marry you all over again."

The agents behind Jing looked up from their late dinner. One elbowed a neighbor. Nitro clapped me on the shoulder. The lone American agent in our cave of wonders tapped her watch, less from her own impatience than the realization the Chinese had had enough of us.

"Zee, we can talk about this when you get home," said Jing, who was now sitting in front of her laptop.

"You won't have to do a thing. I'll find a preacher and a private strip of beach on Hilton Head. Jing, let me do this right. I wrote you a song. I was gonna play it for you on the Martin, but…anyway, here it is."

I took a deep breath and slipped off the respirator. Jing's eyes grew wide as agents came in close around her to listen.

I sang for her. I sang for our marriage. I sang for my family and the hope that all the memories we'd gathered over the last eighteen years were not on fire now. I sang for my beautiful Jing.

> *Make this mistake*
> *Regret it in a thousand years*
> *Scream out loud and face your fears*
> *Make this mistake.*
>
> *Love was never bout playing it safe*
> *Old is the last thing you get if you wait*
> *I never promised we'd get out alive*

All I'm sure of is you own my mind

Make this mistake
Lay it down, forget all you knew
Make this mistake
If I hurt you, I die, die, die too

I don't know if I got all the notes right, I was so strung out on lack of sleep and everything else. I only know that I wanted my music to work its magic.

"I want us to try again," I told my gal.

Two agents who were hauling off one of the fancy microscopes from the lab downstairs glanced at Jing then quickly looked away. Feet shuffled nervously on the platform in Xi'an.

Jing said, "Zee, too much has happened. You were my dreaming man, but I'm not the one you dream of at night. Look, I'm not blaming you. It's my fault too that we don't connect like we used to."

"Us! It's *our* fault and our responsibility to fix it. Jing, we can do this. We've made mistakes—hell, I've screwed up, but, Jing Angell, will you mar—"

"No, Zee. Just no. *Wǒ ài nǐ*. I'm sorry."

Jing stood up, took a breath, composed her face, and turned off the video link.

THE WEIGHT OF
WHAT'S MISSING

THERE ARE MOMENTS WHEN you're young and you can see your life before you in full detail, and the image is so intoxicating you ignore reality to try to *will* your vision into reality. I'm sure this is a common situation.

Lily and I were close in college. We went to artsy movies and shopped on the weekends for silly stuff and talked about everything that was wrong with us. We both had issues with our parents. Just talking to her made me feel better, and I hoped I could help her too. We used words that would stick with me for a lifetime. She wrote the words into a book she gave me. I treasured that book as I treasured her picture before it got lost. I was the problem. I wanted more, and she didn't want that with me. She said she could have lovers but needed a friend. I pressed her. Just before winter break of our senior year, she said she would...once we returned. I bought her a pearl ring. I left it for her to find when she got back to her dorm. I did not hear from her. I left message after message, but she wouldn't talk to me, wouldn't meet my eyes when I passed her on the quad. I saw her early one morning, returning to her dorm with some puffed-up jackoff on a Harley. And I knew: *anyone but me.*

My nerves were shot. The campus nurse gave me a few pills, and that helped get me through finals without jumping from a dorm tower window.

After graduation, Lily wrote me as if nothing had happened. I wrote back often. We occasionally exchanged pictures in the years that followed. I would like to have seen her again, but life got complicated. It was hard to balance things. Marriage and other feelings, I mean. As my career improved, my salary provided options. I dared imagine a different kind of reunion. Such relationships were the privilege of the successful, right?

I was never dishonest with Lily. I don't think I can say that about anyone else. She, in turn, told me about her life: jobs, teaching in London, fun things. I could sense there were areas that were off-limits, but that was okay. We shared something deep, real, unique. I'd write about my feelings, and she'd send back news of her happenings. It was good, but I wanted so much more. My heart wanted to be there.

The reunion never happened.

A couple of years back—this would have been shortly before I left *Daniels, Foye, and Kaiser*—I was spending time with Jessa and Zack one day. We were having a good time at the Legoland at Phipps Plaza in Buckhead; he was still young enough, and she liked helping me keep an eye on him. Anyway, as we got home, I had her pluck the mail out of the box. Jessa was my little helper. We got inside, and she handed me a letter. It was from Lily.

Jessa fixed herself a snack from the fridge while I glanced at it.

> *I will make this brief. I don't think it's appropriate for you to send gifts or letters any longer. I am a married woman now. I will never forget the times we shared. I wish you the best.*
>
> *Your friend,*
> *Lily*

I hate the word "friend."

I did not show Jessa how I felt. It was important to show a brave face—stoic. We spent the rest of that Saturday afternoon playing High Low Jack and chasing Damn Kitty around the living room. The cat would scoot away and then immediately come to me to be stroked. The kids were having a great time.

That night, I was killing a few beers and rereading Lily's letter for the fifth time when I heard Jessa talking to Jing down the hall. She asked, "Why is Dadda so sad?"

I tried and tried to think it out. Sometimes you see your life before you in full detail, the life you deserve, the full promise. I didn't know who took that life from me...maybe God, maybe me. I hated both.

STUFF AND NONSENSE, ODDITIES AND ENDINGS

I GOT DRUNK ON the flight home.

China's first emperor followed me. I liked his travel ensemble: a modest silk cap, loose robes, and UGG slippers. Comfortable, sensible for flying. He'd stored his sword in an overhead.

Nitro had the window seat next to me. I was in the middle, blocked in by an agent. Emp appeared in the window seat whenever Nitro got up to pee, escorted by the other agent assigned to us. Nitro got up to pee a lot.

Emp didn't speak aloud, so I didn't have to answer and look like a psycho, but we shared our thoughts.

I cannot see my Wall. Are we in space?

We're flying…around thirty-eight thousand feet, I answered, reading the figures off the screen set in the seatback in front of me.

Flight must make for a great weapon of war.

And tourism. Sometimes tourism is used in trade wars, so…

Good. Good.

May I ask a question?

Amuse yourself, American.

You said the Onyx Pagoda was a trap only. Where is the secret of your elixir? The mercury elixir that had killed him or made him immortal or some weird-ass thing…but that also held a special ingredient that was the missing key to Tiger Pep.

The secret is in a secure location. You've seen it. His huge belly shook as he chuckled like Evil Chinese Santa.

I don't remember—

Nitro returned from the restroom and made his way past the agent's knees and mine.

Emp started to fade before my eyes, and I was certain he was going out like the Cheshire cat, grin last, taking his secret with him. He surprised me, speaking as he went, *Of course, you remember. I showed it to you. The ingredients and instructions are engraved on the inner surface of the Heirloom Seal of the Realm, hanging there on my crypt.*

*****

Back in Atlanta, Emp was my sporadic companion. He appeared when he wanted to, usually when things got quiet and I had time to reflect. He remained taciturn, complaining about missed potential. I wasn't sure whether that crack was aimed at the modern world or me. As for my breakup with Jing, he said, "It is weakness to let a woman hold power over you." *Is having forty concubines really better?*

He was a lousy roommate. The Son of Heaven drank tequila and watched internet porn until dawn; his singing was atrocious; and I'll never be rid of the image of Emp sunbathing nude on the balcony. Anyway, he skipped my interrogation.

It was at noon. Agents picked me up in a big black sedan at eleven-fifteen sharp. I brushed my teeth at eleven-ten, after chugging one last beer around eleven-oh-five. There was peeing in there too, but that's probably not important.

The agents called it a debrief. *Whatever.* They ordered out for Chinese. A joke, I think.

"So you were the mastermind?" one asked.

"Yes," I said, my mouth full of food. *I love General Tso's Chicken, but Jing says it's not authentic Chinese.*

"And you...what? Made presentations for the sale of..." He read from his notes with just the hint of a condescending smile. "Tiger Penis?"

"Tiger Pep. That was the idea, yes. At that point, it was just a stiffy pill. Herbal."

"And did you actually make any presentations?"

"Not actually, no." *Spring rolls!*

"Did you know the code was going to be something simple, something you couldn't possibly forget?"

"Um, sure."

"Your telephone number, social security number, a kid's birthday, your anniversary, something foolproof. Her computer randomly selected one from a database of familiar numbers and showed it to you but *reversed* it to throw off anyone else. Did you realize that?"

"Jing is very smart." Last I saw, the Chinese had my phone, which was dead anyway. Even if forensic techs found the process, it was worthless without a fresh supply of Emp's secret ingredient. They'd get that when they recovered the jade seal doughnut in a few hundred years.

"Did you know Dr. Angell was skimming funds from ValKnut Pharma?"

"I did not know that," I answered truthfully.

"Your wife is cooperating with us. Fortunately for her, she never received the final payment. Otherwise, she'd definitely be looking at serious prison time instead of wearing an ankle bracelet for a year. As it is, she's provided us with a great deal of information that confirms what we've learned from our other source or helps fill in missing pieces."

"Source? You mean one of the two Chinese officers?"

"I don't know. Maybe. This source sent us e-mails from a dummy account with names, locations, and the time of your big meeting at the emperor's mausoleum. Not sure why they didn't send it directly to the Chinese, but we passed it along on condition one of ours join the fun in Xi'an."

The agent took a sip of his coffee with his meal. He broke open a fortune cookie, again, not really Chinese, though restaurants serve them to please the *dabizes*.

The agent said, "Huh! It says I'm going to solve a mystery." The two agents laughed at that. "Finally, Mr. Angell, Dr. Angell has stated that she expected you to screw everything up, though she didn't figure on Mr. Baine calling for outside help. Did you know your wife set you up to take the fall?"

"I do now." I didn't feel the sting of betrayal because I couldn't feel anything.

So they cut a deal with Jing. She was willing to throw Frank and Gillian under the *Hindenburg* after seeing them together. *My little dragon girl!*

I offered to spill everything I knew. After ninety minutes of interviews, the agents concluded I didn't know jack. For a split second, they let me think I was home free. Then they told me they were freezing my bank account. The sixty thousand dollars Gillian had given me was evidence. I could get it back once the trial was over, in three or four or ten years.

*****

A few weeks later, I took MARTA from my crappy apartment on the Northeast Expressway and met Nitro for my first AA meeting in…a while. It was at our old clubhouse on Briarwood.

I wanted to go. I figured I was ripe for a white light experience since I'd already gotten a blue light experience after parking the Corolla in a neighbor's swimming pool. The judge ordered me to go to AA. So anyway, I got to a meeting.

The familiar aphorisms were posted on the wall, just where I'd left them: *One Day at a Time… I Can't, We Can…*and the Serenity Prayer. These were things a child knew, but I had forgotten. I'd read them each a thousand times but lived them zero times.

At the end of the meeting, I reached into the breadbasket we used and picked up a white plastic poker chip with the AA logo on it. The surrender chip. Nitro slapped me on the back and shook my hand and showed me his own aluminum thirty-day chip.

I had my old haversack with me and pulled from it a framed brass coin, the fancier anniversary version of the chips we got early on in sobriety. I asked the meeting runner if it would be all right to hang the coin on the wall. I explained that it had belonged to another member who attended meetings here years ago.

Nitro said, "His name was Reverend Q, and he was a good man."

The meeting runner asked me, "Did you want to explain why there's a bullet lodged in the middle of the coin?"

"No, not really," I said with rigorous honesty.

*****

There was only one place to go from there. Nitro's son drove us.

In the car, Nitro said, "The other day, I drove past Gillian's great big house. There was a 'For Sale' sign on it. Who'd buy a white elephant like that? Who could afford the thing? I guess Gillian's got a lot on her plate with the charges…and losing

Kevin in that stupid drug shootout. I can't blame her if she doesn't want to live there anymore."

I hadn't thought of Gillian in weeks. I hadn't thought of anyone but myself. It was good to see Nitro and focus on someone else.

"And what about you? How are all your women? Doris, Hattie, Rihanna, Beyoncé?"

"You a damn liar! I got me one woman. Never was another, not ever." Nitro was still my favorite liar.

"I stand corrected. So are you and Bessie getting married?" I asked.

"I don't know. I got things to consider." His face took on a twist of childish mischief. "I've got her on probation. I told that woman after she set me up like that and fed me crazy drugs, I needed a show of faith. I made her donate money to the Metro Atlanta *Task Force for the Homeless*, in memory of Reverend Q. You know, he was my old pastor, right? Mt. Golgotha AME. I been trying to get back there on Sundays. They got a nice little spot for cremains that I got my eye on."

This I felt. The candy or the mercury exposure had given Nitro kidney problems and a compromised immune system. His hands trembled noticeably. I didn't dare ask him for his latest prognosis. For right then, it was just good to see him.

"You need to find a church, Zebulon."

"I don't think so. Religion and I don't mix."

"I know. That's your problem. You don't mix with anything or anyone. You know what they say in the meetings. You're so 'terminally unique' you can't let other people help you with your problems. A church can do that."

"I don't believe in God."

"Fine. He don't care you don't believe. Show up anyway! You gotta let something shine a light on your darkness."

"Maybe when I get out."

"It starts when you start it. Zebulon, I know what you're feeling. I felt it after I got out of the Navy. You're full to bustin' with harsh truth. You're so hurt you look at others and think they're less than you because they don't hurt as much as you do. You know what? That's bullshit. You're just cynical, that's all. Life is not that awful. You live, you have some fun. I wish you could do that, Zee."

The car pulled up to the admissions entrance. *Rehab.*

We went to the desk, and Nitro's son helped me fill out the paperwork. My hands shook, from the DTs, not mercury. Anyway, it wasn't the first time the staff had seen someone as wrecked as me. It wasn't even the first time they'd worked out a deal with the feds to accept payments backed by frozen assets.

I couldn't bring myself to say anything. I was so scared of this place. Mostly, I was scared that I had come to this point. I started crying and could not stop.

As the orderlies came to take me, I tried to thank Nitro, but my mouth went so dry I literally couldn't form words. "That's okay. That's okay," Nitro said. "You can tell me later. I'll be here when you get out."

I wanted to believe him.

*****

Rehab was interesting. I always thought guys howling at the moon was just an expression. Turns out it's not. *Live and learn.*

After a few days, my hands stopped shaking so much. I only cried in the mornings and at night. At lunch, I sulked.

The staff monitored me but didn't let me do much at first.

We started group sessions about ten days in.

I listened and shared. Well, I meant to share. I said a word or two. What I wanted to do was tutor some of the other patients. They were mostly teenagers and twentysomethings, dealing with addiction in one form or another.

I offered to do a class on *Mockingbird,* how it really was about empathy, and these people could benefit from seeing the stark differences between—

An attendant stopped me cold. She said, "You are not in charge. You are not the teacher, or the policeman, or the sage leader for everyone else in the group. What we need for *you* to do, Mr. Angell, is to focus on fixing *you.*"

*****

After lunch each day, they let us watch TV. It was mounted in a corner, up near the ceiling, so it hurt my neck to watch for very long. An attendant picked the channel. Most of the time, we had to watch a guy with a simian hairline use his nasal voice to lavish praise on the president, but once in a while, the TV showed a sports network. I was staring out of the window one day when half my brain heard the sports gal say, "Set to be a major figure in this emerging sport. After coming back from injuries that would have ended the career of a lesser sumo, Tatsuo Nagasaki—" I immediately looked over at the TV. The sports gal had mispronounced her name, but it had to be! "Has won top honors at the Dragon Tournament." I stared at the screen. The video was shot from a distance, showing two powerful women in the dohyō. I couldn't see her face. Maybe I was crazy, but there couldn't be two women sumos named Tatsuo who entered this tournament that she had talked about.

And if she *had survived the fall from that train, then...*

My mouth hung open. I looked around me, at the staffers and the other patients, eager to shout my news. I said nothing.

Who could I tell?

*****

Emp said goodbye one night after I'd been in rehab for a few months. He said he didn't care for my world and thought he'd go back to sleep until things improved. I wished him a good trip and told him to take Delta Flight 888 back to China. Eight means "prosperity," but of course, he knew that.

*****

My group met in the circle every morning. New sad faces joined us, occasionally a calm face disappeared. We talked out our stories. I listened. I heard things from others about letting go of the wreckage of our past. I learned how old failures could haunt the present as surely as huge dreams of the future. "When you have one foot in yesterday and one in tomorrow, you piss all over today." It got a laugh in that room. *It's funny because it's true.*

My turn came around every session. Most days, I talked about how grateful I was to be there, eating peanut butter sand-wiches and not killing people with my car. It was true enough. One day, the group leader asked if I would tell my story.

In my mind, it ran like this: *Once upon a time, a selfish ruler dreamed of ultimate power and immortality and ended up killing himself trying to get it. Later, a man with lots of money hungered for more money, and it ruined him. Finally, a cranky little man with a very nice life forgot to be grateful. He selfishly sent himself off on a wild adventure hoping to become important, and he barely survived. That* was the story. That's not what I said, of course.

All I had in me was a list. I needed to "let go of the face in the driftwood frame who didn't choose me...because *she didn't choose me* and not because I did anything wrong. Maybe one fine morning I'll kiss my scars and stop wishing for a better past. To get to that day, I need to let go of resentments... and fantasies. I need to let go of my hurt for Dad, Jing, booze, bosses, self-importance, my nonstart music career." I had a lot to let go of, my own shadow army. This would take time.

"And what will you keep?" the group leader asked.

I had no answer on that day. I thought about the question for weeks. I started to hear words coming from outside my own brain, telling me to stop blaming others and start living life. I told my handlers I wasn't sure I could do that, and they said I might, in time.

*****

Empires fall—or change hands. And then they stink. I learned this in school. The Chinese learned it long ago. Their history is a flowing tapestry of brilliant dynasties. The Yuan Empire soared. So did the Qing until it faded away in 1912. The Romans had a great empire. It failed thanks to a big split, over-reliance on slavery, syphilis, and other bad stuff. The sun never set on the Brits until it did. Imperial Japan, the Spanish, the Portuguese, the French, so many others. There are empire-minded people today who refuse to learn the lesson, but they will. It's only a matter of time.

A king at thirteen, Qin Shi Huang immediately ordered the construction of a fabulous necropolis covering thirty-eight square miles. He also went on to unite seven Warring States, declaring himself China's first "emperor" (a title he created) at age thirty-eight. To say he was a great man is to miss the fact that he did it for himself. So vain was he that he became obsessed with finding the cure for mortality. He coerced scholars, apothecaries, alchemists, and court magicians into creating an elixir. They did. Believing mercury held mystical properties, they threw it in. The emperor took dose after dose. On September 10, 210 BCE, Emperor Qin Shi Huang died at the age of forty-nine.

At the time, he was touring his expanding China. His death literally raised a stink. Wishing to conceal the emperor's demise, his prime minister and a small group of eunuchs tied wagons of salty fish in front and behind the wagon containing the decomposing Son of Heaven so that the strong fish odor would mask the truth. They lowered the shades, changed his clothes, brought him food, and took him messages from his subjects. They did this for months until they got back to Xi'an, where they finally admitted he was dead. They took Qin Shi Huang to Mount Li, buried him in a fabulous, sealed city, and hatched their schemes to seize power. This last bit worked out about as well as you'd expect. Somebody plotted, and somebody tried to kill somebody, and then his heir sat on the throne for like a minute. *Hell, I didn't know the details. I studied history with Professor Jack Daniels.* Basically, the Qin dynasty crapped out fast.

Here's my point: empires fall. Forged by armies or by daydreams or by discontent and an unquenchable lust for more, all empires fall. If a man who lived without truly connecting to others could die happy knowing he was leaving behind a great big wall, roads, a canal system, and a buried monument to his own ego guarded by thousands of clay soldiers…then I guess Qin Shi Huang died happy.

I had my doubts.

FROM NOW ON...

I'VE GOT PROBLEMS. THEY show up like mail every morning, and I spend the day working through them. Next day, same thing. It's okay. Problems are good practice. One day, I'll get back to some kind of a life. I've got to learn to take on challenges. Get a job. Find a place to live. Stay sober.

It's Valentine's Day, 2019. The year 2018 feels like someone else lived it and sent me the bill. The staffers here in rehab have been promising for a week they'll let me use a phone unsupervised. Today is the day. It's like they're going to sew my arm back on. My attendant says there's a surprise. He hands me the phone, saying, "Someone wants to talk to you."

There's no caller ID, but I think I know the number. "Hello?"

"Hey!" We say "hey" in the South.

"Jessa. Hi, honey."

There's an awkward silence on the other end. I guess silence takes two ends to be silent, but whatever. After a beat, she says, "How are you?"

"I'm fine. I'm good. Hey, I lost twenty pounds. Not sure I'd recommend the diet plan, though."

She forces a laugh. "You sound good. Happy. Are you keeping busy? What do they have you doing?"

I give her a rundown of my routine, which is pretty dull. This part of the conversation goes on for a while, and I'm fine with the small talk. Then I ask about her mom.

"She's kind of bummed. It looks like she's going to lose the house, but the other legal stuff is moving along. She hopes she'll have the fines and court appearances sorted out by the end of the year, and then it's just probation. She says, '2020 is going to be a great year!'" I'm grateful that Jessa's willing to be a bridge between me and Jing. I promise myself not to abuse the privilege. Jessa takes a moment to continue. "MawMaw is fine. She's got a boyfriend. He's kind of a dork, won't let her drink, but she laughs when he's around, so that's good."

"Really? With both me *and* Ma sidelined, the liquor industry will collapse." She giggles. I press my luck. "What about you? Dating anyone?"

"Nice try. We're not talking about that."

"Fair enough." Now a tough one. "And how's Zack doing?"

"Yeah. He's...okay, I guess. He's decided not to do the Marines." She said it like he wasn't going to "do tennis camp." The Marines? When had that been an option? "I think Kevin messed with his head pretty good. Don't hate me, but I'm not sorry Kevin's... Anyway, Zack's going to take some time and sort things out. Find out who he is and all that good stuff."

"I...I hope he can. I should talk to him. I mean when I get out of here. They say that could be in April. I'll move to the halfway house."

"That's great! Don't worry about us, though. We're okay, really." Okay without me. My heart sinks. "Give Zack some time. A big part of his world got pulled out from under him. He has some things to think over...about who he is."

"I should talk to him."

"Not right now. Soon. First, let him figure out how he feels about you."

At this, I have to think for a minute. In the meetings, they say, "When you feel like you are most in need, give." I need to give time to my son. Jessa is waiting patiently on the other end of the phone. Finally, I say, "Please tell Zack I love him and support his choices."

"Will do. And don't worry. He's not angry anymore. We're all getting our heads together."

"Yes. We are."

This is a lot to take in. I can see now why the doctors don't let patients speak to the outside world for a long time. It feels rough but in a good way, like working a muscle after the cast comes off. There's only one thing I need, and that's a kind word.

"The main thing is that you get better, *Dadda*."

That word, *Dadda*, is the one I need to hear. I need to keep hearing it, in all the forms it takes—*Dadda* or *hey you*! or even my stupid name, Zebulon. Words, real words, connect me to other people and let me know there's a reason I'm on this planet and not just focusing on myself. That word, *Dadda*, comes from a world where love still means everything. I can live in that world.

ABOUT THE AUTHOR

CHRIS RIKER IS AN author, father, and journalist. He grew up in Rhode Island and now makes his home in Georgia with his wife, Ping. He has always loved books, from science fiction and fantasy to historical novels and biographies. Building on a background in broadcast news, including a stint at CNN, he is now focused on telling stories with strong characters and moral resonance. Chris Riker's premiere novel, *Come the Eventide*, focuses on a world after the fall of civilization and a dolphin named Muriel who is trying to save mankind from extinction.

CPSIA information can be obtained
at www.ICGtesting.com
Printed in the USA
LVHW092108301121
704812LV00002BA/107